Praise for Dog Days

"*Dog Days* is everything I love in a book—funny, tender, beautifully crafted, and cleverly plotted, with a perfect twist of an ending I didn't see coming. The touching tale of two lost souls finding each other has been given fresh life by the talents of the very gifted Elsa Watson."
—Susan Wiggs,
#1 *New York Times* bestselling author

"Drop eve   Watson's rendering   h-perfect. We all wo   if they had thumb   Jessica are an unforge   take on the buddies-by-accident   Brava!"
—Susan Wilson,
New York Times bestselling author of
One Good Dog

"I savored *Dog Days* for its humor, beautiful prose, heartwarming story line, and quirky, unusual perspective. Elsa Watson writes with compassion and deep insight."
—Anjali Banerjee,
author of *Haunting Jasmine*

TOR BOOKS BY ELSA WATSON

Dog Days
The Love Dog (forthcoming)

Dog Days

—ELSA WATSON—

TOR®

A TOM DOHERTY ASSOCIATES BOOK
NEW YORK

For Kota,

who has an excellent sense of humor.

This is a work of fiction. All of the characters, organizations, and events portrayed in this novel are either products of the author's imagination or are used fictitiously.

DOG DAYS

Copyright © 2012 by Elsa Watson

A Tor Book
Published by Tom Doherty Associates, LLC
175 Fifth Avenue
New York, NY 10010

www.tor-forge.com

Tor® is a registered trademark of Tom Doherty Associates, LLC.

ISBN 978-0-7653-6808-9

First Edition: June 2012

Printed in the United States of America

0 9 8 7 6 5 4 3 2

Acknowledgments

The wonderful thing about writing a book about dogs is that, if you're lucky, you get to be surrounded by talented people who also love dogs—people who appreciate wet noses and wagging tails. Many, many thanks go to my editor, Kristin Sevick, for her clear-eyed wisdom and excellent sense of humor. Time and again, Kristin has steered this book in a better direction, bringing out more in the characters, the story, and the setting. I'm grateful for the work of everyone at Tor/Forge who helped make this book a reality. I'd also like to thank my agent, Kevan Lyon, rescuer of West Highland terriers and lover of novels. Kevan is an absolute joy to work with, and I feel lucky to be one of her clients.

Many readers helped me find my way as this book evolved. I can't sufficiently thank Suzanne Selfors for her cinematic vision and willingness to talk about this book again, and again, and again. My amazing critique group—Susan Wiggs, Sheila Roberts, Kate Breslin, and Anjali Banerjee—endured version after version of this book, offering insightful thoughts at every turn. Sarah

Kostin, Barb Martin, and Dawn Simon all read early drafts and gave me terrific feedback. Thanks also to Judy Hartstone for the phrase "forever family"—a concept she illustrated beautifully through the love she gave her charming rescue dog, Sadie. I'm indebted to you all.

It goes without saying that this book wouldn't exist without the help of our dogs, Lucky and Kota. Kota is the inspiration for Zoë—they share the same love of good jokes, yummy treats, and going through doors. Last, but certainly not least, I'm eternally grateful to my husband, Kol, who not only introduced me to the fascinating world of dogs, but who has always believed in me even when I've been filled with doubts. Kol has buoyed me up at every turn. If anyone deserves to be happily tackled and licked on the face by a dog named Zoë, it's him.

Prologue

Zoë

I'm following my nose, sniffing every curb and corner, but nothing smells like home. Which is upsetting. Home has so many smells that I should be able to detect something, somewhere, but I don't find anything familiar on this street. Or the next one. I stop and pant and wonder where I am.

Wherever it is, it's *not* home.

For one blissful moment, I'm distracted by a robin that I chase down the sidewalk. I run, feet flying, overjoyed to feel the wind in my face. Happiness fills every part of me, out to the tips of my hair. I dash past people and doors and cars. I'm a blur of dog. Nothing can stop me! Nothing! Until the robin disappears and the street comes back into focus.

Then I remember that I'm on a strange street. And now I'm thirsty.

The wind still rustles my fur, but it doesn't please me anymore. I see a man carrying two big boxes, and I run in the other direction. I don't know why I do it—usually

I love people. But it's one thing to love strangers when things are the way they should be, when I'm at home and everything feels safe. Out here, on these breezy streets, I'm too nervous to trust anyone. A gust shakes a plastic bag, and I jump away.

Looking around, I see that I'm in a big, square, paved place with only three trees in it. I check all the tree trunks for smells, and I pee by the most popular one. There. Now my people will be able to find me by smelling my scent. That's good, because I think I might be lost. My tail droops behind me.

Then I see a dog sitting in the middle of the square. Sitting still. I go toward him, and then I stop because there's something odd about this dog. I can't smell him, and he doesn't move. Maybe he doesn't see me? I edge up closer and sniff, but there's nothing. What kind of dog has no smell?

He still doesn't move. I get really brave and go right up to him. I can put my nose *right on him*. He has a doghouse and a bowl with water, so I take a long drink.

Then I sit down and think about home.

1

The Day I Became a Dog

 Jessica

Rain splashed down as I dodged puddles, wishing I'd worn something more sensible than heels. I pushed myself to go faster, thinking of the importance of my mission. Our café staff, including my wonderful business partner Kerrie, was counting on me—I couldn't let them down.

A quick sniff of salt-sharp air told me that the tide was out. For a second, I let my mind wander away to the beach that skirted our little town, picturing the washing waves and gray gulls dancing on the wind. Then I pulled my attention back to the task at hand.

The Northwest Electric office was right next door to the official entrance to the town square, an arch that read A HAPPY DOG BRINGS GRACE TO THE WORLD. Bright yellow posters covered the arch, advertising our big festival, Woofinstock, which started the next day.

I burst in through the Northwest Electric office's double doors, panting from the weather, and shook off my raincoat so I wouldn't drip on anyone's paperwork.

The lobby was ringed with cubicles and office doors, and the wall outside each one boasted one of the yellow posters, showing a grinning dog and the words "Woofinstock! A full weekend of fun, celebrating dogs in all shapes and sizes. Proudly sponsored by the town of Madrona, Washington, a wonderland for dogs." Woofinstock always fell on the first weekend in September—it was a tradition you could bank on.

I took a deep breath and headed up to the counter. A woman in her fifties with short blond hair and a nametag that read MARGUERITE stood on the other side, snapping her gum. A dolphin tattoo peeked out above her shirt's neckline.

"Can I help you?" she asked.

"Yes, please," I said, realizing I had no idea what I was going to say. "I'm one of the owners of the Glimmerglass Café over on the square. We've been late with our bill. . . . I'm really, really sorry about that. But our lights just went out, and if we can't stay open for Woofinstock, we'll never make enough to get on our feet again. I'm uh—" I bit my lip. "I guess I'm here to beg."

Marguerite nodded, snapped her gum again, and turned to her computer, typing in our information. I hated to stare at her while she worked, so I looked down instead at the Woofinstock flyers lying on the counter. My stomach clenched as I scanned the familiar list of activities that made up the weekend: the Pet-and-Person Beauty Contest, the Agility Contest, the 5K Run, the Obedience Trials, Microchipping, the 2-Mile Walk, and the Closing Ceremonies on the green. Throughout it all, restaurants like mine were allowed to run a booth where we handed out cou-

pons and free samples, and sold our signature espres-
sos. If we didn't have electricity in the café, all that
promotion would be pointless.

Marguerite looked up from her screen. "The Glimmerglass Café? You owe two hundred forty-nine dollars and thirty-six cents. Obviously we can't turn your
power back on until you pay that."

I pulled out my personal checkbook and started
writing. "Once this is paid, how long will it take to
get the power back on?"

Marguerite shrugged. "Should be on by tomorrow
afternoon at the latest."

My mouth went dry. "Tomorrow afternoon? But tomorrow is the first day of Woofinstock—do you know
how much business we'll lose if we aren't open first
thing in the morning?"

Another shrug. I took a deep breath and tried to
calm down.

"Please. Is there anything you can do to speed things
up? I know we were late. I know we're the ones to
blame. But our café's really in crisis here—if we don't
do well this weekend, we're going to have to close.
Please, is there any way you can help?"

Marguerite glanced at the computer screen, then
down at my check. "Jessica Sheldon, that's you?"

"That's me." I held my breath. I could almost hear her
mind clicking back over past articles in the *Madrona
Advocate,* remembering where she'd heard my name.
"Aren't you that dog hater?" She looked up at me, right
into my eyes. "Yeah, the Glimmerglass Café—that was
you who screamed at those little dogs, wasn't it?"

I swallowed hard, a difficult thing to do in the face

of her obvious disgust. "Yes," I said quietly. "That was me." As I lowered my gaze, I spotted a magnetized photo of two miniature Chihuahuas, stuck to Marguerite's monitor. My heart sank. I waited for her to yell at me, or at least launch into a forty-five-minute lecture. Instead, she narrowed her eyes.

"What really happened? I mean, you don't really hate dogs, do you?"

I shook my head, sure she wouldn't believe me. It was hard to explain exactly what had occurred. My dog disaster had happened in the middle of last year's Woofinstock, when we were up to our eyeballs in customers. Kerrie was acting as hostess, shuffling customers around like a dealer in Vegas. Our servers dashed from the kitchen to the dining room, scarcely pausing to look before they rammed through the swinging doors. I flew from one emergency to the next. Seconds after I plugged up the spewing espresso machine, a kid vomited on table six, and two servers collided, spilling tomato basil soup and crab dip all over the diners at table eleven.

Just then, a fresh ruckus drew all eyes to the front door. An older woman in a pink hat had entered with four Pomeranians and a Great Dane, all on leashes.

Generally, the Glimmerglass's policy on dogs was the same as all the Madrona restaurants. If the place was quiet and no one seemed to mind, we let well-mannered dogs come in, despite what the health codes said and the amount that they terrified me. However, if we were crowded, all dogs waited outside, no matter how delightful their manners.

I was already on edge, so I was on my way to ask her to move the dogs outside, when the woman lost hold of all five leashes. The dogs sped off like they were part of a jailbreak. One shoved its nose in a lady's lap at table nine. Another raced into the crowd and disappeared. Instantly, I imagined the worst. Carnage. Violence. Brutality. Children missing fingers and customers with flesh torn from their legs.

Out of the corner of my eye, I saw the Great Dane with its paws on top of a table, licking soup out of a little kid's bowl, while the child shrieked with laughter. One of the Pomeranians dashed past me with a dinner roll in its mouth, and I lunged after it but missed badly—I was too frightened to really try to catch it. Seconds later, I jumped about a foot in the air. Something was licking my ankle!

Around me, the room spun in a kaleidoscope of faces, some laughing, some staring. One woman had a Pomeranian in her lap, and I lunged for it, hoping to knock the little dog away so the woman would be safe. It was clearly about to go for the jugular. Before I could reach her, the Great Dane came loping toward me, drool hanging from its snout in long cords. The drool of a man-eater.

I screamed. It was one of those horror-movie screams, the kind that ripples with terror. Everyone in the café could hear me, but it didn't matter. Even if I'd tried, I couldn't have stopped myself. "Get away from me!" I bellowed. "Get away, you vicious, evil beasts! I hate you! *Hate you!*"

Right then, a flash went off in my face. When the

spots cleared from my vision, I blinked and found myself face-to-face with the *Madrona Advocate*'s newest
reporter.

The following morning, I opened the paper and
saw my worst fears realized in newsprint. The photo
showed me at my most hideous—dark hair frizzed
around my head like raised hackles, mouth twisted
midshout. I had a spoon in my hand that I was aiming
at the Great Dane like a sword. Underneath the photo
ran this caption: *Glimmerglass owner Jessica Sheldon
berates visiting dogs in her restaurant. The dogs are
owned by Mary Beth Osterhoudt, owner of Oster
Organic Dog and Cat Foods, Woofinstock's premier
sponsor. Mrs. Osterhoudt says she is now unlikely to
continue her support of Madrona's showcase event—
support that has amounted to over $10,000 annually.*

It was one of the worst moments of my life.

I knew immediately that it was all my fault. As
Kerrie put it, the dogs were just being dogs. And I was
being crazy. I was the one who'd caused all the trouble. It was me—my paranoia, my paralyzing fear of
dogs—that had caused the disaster.

The last thing I'd wanted to do was put the town in
jeopardy, but of course all of Madrona detested me
for the lost support. The café's phone reservation line
stopped ringing. People pulled their dogs away when
they saw me coming down the street. The shopkeepers
worried about their businesses, the city council worried about our reputation, and Kerrie and I worried
that the Glimmerglass would have to close. That saying about there being no such thing as bad publicity?
Not true.

I couldn't bear the thought of losing the café—it was the one place I had that felt like home. It killed me that I'd been the one to put all that in danger. Thankfully, Kerrie sat me down with a cup of tea and helped me make a repair plan—a plan that I flung myself into.

I went before the city council and apologized. For a week, I stood next to the statue of Spitz, our town hero, and handed out free dog cookies. Spitz was a Doberman who saved two Madrona children from drowning twenty years ago. When he died, the city council commissioned a bronze likeness of him and matching doghouse that they placed in the center of the cobblestoned square. It was a town gathering point, the perfect place to do penance.

As my final act of contrition, I volunteered to head up the business owners' committee for Woofinstock, a job that required me to tromp around town asking my fellow entrepreneurs for sponsorships and donations. I would also have to make a speech at the big closing ceremonies.

Woofinstock weekend was going to be torture, and I frankly had no idea how I was going to pull it off without cloning myself. Aside from the speech, I was in charge of the Glimmerglass's espresso stand on the green. And I intended to hand out coupons and menus at every Woofinstock event I could get to. As Kerrie put it, my job was to "go out there and bring us back some business." But without electricity, there was no business to be had. And, even if Marguerite could help me, I was still petrified of dogs—and I was about to spend a weekend surrounded by them.

* * *

"*B*ut I don't hate dogs," I told Marguerite. "I really, really don't. I'm just scared of them. They're so unpredictable—and I get so nervous around them. When those little dogs swarmed me, I just . . . I guess I freaked out."

Marguerite was quiet for a long moment. Then she said, "Do you like living here?"

That caught me off guard. "Sure. Of course I do."

"Then you're going to have to get over this dog phobia. Starting today. If you can't do that, then you should seriously think about moving away. You'd do just fine anywhere else in Kittias County—you just don't seem like a fit here."

I laid my hands flat on the counter, waiting for my heart to stop pounding. I loved Madrona. I could spend hours watching the gulls ride on the wind and the sailboats that filled the water with their sails on race days. This was where my best friend Kerrie was. The Glimmerglass, the café we'd built together four years ago, belonged in this town. Kerrie and the café had always been there for me—that was why it was so important that I get the lights turned back on, so we could give our business one last chance.

Besides, Madrona was a pretty little town, filled with lacy vine maples and old brick buildings. Six years ago, when I was twenty-two and fresh out of the University of Washington, I visited a friend here and fell in love with the place. When the rhododendrons bloomed in the spring, it was as if a rainbow ran through town. Madrona had exactly the small, homey feel I'd always longed for. I didn't want to move away.

But I couldn't deny the truth in what Marguerite said. Madrona was dog crazy, and I was dog phobic. The rest of Kittias County thought Madrona was off its rocker, even though our little town did really well with events like Woofinstock. When Madrona voted to let dogs enter into its shops and businesses, the county's animal control team went berserk, but there was nothing they could do. Madrona had chosen its identity, and it definitely had a wet nose.

"I love it here," I said softly. "I don't want to leave."

Marguerite folded her arms in front of her chest. "The first step to recovery is admitting you have a problem. You have to work on this. If you ignore it, your life will get smaller and smaller and smaller. Fear is like that. It will kill your life."

Zoë

I'm hiding in the doghouse that belongs to the shiny dog, keeping my ears low. I've run everywhere today, but now I'm tired and hungry. So I'm taking a nap. Only things keep waking me up. First it was a cloud of leaves shaking on a tree, then it was a flower rolling across the ground in front of me. Then I thought I saw a dog! But it turned into an umbrella.

It's raining, and I like rain but people don't. A woman in clicking heels walks past me, hiding inside her coat. I stick my nose farther out the doghouse door and sniff, sniff, sniff as hard as I can. She smells friendly. Like a warm house. And she looks nice, though she's moving fast. But I'm faster. I slink out of the doghouse and trail behind her. Maybe she'll help me get home. Or feed me. Or dry me with a big fluffy towel.

She's heading toward a door, which makes me excited. I love doors! I hope she'll let me go inside with her. My parents might be behind that door. They like being inside. I like it in *and* out—both places.

We're almost to the door, her in front and me in back, when a big flash stings my eyes. I spin around, tuck my tail between my legs, and race back to the shiny doghouse.

☕ Jessica

I walked back across the square, my head hung low. The rain fell steadily, and I huddled inside my hood. How was I going to tell Kerrie the power might be off all day?

I was almost to the café when a searing flash blanketed the sky. The stormy grays around me blanched into overexposed pastels. I reeled as if someone had taken a flash picture right in front of my face. At almost the exact same time, thunder boomed, boxing my ears.

I ran without hearing or seeing. By sheer instinct, I raced straight to the café door. I wrenched it open and squeezed inside, panting hard.

Goose bumps covered my skin. I pressed my back to the door, then cautiously turned my head and looked back outside. The square was dark—strangely so for a late summer morning. There was no sign of lightning.

How odd.

I turned back around to the dark café and felt my heart sink. It was 8:20 in the morning and our lights were off—a café owner's worst nightmare. Someone had turned the sign on the front door to CLOSED. We usually had a nice morning coffee rush at about this time, but not today. We couldn't do much without electricity.

With a heavy sigh, I let the hush of the room pass through me, glad to see that at least the place was spotlessly clean. These sixteen hundred square feet felt more like home than my apartment. The café was split into two halves, divided by the front door and hostess station. To the left was the dining room, where fifteen oak tables sat empty, waiting for a rush that wasn't going to come. To the right, the espresso counter and pastry case held the cheaper, faster items that had been our best sellers lately. Except today, when even that was closed.

I shook myself out of my reverie and went in search of Kerrie, making a detour to the bathroom to splash some water on my face. Someone had lit candles in all the back rooms, and the light of one glowed from under the door. As I entered, I heard Naomi, our sous chef, talking on her cell phone. "Yeah, I don't know," she was saying. "It's sinking fast, that's for sure. They couldn't even pay the electric bill. The smart thing would be to look for another job now, while I still can . . ."

She stopped midsentence when she saw me. "Uh,

gotta go," she said, clicking her phone shut. We looked at each other, both feeling awkward.

I opened my mouth, then closed it again. I longed to reassure her, to tell her she was wrong, that the Glimmerglass was going to be around for the next hundred years and she'd always have a stable paycheck. But what could I say that was true? I didn't want to lie. It killed me to see my own employees worry like this. Naomi had two kids. She had rent to pay. School lunches to buy.

"I'm sorry, Naomi," I said, knowing my voice sounded rough with emotion. A sick feeling swam in my stomach. "I'm so sorry. We're doing the best we can, but it doesn't look too good. If the power comes back and we can have a good Woofinstock, then it just might work out." I smiled, knowing how pie-in-the-sky this sounded. Was it unfair to keep her here, working on this sinking ship, when she could be investing her time and energy in something new? We'd already expanded her job. With the dining room so quiet, Kerrie had her doing all the baking for the pastry case. It saved us money on our baked good orders, but baking wasn't the job Naomi had been hired to do. "We'll do everything we can to keep the place open. I don't want you to lose your job."

Naomi put a hand on my arm. "Gosh, Jess, I know all that. You know I'd rather work for you and Kerrie than anyone else in the world. I'm just trying to be practical, that's all. You know, for my kids. You guys are the best bosses ever." She gave me a hug.

When I pulled back, my eyes were wet. "We'll get

through this," I said, praying that it would be true. "Thanks for sticking with us."

"Absolutely," she said with a we're-pals-again twinkle in her eye. "And don't worry, Jess. I'm sure we'll get this all fixed in time for Hot Max to come in."

I blushed. Hot Max, our unbelievably gorgeous customer, came through the espresso line every morning at nine. He brightened my day like a supernova—if the lights didn't come back on and I couldn't see him, this day was going to be one big pile of misery. I glanced at my watch. Just half an hour to go.

Ah, Max. To begin with, Max had cheekbones that belonged on a Native American prince. I had secret fantasies about kissing one of those cheeks (which I imagined would be cool from the wind), then traveling down to his mouth, neck, and places beyond. Just thinking about it made my toes curl.

There was more to Max than just cheekbones, of course. He was tall—often the tallest customer in the café—and he had jet-black hair and sideburns that he always kept neatly trimmed. And dark eyes that you could fall all the way into if you weren't careful.

Naomi and I left the bathroom together and ran into Kerrie, who was coming down the hall, candle in hand. My partner had real talent with food, but what struck people first was her sense of style. Kerrie was in her midforties, with blond hair cut in a sharp wedge, and she owned about fifty different pairs of glasses, each more dramatic than the last. Today her glasses were thick-rimmed and green to match her malachite earrings. She took a look at our faces and said, "Hey, no moping, you guys. Not without me, anyway. It's way too dark for that."

At that very second, the lights flared on. We all blinked in the onslaught of brightness.

"Hey, lights!" Kerrie beamed at me. "Good work, Jess—you did it! We'll be serving today after all."

"Hooray, hooray!" I sang, making a mental note to send Marguerite a free latte card in thanks. I scurried to the front of the house, anxious to flip over the CLOSED sign and get the café revved up again. Sahara, our barista, appeared at my elbow, ready to start brewing and steaming. In the kitchen, I knew Naomi and Kerrie were popping croissants and turnovers into the oven. Gradually people trickled in, and I began to breathe again. Selling coffees and lattes would never keep us in business, but in our position, every little bit helped.

It was 9:35 when Max came in. Usually, I spent the whole morning watching for him, but today I was so busy he surprised me, bursting through the front door right after Sahara left to help Kerrie in the storeroom. I generally liked to see him coming so I could check my hair and get myself into a good position, engaged in a task that would let me watch him come in without being noticed. Steaming milk was perfect. So was wiping tables. I could observe him, flicking my gaze up and down, catching little glimpses of those cheekbones before turning back to the safety of the steamer or the tabletop. Once he reached the counter, I kept my eyes down the rest of the time he was in the café. I couldn't make eye contact with him. Ooh, good heavens no.

It's not that I was a chicken or scared of men or anything like that. With other guys I could flirt and chat, no problem. It's just that, with Max, there were special circumstances. Very special circumstances. Max was not only the town hottie—he was also the town veterinarian. And since I was Madrona's resident dog hater, that made me public enemy number one where he was concerned.

When he walked in, I was all alone, and I felt myself turning pink before he even reached the counter. In a panic, I checked my hair in the stainless steel side of the espresso machine, but all I could see was a steaming blur. Max wore a dripping green raincoat over his red-and-white Manchester United jersey, and as he pushed his hood back, I saw that his black hair was still damp from the shower. Or the rain. No, definitely the shower.

He usually spent some time looking over the pastry case before placing his order, but today he walked straight up to the counter. I glanced around, half wishing Sahara would materialize and take Max's order for me, but she was nowhere. I was in this alone. With very damp palms.

"Hi," he said. His smile made his cheekbones pop and his eyes glow. My insides fluttered. "I'm not sure we've met. I'm Max Nakamura."

Obviously, I knew that already. "Hi," I said, working hard to regulate my voice so it wouldn't squeak. "I'm Jessica. Jessica Sheldon." I mumbled my last name, but by the way he nodded, I was pretty sure he caught it. His eyes lingered on my face, making me blush.

"You're one of the owners here, aren't you?"

I nodded, feeling the blush creep down my neck. If he knew that, then surely he knew all about my infamous dog incident. Everyone did. Was he introducing himself to me because I was the enemy? A sick feeling coiled in my stomach as I concluded that he already knew all about me—he must. This was our first conversation, if you could call it that, and he already hated me. Better to serve him his double-shot Americano now, regular sized but in a large to-go cup, and be done with it.

"I'll take a double-shot Americano," he said. "Regular sized, but in a big cup."

I smiled weakly. As I busied myself near the espresso machine, I hoped the steam would explain away the redness of my face. "I like this place," he said.

I jerked my head up. Wait, was he making conversation? With me? He, the town's best-loved veterinarian, making small talk with a woman of my reputation? *Well*, I thought. *Maybe he doesn't know after all. In which case, I should really say something in return. For goodness sake, don't say anything about dogs!*

"Thanks," I said, grateful for his compliment of the café. "The Sounders are sure doing well this year," I said. Under the counter, I kicked myself. Lame, lame!

Max's eyes brightened. "Do you follow soccer?"

"Um, not really." That's why it was such a *lame* thing to say. I knew how he felt about soccer, but that was no reason to jump into a topic of which I was utterly ignorant. "I saw your jersey and thought you might be a fan. I . . . uh . . . I don't know anything about soccer."

"Oh," he said, taking his steaming large cup from my hands. His index finger brushed my pinky—his skin was surprisingly warm. He smiled again, but he clearly had nothing to say about my sports ignorance. He hoisted his cup toward me in a good-bye salute. "Thanks."

Thus ended our first, and probably last, exchange of syllables. *Way to go, Jess. Way to go.*

As he turned away, I looked at the golden skin on the back of his neck and saw a few droplets of water fall from his wet hair onto his collar. *Oh, Hot Max. What would you think if you knew how much Madrona's number-one dog hater wanted to kiss that neck?*

I watched him walk out the door, pulling his hood back over his head, and felt my heart drop into my shoes. Just outside, he bumped into Leisl Adler, the owner of the competing café across the square, and my heart shot all the way to the floor. After my dog-hating incident, Leisl had been the first one to stomp into the Glimmerglass and accuse me of ruining Woofinstock forever. I was pretty sure she hated me.

As Leisl stopped to talk to Max, I saw her gesture to the café, her face dark. I turned away and pretended to clean the espresso machine, my eyes stinging. It was done now. Over. Kaput. Leisl would tell him everything, the whole ugly truth, and then Max would never speak to me again.

2

The Dog Hater

 Jessica

I shook myself out of my Max-induced dreams. He was a wonderful distraction from real life, but I didn't deserve an escape. I deserved to work on the bills. I was heading to the back office when I ran into Kerrie, who caught me by the arm, spun me around, and steered me toward the espresso counter.

"C'mon, you. You've got to taste something. I had the best idea for a new Woofinstock drink and I need a taster. What do you think of a shot of espresso with whipped cream on top—called 'Bark Worse Than Its Bite'?"

I nodded. "Brilliant, I love it. But I was going—" I pointed toward the back office, an area we'd started calling the Pit of Death.

Kerrie shook her head. "I know you were going to work on the bills. But they'll still be there in ten minutes. Heck, they'll have reproduced and had grandchildren in ten minutes."

At the espresso machine, she started packing grounds

into the metal filter, then turned her back to me as she dripped mysterious combinations of flavored syrup into one of our little white enamel cups. "You need a break, Jess. You've been closing and opening the café for the past week. And we both know you're doing two extra jobs besides your own, running the espresso counter and serving at night. You have to ease up or you'll never make it through Woofinstock. Speaking of which, I got the extra servers from the college for the weekend. That'll give us three up front, two in the kitchen, you doing promo, Sahara on morning espresso, and me as hostess, line manager, and catchall girl. If we can fill up, it'll be just right." Kerrie locked the filter holder onto the machine, set the cup under the nozzle, and hit the button. Toffee-colored liquid dribbled out in a thin jet. "So, right now, let me baby you for half a second."

Baby. The word made me flash on the lilac-colored envelope that had arrived in yesterday's mail. I rubbed the scar on my arm—the one I'd had as long as I could remember—and chased the thought away with a sip of Bark Worse Than Its Bite. "Ooh, delicious. That wasn't just chocolate syrup you added, was it? Chocolate and orange? Pineapple?"

Kerrie was about to answer when the bell over the door jingled, and a woman in a raincoat came in, leading the biggest dog I'd ever seen. The thing looked like Chewbacca on four legs. Its bearded snout dripped with water—or was that saliva? My mouth went instantly dry. Breath came out of me in frantic puffs, and I could feel my eyes growing wider and wider. Before I could start shaking, Kerrie had me by the shoulders, and I found myself moving down the hall and into the Pit of Death with her hand wrapped firmly around my waist. *This is the way she steered her son JJ across the playground that time he fell off the monkey bars*, I thought.

She yanked out my desk chair and eased me into it, then pressed my head down between my knees. "Breathe," she instructed. "In and out. Nice and easy." She bent toward me. "Are you hyperventilating? Should I get a paper bag?"

I shook my head, my nose rubbing against my black skirt. I sat up. "I'm okay."

"You sure?" She crouched down in front of me and peered into my face. "You look really pale. That was one huge dog."

True—the dog was a giant. And it was also true that my sip of Bark Worse Than Its Bite was sloshing painfully around in my stomach. But I desperately wanted to be okay. Kerrie had things to do—these days she was our hostess, line manager, and emergency waitress, all rolled into one. I had bills to pay. We didn't have time for a panic attack.

"I'm fine," I said, summoning up a big smile. "Totally fine. Or, at least, I'll be fine right *here,* doing the bills, in this nice, quiet room with no dogs in it."

Kerrie nodded. "Right on, super trooper." She straightened and glanced down at the six-inch-high pile of bills on my desk. "I suppose we'll have to have one of those serious talks about our bottom line later?"

"Without a doubt," I said, "after the weekend's over. That's when we'll know which way the chips are going to fall. If we can't make next week's pay-roll, then . . ."

I didn't need to finish. We both knew what would happen if we didn't have enough for next week's pay-roll.

*I*t was midafternoon and I'd just finished placing our orders when I heard the unmistakable high notes of Kerrie in an argument. I headed that way, noticing that the storm outside had gotten worse. Rain pounded against the windows. The wind whistled through the square, where the Woofinstock banners snapped like sails.

The second I pushed through the swinging doors, Kerrie grabbed my arm and dragged me to her side of the kitchen, facing off against Guy, our loathsome chef. Naomi was throwing chopped onions into a pan with an angry motion.

"What's going on?" I asked, although I knew per-fectly well what was going on.

"Guy was late this morning. Again." A pair of stress lines appeared in Kerrie's forehead.

Across the room, Guy looked peeved. He was shorter than Kerrie, a fact he made up for by standing as tall as he could get, arms crossed, chest swelled. Guy had a cylindrical head that never failed to make me think of Beaker on the *Muppet Show*. Except when Guy spoke, he said a lot more than "me-me-mee."

"Like it mattered," he sneered. "We were closed, any-way."

"We opened before nine," Kerrie countered. "You were barely here in time for the lunch rush!"

Guy gave us both a smug look. "This place never has a lunch rush. What happened, anyway—did you forget to pay the electric bill?"

My face grew hot. Kerrie jumped in. "You were late, and that made the lunch orders slow to go out. Your tardiness might have cost the Glimmerglass money and customers."

"What d'ya wanna do about it," he asked, his chin jutting forward, "fire me? Yeah, right, that's rich. You can't fire me now, not before this weekend."

Beside me, Kerrie sounded like a teakettle that was about to boil over. I stepped forward, fighting to keep my voice calm. "Guy, I'm sure you remember the conversation we had last Tuesday. When I told you that you were beyond probation, that if you were late one more time Kerrie and I would have no choice but to fire you?"

He swept the toque off his head and beat the stainless steel worktable beside him to accentuate his words. "You've never had a complaint about my food. What about my *talent*? What about my *future*? You think I wanna be stuck in small-town *hell*, working some two-star dive? I'm no hack. I'm the *best chef* you've ever seen."

"In some ways the worst," I said. "It's true that no one complains about your food. But let's get real, Guy—how are you going to make it in a big city if you can't behave yourself? Professional chefs are impeccable in their work habits. That means showing up on time. Not drinking all the cooking wine. Not changing your clothes in the walk-in freezer. Not bullying your kitchen staff until they quit." Naomi shot me a grateful look, then dipped her face back over her roux. "If you ever want to fly this coop for New York or L.A. or even Seattle you'll need a good recommendation from us."

Guy waggled his jaw back and forth. "You people. This restaurant is such a joke." His eyes kept dropping to the front of my shirt, so I crossed my arms in front of my chest. "And you," he turned to Kerrie, "why you think you're qualified to make the menu, I don't know. What do you know about cooking?"

I gasped. Though I couldn't see Kerrie, I could practically feel the blood draining out of her face. Guy had no idea that Kerrie used to be a superb chef, one of the best in the county. She might not cook anymore, but she was still far more qualified than Guy to set a menu. "Kerrie knows more about food than you'll ever learn," I said, narrowing my eyes. "She could cook circles around you."

"Yeah?" he answered, his jaw jutting forward, "well why doesn't she, then? C'mon, she either belongs in the kitchen or she doesn't. And she doesn't. Period. End of story."

For a minute, the kitchen was silent except for the sound of Naomi sautéing rice for her risotto and rain hammering against the windows. It was true that we needed all the help we could get this weekend, but Guy was a five-foot-five font of ill will, spreading tension all over the Glimmerglass. Yes, he was a solid chef. But brilliant, he was not. And insulting Kerrie's skills with food, well, that was just too much.

"Guy," I said in my most professional tone. "I think you'd better leave."

Guy's jaw muscles twitched. "You can't fire me. You'll be screwed if I leave. I'm not the one over a barrel here. Woofinstock starts tomorrow. I can do whatever I want." He tossed his toque onto the counter and gave me a victorious smirk.

"No." This time my voice was so calm it scared me a little. I took a long breath in through my nose. "You can't. You're fired."

Guy looked from me to Kerrie and back to me again, a smirk spreading on his barrel-shaped head. "Huh. You're serious. Well, have a merry Woofinstock, both of you," he said, swiping his toque off the counter. He stomped out of the kitchen, through the swinging doors, and out of our lives.

Behind me, Kerrie blew out a lungful of air and sagged against a worktable. "I can't believe that just happened." Suddenly, she let out a giggle. "Oh, wow— he's gone!" Silent peals of laughter shook her shoulders. She was so giddy her glasses fogged up. "I mean, I know we're in deep doo-doo and everything. . . . But he's *gone*!"

Naomi's smile was a mile wide. Even I let out a shaky laugh as thunder rumbled outside.

"Well, we seem to have an opening in the head chef position. Naomi, Kerrie, want to flip for it?"

Kerrie bit her thumbnail and shook her head. She could do the job, we both knew that—she'd done it beautifully for years. But we also both knew what held her back. Things can go wrong in the restaurant business. Many land mines lie in wait as food journeys from the farm to the table. Sometimes a chef, even one as skilled as Kerrie, could serve contaminated food. It happens. But when it happened to my partner, it frightened her so badly she quit cooking altogether. "Count me out," she said. "Naomi will do a terrific job."

"In that case, Naomi, congratulations—you've just been promoted." Naomi beamed at us both. "Thanks, you guys! I won't let you down, I promise."

The truth was that Naomi wasn't completely ready to be head chef—if she had been, we'd have let Guy go months ago. She cooked wonderfully, but she just wasn't adept at running the kitchen. If we got customers this weekend, the kitchen would be under more stress than Naomi had ever seen. She'd need a seriously talented sous chef behind her.

All the same, Kerrie and I gave her our most supportive smiles as we headed into the hallway. When the kitchen doors swung shut behind us, Kerrie drew me close. "Jess, do you have any time to deal with this? It's two-thirty already. Paul's swamped today— I've got to run JJ to the dentist."

The stress dent was back in Kerrie's forehead. I wanted nothing more than to collapse on the floor and hide until this nightmare was over, but the sight of my stressed-out partner made me summon reserves I didn't know I had.

"No worries," I said. "I've got this. The bills are done, or as done as they can be—I can work on this until it's time to get ready for dinner service. I'll try everyone I can think of. And I'll call Jerry at the

Chamber to see if he has any ideas. I might as well make up a quick flyer, too, and put it up on the bulletin boards. With a little luck, I'll find us a sous chef."

"Thank you," Kerrie said, kissing me on the cheek. "You're a mensch! I'll be back just as soon as I can." She headed for the door, her keys jangling. "Oh, I almost forgot. The mail came. No bills for once, but you got another one of those big purple envelopes." She turned around, walking backward so she could grin at me. "You have an admirer or something?"

Yeah, right. An admirer. If only it was something that pleasant. For a second my mind flashed on Max, and I felt my heart squeeze. Why did he have to run into Leisl, of all people?

Kerrie went through the door, and as it shut behind her, I heard a snap and crash. And the lights went out.

3

Dog Fraud

 Jessica

At least when one piece of our world fell apart, it gave me the chance to improve another. With the power out all over town, the café was closed once again. And since we had no dinner service looming, I was free to spend all afternoon finding a new sous chef.

First, I sat down at my desk with four lit candles and hand-wrote fifteen flyers. Then I ran out into the torrent and posted one on every public bulletin board in the square, squeezing it in between Woofinstock posters and cards advertising yard sales. When I got back to the café, Kerrie and her husband, Paul, were hooking their generator up to the refrigerator so we wouldn't lose any of our food.

I went into the Pit of Death and made calls with my cell, leaving what I hoped was an enticing and upbeat voice mail for Theodore, our former sous chef. I checked in with the two high school students who would be running our Woofinstock booth on the green in the morning. And I called all of our outsourcers, the companies that provided our baked goods, vegetables, fruit, meat, and other foods, and explained that we had a big weekend coming up, so could they please continue delivering to us even though our latest payment was late? I even called our landlord and offered, once again, to give him free meals in exchange for reduced rent. Once again, he turned me down.

In the candlelight, I traded my sopping heels for a pair of Kerrie's espadrilles, pulled on my emergency pair of khakis, and slung on my raincoat. Kerrie and Paul had gone, so I locked the café doors, startled to see how dim it was, even though my watch said it was only 5:30. The sun wouldn't set for another hour, but apparently the storm had cast its own veil of darkness over the square. With a deep breath, I tightened the drawstrings on my hood and set out. Bonita Rialto, an amazing chef who'd recently left the Salish Table, lived just three blocks away, right next to the ice-cream shop. Her place was close, but I'd still have to run if I hoped to stay reasonably dry.

I darted from awning to awning, rain zinging into my face. The town was empty and devoid of light. In the middle of the square, Spitz's bronze statue looked forlorn. Even the pots of late-blooming geraniums that lined the square looked washed out and drab. A branch snapped off a leafless Japanese maple and hit the travel agency's window, its fingers shrieking against the glass. Puddle water soaked the espadrilles after the first ten yards, and they flopped on my feet like flippers.

As I rounded the corner near the bank, I pulled up short. Sitting still, right in the middle of the street and the storm was a giant white dog. I slowed down. What on earth was it doing? Rain beat against its head, but the dog didn't move. Its ears drooped at the tips like lazy tulip petals. Was this one of those cases of weird animal behavior that precedes a natural disaster? Were we going to have an earthquake? A tidal wave? Since when did dogs sit in the middle of the road?

The dog's ears flicked in the wind. It looked like a small German shepherd, only completely white. And its eyes were glued to me.

A gray van turned onto the road at the far end of the block.

"Hey," I yelled to the dog, "get out of the road! There's a car coming."

The dog stared at me. I waved my arms, and the dog opened its mouth in a pant, but didn't budge. The van barreled down the road, far too fast for these weather conditions.

"Come on, move!" The dog was smiling at me now, but showed no inclination to scoot out of the way. Didn't it hear the van coming? I didn't have time to run into the road—the van was too close. I squeezed my eyes shut as the van flew toward the dog. With a screech of tires, it came to a halt, inches from the dog's tail. A linebacker-sized man hopped out, wearing a uniform vest and black hat. He had a pole in his hand with a metal loop on one end.

The letters on the van read KITTIAS COUNTY ANIMAL CONTROL.

"C'mere, you." He shuffled toward the dog, pole extended. The dog turned its panting face to him and lifted one ear. My feet itched with the urge to take off—I was getting soaked—but something kept me glued to the scene. I stepped into the street just as the man lunged for the dog, which bolted up and skipped away, just out of reach.

"You little bugger," he said, moving toward the dog again, faster this time. It darted off a second time, tail up, as if this were the best game ever. Didn't it know what happened to dogs that went to the pound? This could be the last game it ever played.

Mr. Animal Control was breathing hard. With his hands on his hips, he swore under his breath. Then he returned to the truck and came back with what looked like a pair of *Star Trek* stun guns. If the mayor saw this guy, she would have a fit—not that she had any control over the county animal control officers. Until Madrona came up with its own animal services, it was stuck with the county and its Tasers.

"Wait," I called, running over. "Don't shoot it."

He turned on me, stun guns out. "Keep back, lady. I got a feral dog here. This is a dangerous situation."

"Dangerous?" I looked back at the dog. It didn't look dangerous. Frankly, for a dog, it seemed remarkably clean and calm. Compared with those Pomeranians in the café a year ago, this dog was as mellow as Jell-O.

"You don't wanna mess with wild dogs. I just transferred here from Denver, and let me tell you— people here don't know from being bit. I been bit five times." He brandished his stun guns. "It's legal for me to carry these Tasers. County ordinance." He looked like he expected me to argue, but I had nothing to say. "I'll use 'em, so help me, I will. You just keep back and let me handle this."

Of course I was tempted to do just that. I could dash away down the street and never look back. But wouldn't that just make me the dog hater everyone said I was? I glanced at the dog again. It watched us from twenty feet away, waiting to be chased. I saw a flash of a red collar at its neck. *Wild dog, my ass.*

"It's not wild," I blurted, surprised by the force in my own voice. My heart hammered against my rib cage. "I own it—uh, her." This was a guess, but she just seemed female. "She's mine."

Mr. Animal Control frowned at me. "Yours?"

"Uh-huh." *What was I saying?*

He pointed a Taser at the dog. "It's not on a leash. You've gotta have all dogs on a leash or under voice control. It's a law."

Voice control, huh? I turned toward the dog. With my heart in my mouth, I bent my knees and spread my arms wide, like I'd seen the mayor do with her rescue dogs. "Come, sweetie—come!"

Be careful what you wish for, right? Amazingly, the dog trotted over. I held out a shaking hand, my mouth dry, and she came close enough to sniff me and even let me take hold of her collar. *Please don't bite me,* I prayed. *Please.* Her wet fur clung to my fingers.

"See?" My voice trembled, but he didn't notice. "She's my dog. I promise she won't get into any more trouble." I stood there, half bent over, holding the dog's collar like it was a snake. The dog panted, her eyes bright. The animal control officer shook his head and climbed back into his truck.

The second the van was out of sight, I let go of her collar and pressed the heels of my hands to my forehead. "Boy-o, that was close. Do you have any idea what could have happened to you if you'd been caught? You can't trust that guy—he's bad news for a dog like you."

The dog cocked her head as if she were trying to understand. I put my hands in my raincoat pockets and took a step back. The rain, which had quieted, picked up its pace again, drumming on our heads. Now that there was a little more distance between me and the dog, I regained the ability to breathe normally. "You're a fine dog," I told her. "Thank you for not biting me. But you should really get on home. It'll be your dinnertime soon."

The dog wagged her tail.

I shuffled farther away. "Listen," I said, "I don't have any dinner for you. You'll have to go home. I'm sure you have a family that loves you." Now that the moment had passed, my knees started shaking. "And I'd better go before I get any wetter. I can't be sneezing and snotty during Woofinstock. I have to make speeches and things." The dog licked her nose and carried on wagging. "Okay. So, I'm gonna go now."

Wag, wag, wag.

I turned away, feeling off-balance, though I wasn't sure why. I'd done a good deed, right? I'd saved her from animal control—wouldn't my fellow Woofinstock committee members be proud?

It wasn't as if I could do anything more. I didn't know where she lived or who her owners were. There weren't any tags dangling from her collar, nothing to tell me who she was. I didn't have a car to drive her home. And, frankly, even though I'd just held her collar for three endless minutes, I was afraid to touch her again.

I squelched my way toward the ice-cream shop, trying to switch my focus back to the Glimmerglass. I needed to decide how low on the experience ladder we were willing to go. A sous chef with a few years of work under the belt was ideal, of course, but in this situation we'd probably have to settle for a talented prep cook looking to move up or a line cook who wanted a change. As I weighed the most likely cases, my mind skittered up, down, all around—and kept veering back to the dog.

What was she doing out here, anyway?

Following me, I was pretty sure. True enough, when I glanced behind me, I saw her white tail bobbing along the street about twenty feet back—close enough to keep up, but not so close as to make me nervous. Pretty clever.

As I turned onto Bonita's street, the world suddenly burst into light. Every streetlight, door light, and CLOSED sign beamed on in the same instant, like the lighting of a giant Christmas tree. Suddenly, the street that had seemed so empty felt populated again, even though I didn't see a single soul. The potted geraniums and black-eyed Susans nodded and winked at me from their baskets under the streetlamps, making a splash of color against the steel-gray sky.

I started walking again, briskly, trying not to think about big white dogs with mouths full of teeth. The rain had practically stopped, and I took this as a good sign. Bonita lived at the end of the block in a brick ranch house, just beyond the white-clapboard cluster of shops and businesses and the ice-cream shop. Now, with the lights back on, my purpose seemed clearer than ever. I was speed-walking, so I barely noticed the door to one of the shops swing open.

"If you're trying to race out of town, I'm sorry to tell you, it's too late. You're still going to have to make that speech." Alexa Hinkey stopped me with a wink. Alexa was one of my fellow Woofinstock volunteers. I liked her because she had never once called me "dog hater"—at least not to my face.

Alexa didn't look it, but she was one of the most powerful women in Madrona's good-works community. She ran the Madrona Foundation, which gave out hundreds of thousands of dollars for beneficial projects in town. I say you'd never know it to look at her because she was always dressed as if she hadn't meant to leave the house that day. Sweats, velour pants, shorts—they all played a role in her work wardrobe. I loved this about her. If I thought I could get away with it, I'd go to work in pajamas.

Alexa was currently wearing an oversized Henley shirt with a pair of black stretch pants. As she came through the door, the rest of the Woofinstock Lost Dog Committee tumbled out after: Mayor Park and Malia Jackson with her poodle, Mrs. Sweetie, in her arms. Each carried an emerald green Woofinstock tote bag with a clipboard poking out the top. Within seconds they had me mobbed.

"Superb timing," said Malia, absentmindedly stroking Mrs. Sweetie, who gave me the evil eye. Malia's mud-cloth tunic and kente-cloth scarf were soft and fluid. Malia taught chemical engineering at the college and moonlighted as the conductor of the town's all-volunteer symphony. "We've just been to see Dr. Max, to confirm him as a judge at the Pet-and-Person Beauty Contest tomorrow. He's the emergency contact for our lost-dog committee. We're out dotting all the I's, as you can see. If any dogs go missing this weekend, we have twenty volunteers ready to deploy."

"Dr. Max is so wonderful," gushed Mayor Park, leaning in close enough for me to see the dog hair that covered her black wool jacket. She'd been elected because she promised to make Madrona free to go its own dog-loving way, no matter what the rest of the county thought—though so far she'd lost most of her battles. She also had three Hurricane Katrina dogs. "My bébés say he's the best vet they've ever had."

Hot Max strikes again, I thought. *He must have groupies all over town.*

The women were engrossed in nodding their enthusiasm over Hot Max, all except Alexa, who seemed distracted by something behind me. "Look," she said, "a dog! Pretty white thing. Where's its owner?"

They all turned at once. My canine friend stood about twenty feet off, looking out from behind a blue mailbox. Malia clicked her tongue off her teeth. "Honestly, some people ought to be shot. Letting that dog wander around on her own—she could be hit by a car."

"Or stolen," put in the mayor.

"Or caught by the county animal control squad. You know they let those guys carry *Tasers*?" Alexa's voice turned honey-sweet as she bent down, her sleeve resting on her knee. "Come here, puppy. Come on—let me take a look at you. Do you have tags, hmm? Want to show Auntie Alexa?"

The dog dropped her head, took a few steps forward, then stopped, suspicious. Instantly, the committee sprang into action. All three women crouched down, trying to woo the dog over with singsong voices. They searched their pockets for cookies, spread their hands wide, clapped, wriggled, and shimmied, but nothing worked. The dog just swung her head from side to side, sizing them up.

At last she took one bold step closer. In Malia's arms, Mrs. Sweetie bared her teeth and growled, her whole body shaking. Malia stood back up.

"Mrs. Sweetie has aggression issues because of her size," she whispered to me. "A Napoleon complex. The world sees an adorable lapdog, but in her mind she's the queen of the Amazons." She chuckled. "I hate to say this, ladies, but I think our stray likes Jessica best."

The dog had edged toward my side of the group, but I'd hardly have said it had anything to do with me. She probably just wanted a buffer between her nose and Mrs. Sweetie. Still, all the other women rose and backed away, as if Malia's comment were too obvious to be ignored. They stood perfectly still. I started to say something, but Malia hushed me.

"Give her a chance to make up her mind. And get low, so you don't look so big."

As I crouched down, I suddenly remembered how big the dog's teeth were. Was I sure I wanted her to come closer? I was scared. My feet were wet. I didn't want to be here, in the middle of this. I wanted to work on the café, on getting a new sous chef.

Still, it almost felt as if the iron-gray sky had me pinned in place, there in front of that dog. Then I remembered what Marguerite had said. I needed to face my problem. I owed it to the town. I owed it to myself.

"I have a problem," I mumbled under my breath. "I have a big, big problem."

Amazingly, the dog took a tentative step, then another, angling her body away from the other three. I kept my eyes on the sidewalk, not wanting to spook her. My pulse pounded. Would she come? And if she did, what would I do with her?

Step, step, step—I felt a damp nose on my arm. Stifling the urge to shriek, I reached out my hands and put them on her shoulders. The ladies exhaled in unison.

"Well done," whispered Malia.

I swallowed hard and slid my fingers across the dog's wet fur. Underneath, I felt the warmth of her body. After a day of bills and spreadsheets, of worrying about an unknown future, this dog felt alive in a way that caught me off guard.

I wanted to do the right thing in front of the committee, but I really wasn't sure how to keep the dog there. Should I grab her collar? Tickle her chin? What?

"Wow, she really likes you," Alexa said. When she stood, the knees of her stretch pants bagged. "Do you know her?"

"I, uh—" I paused, unsure what to tell them. "She

had a little run-in with county animal control. I—
um—I lied and said she was my dog so they wouldn't
take her."

A note of approval thrummed through the air. For
a second, joy swelled in my chest and I dared to
hope that the committee and I were edging toward
actual friendship. Until Mayor Park said, "But you
didn't keep her with you? She was wandering loose—
you hadn't leashed her up or anything? You can't just
let a lost dog go like that! Her people are probably
terrified. Plus, she could be hurt. Hit by a car."

"Or stolen," said Malia.

A blush grew on my cheeks. They were absolutely
right. I shouldn't have walked away from the dog—
that had been stupid and irresponsible. It was the
kind of thing a dog hater would do.

"Oh, come on, you guys," Alexa said, inching closer
so she could pet the dog's back. "Jessica was here,
wasn't she? At the vet's office? I think it's pretty obvious that she was bringing this sweet doggie in so Dr.
Max could get a notice posted."

Hot Max—this was his office? This building right
here? My face turned rosy.

"But it isn't still open, is it?" I remembered that he
knew all about my bad reputation and my stomach
tightened.

"Oh, sure," Alexa answered. "Dr. Max always stays
open late around Woofinstock."

I opened my mouth to confess the real truth—that
I'd been heading for Bonita's—but it was too late.
They were already glomming on to Alexa's idea that

I had been bringing the dog to the vet. Before I knew it, the mayor had borrowed a leash from inside the office, hooked it on the dog's collar, and was ushering me inside. I was surrounded.

"But I was headed down to—" I started to say, but I never got to finish because the air flashed blinding white. A sharp crack ripped into my eardrums. The earth shook as thunder rolled through the air and rumbled our bones. Mayor Park screamed, and Mrs. Sweetie started yapping.

"Good Lord! Was that lightning?" Alexa looked like she was shouting, but I could barely hear her. Malia had her hands pressed over Mrs. Sweetie's ears, her face pale.

"It almost hit us!" Trembling, we all staggered inside. Only the white dog seemed unfazed by the lightning.

Once we reached the front desk, the committee collected itself. There was work to be done, a dog in need, and no little thing like lightning would deter them. They guided the dog and me forward as if I were a mother with a newborn. I held back, not so sure I'd be welcome in this building dedicated to canine health. Would Hot Max even speak to me? Or would he pawn me off on one of his colleagues?

The dog pulled on her end of the leash, and I stumbled to the desk, taking in the reception area with its plastic chairs, magazines, and piles of kids' toys in the corner. Alexa was explaining to the receptionist that I had found a stray. Far off in the back, I heard the mayor and Malia regaling someone with our story in loud voices. I tightened my grip on the dog's leash. Whatever was about to happen, the dog and I were in it together. I hoped she would be good to me.

Someone cleared his throat behind me. "Hi there. I'm Dr. Nakamura. You found a lost dog?"

I turned around, my face flaming.

"Oh, hi," he said. "Jessica, right?" He held out his hand. Up close like this, he seemed taller than ever. I jerked my hand forward, stiff as a robot, and almost jumped when our skin touched. His was so warm, and mine was so cold. And wet. And covered in dog fur, not that he seemed to notice. He folded his hand gently around mine and held it there a half beat longer than he had to.

When he released my hand, I felt like I could breathe again. The skin that had touched his was still warm and tingly. I pulled air in, determined to act as much like a sane person as I possibly could. *Please, please, Jess, just act normal!*

Max was wearing a white coat, and suddenly his soccer jerseys made sense. Under his veterinarian's coat, no one could tell what he had on. He could wear some ratty old tee or a tank top or nothing at all. . . .

Normal—come on, normal.

"So," he said, "you found a stray dog?" Malia and the mayor appeared out of nowhere and hovered at his elbows.

"Mm-hmm, she was sitting right in the middle of the street. That's really all I know about her. . . ."

He checked his clipboard. I watched the way his dark eyes darted up and down the page. "Well, why

don't you bring her in and we'll see what we can do."
His smile was bright and easy. Every woman in the
room watched him walk toward the exam room door.
The dog pulled at the leash, ready to follow. I swallowed hard and headed after him.

As I turned to go, Mayor Park stage-whispered,
"Have fun, Jessica. Dr. Max is single!"

A second blush spread across the first. I walked
through the door, not daring to look at Max. The dog
followed. As the doctor closed the door, he gave the
committee a parting wink and a smile—and the three
of us were alone.

4

Stuffed-Animal Heaven

 Zoë

My new friend goes inside a building, so I go in, too. I love going in doors. You never know where you're going to end up when you go through one.

Inside it smells like carpets and people, old papers, cleaner, and nervous dogs. And *cat*. A dog marked on the floor near me, and I wonder if I should do that, too.

Maybe no.

My friend is making talking noises to the other people, so I look around. Nothing here reminds me of home, and none of these people are my mom and dad. There are chairs, like in a house. But no beds. In the corner is a little table and chair, so small they must be for small people. There are books and blocks and—

I tremble slightly. A pile of stuffed animals sits in a crate on the floor. The white rabbit on top is staring at me, challenging me. I've eaten rabbits like this before—I can already taste its fluffy insides. I'm ready to pounce and rip its head *off its bunny body*!

I wiggle my haunches, preparing to spring, but my friend leads me to another door, so naturally I go through to see what's on the other side. We go into a room that's the size of a car. It has a table and counter and chairs. There's a man there, too, and his shoes make a quiet sound, like breathing in and out. She sits down, then she stands up. He says something and she giggles.

We all sit, and she touches my back. Her hands are gentle, and I relax for the first time in a long time. I sink to the floor and pant softly. The room smells worried, but I'm not worried, not right now. Not as long as she keeps stroking that itchy spot on my back. Her fingers seem to be filling me up with some of my old joy.

A door—not the one we came through, but one that smells more like dogs—opens, and a woman in white comes in. Keys jangle at her waist. She takes my leash, and I go with her because I'm curious to see what's on the other side of her door. We go into a hall, where I sit on a black pad and she tells me I'm being weighed. I try to entice the jangly woman into some fun with a play bow and a big smile, but she doesn't look at me. She looks at the wall and writes something on a paper. Then we go back to the room. My friend is still there, which makes me so glad I lick her on the face. She acts like she doesn't like it, but I know she does.

The jangly woman leaves, and we sit. They are talking. I'm sitting.

Sitting, sit-sitting. Sitting.

I try sniffing all the edges and corners. *Boring*.

Yawn.

The man rubs my special spot, between my shoulders, and I pant. He smells strong, like the medicine drawer, and his hands are brusque. I watch him closely to see what he's up to.

My friend turns to me and tells me the man is "Dr. Max." I knew a dog named Max who had a severe slobber problem. I look at Dr. Max carefully and give him a long sniff. He's lucky to be slobber free.

Max has black hair and calluses on his hands. Underneath his clothes, I smell a hint of sweat. That makes me relax. I like to get a good smell of people, of their real smell. Like the way they are when they get out of bed in the morning, not the way they are after a shower—blank and empty.

He talks to my friend for a while. Max looks at her intently when he speaks. She doesn't meet his eyes, but when he turns to look at me, she flashes little glances his way. When Max licks his lips, she licks hers.

I wonder if Max is an alpha dog?

She might be an alpha female. It's hard to tell. They could be an alpha pair. I think he'll mate with her.

I sit down and wait, to see if they do.

Instead, they come over to me. She holds my body, and Max puts a tiny funnel in my ears. It makes me want to growl, but I don't because she's holding me and I don't want to frighten her. He sets a cold disc on my chest and stares at the floor while she pets my back. Then he shines a light in my eyes.

I've had enough and I squirm away.

As they try to catch me, she and Max bump into

each other. He says some words and puts a hand on her shoulder. They both laugh.

Now they're going to mate. I can feel it.

Only they don't. She wraps her arms around me, and he crouches down and squeezes my stomach. He does it gently, but it feels odd, so I try to shake him off. He touches my foot, and I jump. Then Max rubs my shoulders some more.

I'm completely bored with them. If they aren't going to mate, what are they doing? Why are we here?

When the door opens the next time, I'm more than ready to go. Max gives my leash to the jangly woman and tells me I will be "scanned." This is different from last time, when I was "weighed."

Whatever.

Jangly woman takes me past the black pad that I sat on before, past a row of empty cages. She picks up a black paddle and is about to scan me when I see it. *I see it.*

A cat.

I've seen cats before. One, a gray cat named Gobbler, used to live in the house with me—the place where I lived with Mom and Dad, before I got lost and confused.

In a rush, it all blows back to me, like a scent in the wind. I miss my family so much, the missing stabs me. Mom and Dad. I even miss Gobbler.

I have to get home.

When Jangly woman bends over, I jerk myself free and tear down the hall, away from the room that my friend and Max are in. I skid around a corner and fly past a desk. Someone lunges at me, but I veer away. People are shouting. A man is coming in the front door with a cat carrier, but I won't be distracted. I zip out the door at top speed.

I have to get home.

I'm halfway through the door when someone grabs my collar, and I choke myself, stopping. Jangly woman hauls me back inside. I try to squirm away, but she's very solid—clearly an alpha.

Together we go back inside, past the man with the cat carrier, past the desk. Visions of Dad flash in my mind. Dad and Mom. Mom and Dad. Mom and me.

I blink and they're gone.

Then I start to tremble. I shake because I'm so excited. I can see a stuffed animal rabbit, and it's staring right at me!

☕ Jessica

"So," said Max, "you're giving the closing speech at Woofinstock?" He noted things down on his chart, and glanced up at me between words. "Congratulations." Every time I looked at his hands, I thought about skin, and thinking about skin made me remember how warm his was. And how tingly his touch made me feel. So I pulled my eyes away and stared hard at the back of his chart instead.

"Don't congratulate me until it's over." I laughed. "A thousand things could happen between now and Sunday. I could still skip town!"

"Yeah, sure," he said with a smile that made me

feel faint. The door flew open as a vet tech muscled in, hauling the dog by the collar.

"Here she is—there wasn't any microchip."

"Thanks, Emma." Max clicked his tongue softly, and the dog went to him, burying her nose in his palm. "So, what do you think of Zoë?" he asked, nodding to the pair of white ears between us. I had to drag my gaze away from his hands again.

"How do you know her name's Zoë?"

"It's here, on her collar. No tags, but her name's stitched right on it."

"You're kidding." I reached down and touched the red collar around her neck. Sure enough, it said ZOË, plain as day. "Well. You'd think I might have noticed that."

Max shrugged. "I'm sure you've had other things on your mind." He flicked his eyes up at me and suddenly I had a flash of insight. He knew. He knew all about me. I was absolutely sure of it. My heart sped up a notch. For the first half of the dog's exam, I'd thought maybe he didn't, that I'd miraculously skated free. But there was something in the glint of his black eyes that told me he knew everything. And when he said I'd had other things on my mind, I knew he meant the overwhelming multitude of things that went with a dog-phobic person trying to make amends with a giant white canine named Zoë.

For a minute, I felt positively naked. How could he have understood so much about me when we'd only spoken for the first time that morning? To shield myself, I bent down and looked more closely at the dog's collar, then touched her shoulder with two fingertips.

Max rose and stepped back, put Zoë's chart on the counter, and folded his arms. "Now let's talk about Zoë. She might have a family out there somewhere. I can get her posted on websites and in the paper, but where can she stay in the meantime? Can you take her?"

Me? Me—take a dog? He had to be kidding. Didn't he know I was renowned as a dog hater? I waited a minute, but no one laughed, not even the dog.

"Um, I think you know that I'm not really a dog person."

Max chuckled softly, then his face turned serious. "Well, we can board her, but it might be rough. Even the most stable dogs have a hard time being boarded. Foster families just work so much better, especially for people-loving dogs like Zoë." He paused for a second. "If it's about having enough time, I could help you out. This must be a busy weekend for you. I could take her for a couple of hours every day." He ran his hand under Zoë's chin, and she looked at him adoringly. "I think Zoë would do a lot better in a home than she would at the kennel."

I froze. The walls seemed to be closing in. While I hesitated, Max studied my face in a way that made me squirm.

I have a problem, whispered a voice inside my head, *a big, big problem.* Marguerite had said I needed to fix my problem. But *now*? Did it have to be now? With the café in such a fragile state and Woofinstock staring me right in the face? I looked down at the dog, and she looked up at me, her brown eyes filled with light and hope. And I caved. Just like that. This dog terrified me in fifteen ways, but at my deepest gut level, I felt sorry for her and wanted to help. And that's the level that did the talking.

"Okay," I said, so quietly I could barely hear myself. "Okay. I'll try."

"And I'll help." Max gave me a cheekbone-arcing smile that was a reward in itself. Still, my mouth went dry with panic.

"How hard can it be, right?" I asked nervously. "I'll just get some dog food on the way home. And, um, a leash."

"I can take care of that part," said Max, standing. He reached into a cupboard and produced a red fabric leash that he snapped on Zoë's collar. "There." As he held it out to me, his fingers touched the back of my hand. An electrical charge shot through me, all the way to my core. If he touched me one more time, I was pretty sure I would melt. "You're ready to go," he said softly. Then, just as I gathered my wits and began to take the leash, he pulled it back. "You really aren't a dog hater, are you?"

"Of course not." I laughed, praying that I sounded sincere. "Just a little scared of them. I was having the worst day, I swear." His dark eyes followed me, but I couldn't tell what he was thinking. I swallowed, and not because he was so cute. "I really want to make this work. I'll take good care of her, I promise."

"All right." He held out the leash again, and I took the other end. For a second, we both stood there.

"Um, are there directions?"

He grinned. "You'll do fine. Just pay attention to her. She'll let you know what she needs. And be sure to take her outside for plenty of potty breaks. She's old enough to be house-trained, but you never know."

He let go of his end of the leash, and he and Zoë both looked at me expectantly.

I licked my lips. Was it too late to back out? "This is just until we hear from her family, right?"

"Right. It's not forever. Just for now."

I took the leash, feeling like he'd just handed me the keys to the *Titanic*.

 Zoë

We go through a door and it takes us . . . outside! I love all doors, but my favorites are the ones that lead outside. I'll never understand why people insist on spending so much time indoors. Don't they realize how alive the wind and sun make you feel?

The second my friend opens the door, I feel a rush of cool air on my face, making my breath quicken. It's windy, and the wind tickles my nose. It'll be dark soon.

I sniff the bushes and look for the best places to leave my mark. People act as if dogs can just go any old place, but they don't understand that peeing is only a piece of the process. Leaving my scent behind in a place where another dog will find it—that's the real goal. I hunker over a patch of marigolds, some brown grass near the door, and a pile of gravel that carries the scent of about fifty dogs.

Just to make sure everyone knows I was there, I scratch the gravel, rubbing my paws carefully on the ground as I kick it up behind me. Now no one can miss my mark, even if they're in the middle of chasing a squirrel.

Hmm, squirrel? My heart skips as I check the parking lot for squirrels. I check every bush and shadowy corner.

No squirrels here.

Now that the marking is done, I take a look at my friend to see what's going to happen next. So far she's taken me on a long walk and brought me to meet the man who smells like dogs. I think she might give me a cookie next. Or pet me some more. Especially if I put my extra-cute face on. Cocking my ears gets people every time.

My friend seems nervous, though, and distracted, like she's thinking about something else. Maybe she misses her family, like I do. I look around to see if they're here, but they're not. And still no squirrels. So I sit down with a sigh and watch my friend, who's fiddling with my leash. If I could talk, I'd tell her it's just a leash, not a life-or-death decision.

"I wonder if I've made a huge mistake," she says. I come closer and lick her fingers, which makes her smile. "I don't even like dogs. What am I doing with you? I don't care if I am just a foster parent or whatever they're called—here I am, leashed to a dog. No offense—this isn't about you, personally. It's just dogs. Dogs and I don't really blend. You have all those teeth, and I never know what you're going to do next." She sighed. "Just be nice to me, okay? Please?"

I have no idea what she's talking about, but I listen patiently. And cock my ears even farther, in case there's a cookie coming.

She sighs and stands, the leash dangling between us. I lift my head and give her a long look. Her body language is unclear, like she's trying to communicate fifty things at the same time. I wish I understood people better.

When we start going, I trail behind her heels because it's dark and I want to keep one eye out for squirrels. It isn't raining very much, but it's windy. Sometimes thunder booms and makes us both jump. When lightning flashes, she gets scared. I'm not normally afraid of lightning, but seeing her look so worried makes me nervous.

She leads us down a street that smells like rottweilers, then up one that smells like cats. The next road has pee spots from a Westie puppy and a pregnant dog. We're in the big cobblestoned square with a metal dog in it, and the wind is so strong, it knocks branches out of the trees. One almost hits me, so I dash ahead, pulling her with the leash. She says something, but I'm not paying attention. I want to get to that metal dog and hide inside his doghouse.

Thunder crashes and I change my mind about racing ahead. I run up to her legs, my ears pressed back against my head. She puts a hand on my back. I lean in closer.

On the other side of the square, a tree falls down and the ground shakes. I bark one time, then a second, and a third, just to be safe. I want to run off, but she holds my collar and keeps me close. Okay, now I'm scared. It's too dark to see anything except the metal dog and his metal eyes.

At least I'm not alone.

Without any warning—not even a growl—a blast
of pain sears through my feet. There's a flash of light
that's so strong, I can't see.

Then I fall. And the world turns black.

5

On the Other Paw

 Jessica

I woke up on the ground, my muscles cramping with pain. Everything about me felt pummeled and crushed, like I'd been squashed by a stampeding cow. Somehow, I was able to move. I stumbled to my feet, utterly blind. My eyes were open, but all I could see were the shimmery remnants of a brilliant flash.

What happened?

I remembered a hot bolt of pain, then a flash and the sense of being riveted to the ground. I knew I was in Midshipman's Square, halfway home. My mind flicked through memories, trying to piece it all back together. I remembered talking with Max—had he actually touched my hand? I could recall firing Guy, leaving the café, talking to that strange white dog. The last thing I remembered was looking down at a leash in my hand. Right, the dog was with me and her name was Zoë. Had I really agreed to care for her until her family appeared? Apparently, I had. But that was in the past—what had hurt me so badly?

My vision was improving—I could make out the blurry outlines of vine maples around the square. As my ears recovered, I heard the wind whistling around the buildings' corners. The air seemed thick with smells. I detected mud, wet newspaper, meat grilling, and . . . bubblegum? My nose couldn't stop sniffing. I lifted my head and looked for Zoë, blinking hard, but I couldn't spot her. All I could make out was a human form on the ground wearing khakis and a blue raincoat. And . . . espadrilles?

I tried to run to the fallen body, but my feet weren't working. Every time I straightened my legs, I stumbled onto my face. Did the flash break my legs? Was I paralyzed? I looked down to see what the problem was, but my eyes had wigged out again—all I could see were two hairy paws.

Dog paws. Where my feet were supposed to be.

I reached down for them, but something was wrong with my hands—they felt like they were already on the pavement—and my face was uncomfortably close to the ground. This was not right, not right at all. I reached out for the ground again and saw the right paw slap the pavement in a rhythm that matched my movement.

Whoa.

I sat back down and squeezed my eyes shut. I heard my own breath and tried to concentrate on that and nothing else. *You're alive. It's okay. You're going to be okay.* Still, even as my mind whispered the words, I could tell something was different. The air had changed around me. It was several degrees warmer and full of smells—rich, soupy smells—like I'd just landed in a tropical country. My eyes flew open, relieved to see the familiar square with its sleeping storefronts. I turned my gaze upward. There was Orion, the hunter constellation with his sagging belt, peeping out between two clouds. To my right I could see the clock over the jewelry shop, and Spitz's bronze head. Yes, I was definitely still in Madrona.

Then I made the mistake of glancing down at the white paws again. They were still there, toes curved toward the cobblestones. White hairs covered them like feathers, all tidily brushed in the same direction. They might have been pretty if they hadn't been where I expected my hands to be.

Air came out of my mouth in frantic puffs. *Don't freak out, don't freak out.* In a rush, I tried to stand up again, but apparently I was already on my feet. The second I realized I was standing on four legs instead of two, I went ahead and freaked all the way out.

Dog feet—why am I on dog feet? Why am I so low to the ground? Is this a dream? Am I dead?

I didn't feel dead. I felt very, very alive in this scent-filled world. So it had to be a dream. After all that time at the vet's office, I was dreaming that I *was* a dog. That was it. Simple psychology, right?

Still, if I was dreaming, why was the rain getting me wet? Why did I have to pee? And why was the wind so cold when it ruffled my . . . fur?

Oh no. I'm going to throw up.

I must have injured my head. That was the answer. When I fell, I hit my head and now I was seeing things that weren't actually there. I'd read about crazy things happening to people after accidents, like losing all their short-term memory and forgetting how to talk. I must be imagining things. I'd probably snap out of it in a minute or two, right back to normal.

If I could just get home to rest, this would all be okay. I just had to get moving—that was the first step.

Moving turned out to be easier than I'd expected. Maybe my head injury wasn't so severe after all? My feet were clammy, and I was panting hard, but I went forward without any problem. A part of me knew that, as a good citizen, I should check that fallen body, but I was too afraid of what I would find. Instead I hurried toward the edge of the square, trying to keep my eyes focused forward. If I looked at the ground and saw those white paws flashing, I knew I'd throw up. Moving felt good, so I concentrated on action. Without thinking about it, I found myself jogging to the Glimmerglass, right up to the glass French doors. With the glow of a streetlamp behind me, I could get a rough view of myself.

That was when I felt genuine fear. The image in the window rippled, illuminated by the streetlamp, the stars, and the quarter moon that looked down from the ink-black sky. A shudder passed through me, and I tried to look away, but my eyes were drawn back, sickly fascinated.

I saw white ears, a white face, and a long, white, tapered nose. My teeth curved like meat-tearing machines. A damp black nose quivered as I exhaled. My breath cast a foggy cloud on the glass.

I gave in to panic and peed.

*I*t took me a long time to work up enough nerve to investigate the body in the blue raincoat. Even from a distance I could recognize my own limbs and torso. Those were my hands flopped across the zipper. It was my dark brown hair that splayed around the turned head. But if I was here, then what was there? A blob of goo? Some kind of monster? Nothing at all?

What if my body was dead?

Or maybe none of this was real. Maybe I was hallucinating, seeing the world through a haze, even though everything looked perfectly sharp. This could be a side effect of the head trauma.

No matter how scared I was, I decided I needed to check on that person. They could be badly hurt—I could help. I had to investigate, even if I was seeing things that didn't exist.

My heart rammed against my rib cage as I edged up sideways and nudged the raincoat arm with my nose. It lifted and fell the way a human arm would. Panting hard, I stepped forward for a better look.

There lay my own face, cheek resting on the pavement. I exhaled a thick breath, trying to work through my panic. There were my eyes, set above my cheeks and mouth and chin. My hands were crumpled at my chest. A little frisson slid through me as I watched myself breathing.

This is too weird. I really am going to vomit.

Still, I couldn't look away. It couldn't be true, I reminded myself. Unless I was dead, there was no way I could be looking at my own body. And so far, I did not feel dead.

I bent down to peer at my face. Wow, did I have a funny-looking nose. Who knew it was so . . . pointy? I trotted around to my body's other side, so I could see myself face-on. I looked different than I did in the mirror—my face was narrower and more off-kilter, as if I was looking with one eye shut. A smear of hair covered my cheek. I reached down and nudged the human face.

6

One Paw Forward

 Zoë

I wake up and can hear myself whining.

Owww. Everything hurts.

Ow, ow. Maybe I should sleep some more.

I try to, but something keeps licking my face. I paw it away, and it yelps.

Good. I hope it leaves me alone so I can sleep.

Except now I'm awake. I stretch and roll over onto my belly, then try to stand up. Only something's wrong. When I stand up, my butt sticks up in the air. And my paws are cold. Freezing cold. They feel strange—soft. I drop my head to take a look.

These are the wrong paws.

 Jessica

I'm in the worst horror film of all time.

I just saw my own body walk up to me on all fours, its bottom stuck up in the air like a mutant crab. I knew this had to be my head playing tricks on me, but I couldn't help it—I yelped and ran behind Spitz. No creature from the deep was eating me for lunch, even if it was just a figment of my imagination.

A sick feeling swirled around my belly as I watched. The body froze in downward-dog position, staring at its hands. Then it pushed off hard, bounced into the air, wavered, and fell, flat on its face. If I was hallucinating, I was cooking up some wild stuff.

Just then, my neck developed a vicious itch. I mean a fiery, devastating itch—the kind you couldn't ignore if your life depended on it. I tried scratching with one hand, then the other, and, weirdly, had to settle for using my right foot. I was surprised by how healthy I felt. Maybe I was in shock? I'd thought an injury like mine would have left me crumpled on the ground, not spry and flexible.

When I checked on the body again, it was up on two feet, lurching around like a zombie. It seemed to be aiming for the Glimmerglass, but it veered off course and accelerated across the square, until one foot tangled up with the other. Down it went, face-first.

This had to stop. No matter whose body that was (and it couldn't *really* be mine—could it?), I had to help it before it broke its nose in fifty places. Maybe we should both go to my apartment. We could re-cover there in safety. Maybe if I could sleep or sit down or meditate or something, I could straighten out my brain.

I suppose it might seem weird that I considered taking this stranger home with me. Injured or not, she could have turned out to be a crazed psycho killer. But what can I say—I wasn't really thinking clearly. And besides, she looked like me. Exactly like me. I couldn't leave her out there in the square.

Summoning my courage, I left my hiding place. The body was halfway up to standing and making good progress, but when it saw me, it lost its balance and flopped over again.

I sat down to wait. Once the body was almost stable on two feet, I ran across the square in the direction of home and then ran back to the body, trying to get it to follow. It lumbered forward, arms flailing. I zipped from one side to the other, nudging it a little to the right, a little to the left. And once, when it almost fell, I let it catch its balance by using my head as a prop.

We set off down the street. I tried hard to not be creeped out by the whole situation—for now, at least, I had to stay focused. The body alternated between walking straight into storefront windows and wandering into the street. I did my best to keep it on the sidewalk, but, to be honest, I was having a hard enough time with my own feet. Walking went well enough as long as I forgot to think about what I was doing. Once my mind engaged—and started thinking about how many feet I had and what part of this was a hallucination—I got all twisted up.

Amazingly, we managed to cover the two blocks between the Glimmerglass and my apartment building without seeing anyone. I led us around the back, trying not to watch as the body hit its head on a low-hanging branch. Together we made it across the building's little courtyard and up to my sliding glass door, which my body walked straight into. Like a stunned bird, it reeled back a few paces, caught its balance, and came trucking forward for a second try.

Oh, no.

Heart pounding, I heaved up onto my back feet, put both front paws on the sliding glass door handle, and pushed with all my might. The door slid open just as the human body stumbled through and fell head-long onto the couch.

*H*ave you ever had one of those nightmares that clings to you even after you've opened your eyes? I had one of those—a bizarre, *Twilight Zone* kind of dream that was so vivid it felt even more real than reality. In my dream, I was a dog. Only it wasn't like dreaming that I was a dog—I actually *felt like* a dog. I saw my own fur and paws and everything. And that was only half of it.

It was only a dream, I told myself, trying to shake off the residual echoes. *Only a dream.*

I yawned and looked around. I was at home, in my own apartment. A pale beam of morning sunlight splashed across the living room floor, where I lay. And I itched all over. I reached up to rub my eyes and was surprised to get a paw in the face.

Oh, no.

No, no, please no.

Horror pumped through my veins as I jumped up and paced the kitchen floor, my nails clicking. This couldn't be happening. *Couldn't* be. Why was I still seeing things? Maybe my head wound was really deep—so severe that I'd blasted away all my nerve endings and couldn't even feel that I was injured.

I wasn't in pain, but everything about me felt awkward, like I'd been taken apart and put back together by Dr. Moreau. My legs were too short and turned oddly, so I had to go on all fours like a gorilla. My wrists were bent at a funny angle. Everything had a dim, washed-out look, as if I'd stepped into the black-and-white part of *The Wizard of Oz*. And something furry—a tail?—kept slapping the backs of my legs.

It was one thing, I thought, for my brain to whip up false visions. But if this was all just a hallucination, then how could I feel the fur bristling on my body? How was I walking on four feet? It really seemed like I could move that tail around at will. This didn't feel much like a hallucination to me.

In fact, it all felt incredibly real. My apartment was thick with smells. I could smell the shampoo I'd used the day before and my lemon-and-lavender dish soap. Shoot, I could even smell the *carpet*.

If I could have wept, I would have.

Jess, you just need to calm down and think this thing through. I tried to replay exactly what had happened the night before. I'd been walking home with Zoë when we were hit by lightning. That much seemed based in fact. But what had happened in that blast? Either I was dead and trapped in my own twisted circle of hell or I'd been badly injured and was dreaming all of this.

Of course, there was another explanation, but it was so ludicrous I didn't even want to voice it to myself. I could have experienced some bizarre, cosmic disaster, some kind of intense out-of-body experience. But that just didn't seem likely.

I padded around the kitchen, trying to figure out what to do. Should I call the doctor? Try a shrink? Alert the federal government? *So hard to know what's best.* And hard to concentrate. An amazing smell kept distracting me. What was that, ketchup? Tomato sauce?

I lowered my nose, inching along the space where the cabinets met the floor.

The tomato smell was stronger there, touching off highlights and lowlights in my nose like a fine wine. The bouquet was so strong that a blazing image of a tomato was all that fit into my brain.

I pressed my nose farther down the tiles, stretching my body and pushing with my hind feet. There! A shriveled, rock-hard cherry tomato sat forlornly on the tile. My mouth was halfway to it when I stopped myself. *No, Jess—no eating things off the floor. Come on, get a grip!*

With incredible self-restraint, I pushed myself up off the floor and steered my four feet to the couch. That tomato might be calling, but I had bigger things to consider. It was time to see what that body was up to.

 Zoë

I'm so comfortable. I'm dreaming that I'm on the world's biggest dog bed. Billowing cushions cradle my shoulder blades. Ahhhhh.

I roll over, rubbing my spine into the sofa. Roll,

roll, roll. I stretch out and give my legs a kick, enjoying how long I am. I'm the longest dog in the world. I'm the queen of longness. And tallness. Longness and tallness combined.

I stretch, feeling soft pillows underneath my body. My eyes pop open.

WOW. Things look *strange*. Very strange.

I stare at the world around me. I see everything perfectly—the poodle-brown walls, the Labrador-yellow shelves, the sky-blue curtains. I'm lying on a RED couch. For a minute I wonder if it's magic. I've never seen red like that. It's so intense and yummy looking.

I go back to rolling. I've never been allowed on a sofa before, and I'm glad to find that it's just as wonderful as it looks.

The cushions massage my spine almost as well as a pair of human hands.

Hmmm.

I'm thirsty. Time to explore.

☕ Jessica

The body looked exactly the same as it had the night before—like my twin. As I watched, feeling slightly nauseous, the body staggered off the couch and onto its feet. It wobbled but held, wavering from side to side. Then it grinned at me and set out for the bathroom. I followed, sure something awful was about to happen. I mean, what good could come of a trip to the bathroom—*with* your body, but not *in* it?

Stumbling across the threshold, my body lunged for the toilet, conked its head on a shelf, and dropped to its knees. With one hand, it pried the toilet seat open. Then it dropped its head—my head—into the toilet and tried to drink.

Ew! I ran in a circle and started to howl, but the body kept on drinking. Out of the toilet. Like a dog.

Like a dog.

Realization hit me so hard I fell backward onto my tail. Could it be . . . ? No. No, it couldn't. No matter how much evidence pointed in that direction, it just wasn't possible. No way. No how.

But . . . could it? I peered closely at the body. It did look exactly like me—me, acting like a dog. And here I was, feeling for all the world like a human trapped in a dog's body. Now my head *was* starting to hurt.

I closed my eyes and tried to sort out the facts. It was absolutely impossible that I had switched bodies with a dog. And yet, as I watched my body try to groom its arm with its tongue, I had to wonder.

The second I opened the door to the idea, a million scary thoughts shot through my brain. How could I be a dog? If I was trapped in a dog's body, what would become of me? Would I ever see Kerrie and the Glimmerglass again? I thought of all the things I'd always wanted to do—play the guitar, go salsa dancing, learn to knit. Someday I'd planned to retire and volunteer with the Boys and Girls Club. I couldn't do any of those things with paws!

Terror made my vision fuzzy. The more I thought, the higher-pitched my internal voice became. How could I date? A vision of Max flashed through my mind and I groaned. I'd never meet anyone and fall in love, not like this. I couldn't kiss anyone. I couldn't run the café. I couldn't even type. Or talk on the phone. Shoot, I couldn't speak at all.

And what about dogs' short life spans? My life expectancy couldn't have suddenly dropped to fourteen. Could it?

I paced in circles, gasping for air. *This is it—this is the end.* I never expected to go out like this. It wasn't as if I had died, I was just . . . hidden. In a furry body. Destined to die young. Talk about creepy.

I didn't want to believe it, but the truth was staring me right in the face. I was in a dog's body. And Zoë was in mine.

Before I could fully process the thought, Zoë was up on her feet again, dancing around like a lunatic. Using my body like a human fun-suit, she chomped my teeth, rolled my eyes, swung my arms in circles, and waggled my knees like a chicken's. She stood on one leg. She did karate kicks and deep knee bends. She jumped and punched the air. Then she lost her balance and fell on her ass.

Enough was enough. *This abuse ends here,* I vowed. *I'm getting my body back.*

Zoë

I have to take a deep breath, because an amazing thing has happened.

I'm a person.

I have *hands.* Hands and people feet and hair that

hangs down off the top of my head. Talk about unexpected. I've never turned into another kind of animal before.

Still, a piece of me isn't surprised. I've always known I'd make a great person. I've been watching them drive cars for years—or at least for both of the years I've been alive. This is going to be great.

She doesn't look so happy about being a dog, though. Which is ridiculous, since she's not just any dog—she's me. And she's in my body, one of the prettiest in the world. Honestly, I can't take my eyes off myself. I'm such an adorable dog. Just look at my ears!

It's clear that I can't spend all day admiring my dog body, though—not when I have a human one at my disposal. The person body isn't as easy to operate as it seemed. How do people keep from tipping over? I don't like standing up so high on just two legs. Honestly, it's a bad design. I'm surprised I haven't seen more people fall on their faces. I've tried going on all fours—hands and feet—but that's wrong, too. My hands get tired and my back end feels weird, sticking up in the air like that. Plus I have no tail. And I'm so cold. Where's my fur?

Also, this tongue is no good at drinking.

I'm doing kicks again when it occurs to me—*maybe I can talk*. Why not? I'm a person, right? Dogs bark, cats meow, people talk. They're always opening their mouths to blabber at each other. People get mad at dogs for barking, but that's only because they've never stopped to listen to themselves. They speak constantly—it's like they can't help talking.

If they can do it, why can't I?

I shift my mouth around. My tongue is different than normal—shorter and thicker. I test my lips by making some shapes. Duck lips, twisted lips, smoochie lips. She's staring at me in amazement, like I just created a hamburger out of nothing. I show her my lip tricks. Then I clear my throat and make a little sound. It sounds like "mmm," which I think is a very good start.

I hum some more to warm up. There. I'm ready to say the words that all dogs have wanted to say since the dawn of time.

"I'm hungry."

I'm so irritated, I'm about to bite somebody.

If there's one thing I know, it's that people always have food. *Good* food, too, not just dried-up kibble. They keep it in the kitchen, the room with the slippery floors. It's always that way. It's a people law.

So here I am, in a person body, standing in the kitchen, yet I can't find food anywhere. This is unbelievable. I feel a million new things flooding into my brain, but they're mostly words. Words, words, words. When do we get to the food? I've sniffed the entire room, but I can't pick up a single scent. Everything smells like lemon cleanser. I can't even see anything that looks edible—just square-shaped boxes that I can't open. Excuse me, but food isn't square. Where does she keep the *good* stuff?

I spend some time investigating the big white cold thing that sits in the corner. It hums, which I thought might mean that it's important. I have to use my teeth and an elbow to get the door open and then I'm blasted with cold. I shiver and stick my head in for a closer look, but there's nothing good inside, just a bag, some boxes, round plastic things, and drawers. No food.

I lean even farther into the big white cold thing and sniff around, but there are no smells. At last, I reach in and grab something—anything—and throw it on the floor. It doesn't break, so I use my foot to stomp on it. Pink goo oozes out. Success! I get down on my hands and knees and lick the pinkness up off the floor.

Mmm, strawberry yogurt. I'm a genius.

Except that I get dust and a piece of dog hair on my tongue.

When I've licked it all, I stand up and go back to the big white cold thing. I have my hands on a sloshy white carton, when she starts barking and prancing around like her tail's on fire.

"What?" I ask her. "What are you trying to say?"

She barks again, and I frown. Barks come in a thousand varieties, but the sound Jessica's making means nothing to me. It's not a play bark, not a warning or a bark of alarm. It's not the kind of showing-off bark you'd give when you're in a car and you see another dog that isn't.

I frown at her. "Please don't do that in public," I say. She looks at me with shocked eyes. I try to explain. "You sound like a person pretending to bark. If other dogs hear you do that, they'll think there's something wrong with you."

She closes her mouth and stops barking. As I turn back to the big white cold thing, I decide that I'm being too hard on her. Barking is more difficult than talking, after all. Of course she'll need to practice before she's ready to bark in public. Besides, even if she did sound like a cross between a horn and a cow, she was probably trying to tell me something useful about the big white cold thing. It might have been about what not to eat.

Keeping my eye on her, I reach into the big white cold thing and put my hand on the plastic bag with bread inside. She doesn't bark, just flops on the floor and sighs, which I take as a good sign. I smoosh the bag against the counter and rip it with my teeth. The plastic tastes like nothing, but the bread is delicious. I eat the whole loaf and a bit of plastic, too.

The rest of the plastic falls on the floor. She gives it a sad sniff.

"Ah-ha-ha, you're hungry!" I say. "Of course you are. Now you can see how it is to be a dog and feel hungry all the time—and watch people eat good stuff like bread and sausages and pepperoni pizza. Well. You're a dog." I can't help smiling. "You can eat what dogs eat."

☕ Jessica

Not having vocal cords is the pits. I'm about to be very depressed.

Zoë clearly thought it would be a good joke to make me eat dog food, but the joke was on her. I didn't have any dog food in the house. Besides, breakfast wasn't my top concern. I needed my body back. Today—Saturday—was the first day of Woofinstock. I didn't have a second to waste.

While Zoë crouched on the floor, looking at the cat figurine I kept near the philodendron, I crept up behind her. This all started with a moment of violence and pain, so it stood to reason that we needed both things to reverse the process. Backing up a few steps, I got a running start and rammed straight into her.

"Yow!" she shrieked as we tumbled and skidded across the floor. "What was that for?"

Just trying to put the world back to normal. Sheesh.

Zoë smacked at my paws. "What's wrong with you? Are you trying to kill me?" She frowned and rubbed her arm. "Don't you know how lucky you are? You're a dog! You have *four* feet. Everyone loves dogs. Why are you like this?"

There's something very disconcerting about sitting on the floor, being lectured by a dog. I don't know anyone who's emotionally balanced enough to take that. I stuck out my tongue at Zoë, but that just made her laugh.

Yeah, well, I can lick my own butt if I want to.

The way Zoë was rubbing her wrist caught my eye and drew my attention to the watch she was wearing. *Oh, shit.* It was eight o'clock already. Eight o'clock on the first day of Woofinstock.

I had to get to the café.

7

Short-Order Dog

 Jessica

I didn't have time for Zoë's shenanigans. There were a million things to do at the Glimmerglass, and they all depended on me. I had to find a sous chef, get Naomi squared away, and make sure our team got the stand set up at the Farmer's Market. At last year's Woofin-stock, we sold over a hundred espresso drinks at the market. And—shit, shit, shit—I had to find out if our electricity was back on.

My stomach's on fire—is this an ulcer?

I wanted to spend my time getting out of this dog body, but that was just going to have to wait. The Glimmerglass came first. Not that I thought I could do much "work" in my furry, four-legged state. I'm not an idiot. But I had to try. I had to hold onto the one thing that still felt normal, and that was work. If I could just get to the café, I could stop panicking for a minute.

I used my paws to push the sliding glass door open and raced outside. Zoë yelled something behind me, but I didn't stop to listen. I didn't have time. Instead, I put my four paws to work. Running fast enough to create my own breeze, I darted up the shortcut to the square. The wind blew in my face, ruffling my fur. The breeze felt delicious, and it made me want to go faster. And then there was that smell—what was it? Fried eggs . . . warm syrup . . . and, oh my God, *bacon!*

Rounding the corner into Midshipman's Square, I nearly knocked down a pair of kids with a shaggy little dog. I veered away instinctively. The dog tried to trail after me, but I ran on. I flew past Spitz, past a group of people handing carrot cookies to their dogs, and up to the Glimmerglass door.

Rising on my back feet, I pushed the door open and darted inside. The power was on! I looked around and spotted two customers in the dining room. Great. Woofinstock had already started and we had a grand total of two dine-in customers. Well, that was two more than we'd had yesterday.

At least the staff seemed calm. Sahara had the espresso counter under control, and our server, Whitney, was chitchatting with the two breakfast customers. I ran around the back of the bar to check the supplies, nudging boxes with my nose. Plenty of coffee, plenty of ground espresso. Whipped cream was getting low. The bin of pumpkin cookies needed replenishing. All under control for the moment, but trouble was just one big rush away.

I turned and headed for the kitchen. Somebody said, "Hey, that's a cute dog," and a customer tried to pet me as I jogged by, but I kept my head down. I shoved my nose between the swinging doors and pushed my way into the kitchen. The smells there were so intense, they almost knocked me over. Naomi sweated over the stove, flipping omelets and browning cottage fries. My mouth started to water. The only thing that saved me was the sight of Kerrie clicking her phone shut.

"She still isn't answering," Kerrie told Naomi. "I'd run over to her place, but there's no time. If we run out of pumpkin cookies, we won't have anything to sell at the booth." She was turning back to the mixer when she spotted me.

"Oh, no, not in the kitchen, doggie. In fact, you'd better go all the way out. If Jess arrives and sees you here, she might be too scared to enter the building." Her voice dropped a notch as she caught hold of my collar. "Pretty as you are."

Kerrie pulled me through the kitchen door. I whined and pawed at her leg, but she didn't give in. Kerrie was a mom—she knew how to enforce a rule once she set it. She yanked me through the front doors and deposited me on the cobblestones. "You stay out here, cutie," she said. "I'll have to talk to the staff about not letting dogs in this morning. We have to be careful, at least until Jess shows up and gets settled."

Ah, Kerrie. How sweet she was to protect me like that. But not right now!

She dropped her voice to a whisper. "It's weird for her to be this late. She must have burned the candle at both ends last night, hunting for a sous chef." My heart sank with guilt. I hadn't found us a sous chef last night. I hadn't fixed any of our problems. Instead, I'd let myself get sidetracked into saving a dog and flirting with Hot Max.

Kerrie crouched down and stroked the fur on my neck. "I worry about her burning out, you know? She works so hard. Sometimes I think she's trying to earn her place here, make herself super valuable so she'll be completely safe. Which is silly, of course, but understandable if you know about her past. Her mom abandoned her—can you imagine?" Kerrie shook her head. "How any mother can do that is beyond me. I could barely let JJ go to preschool without going crazy."

Underneath my fur, my cheeks burned. Kerrie was right—all too right. I did try to make myself irreplaceable at the café, and it probably did have something to do with being left by my mom. Though I didn't think any of it was as straightforward as it seemed to Kerrie. I also enjoyed my work, and I liked helping people. If I could take on a job for Kerrie and lighten her load, that gave me real joy. It wasn't all about my screwed-up childhood.

Still, I couldn't help but think of that darned purple envelope. It was sitting on my desk inside the café. Unopened.

I wish I'd burnt it.

I shook my head to clear my thoughts. More than anything, I wanted to stand up on two feet and march into the Glimmerglass, ready to take the weekend by storm. I was eyeing the front door when my eyes caught sight of a pair of espadrilles flopping across the courtyard.

Kerrie abandoned me in a flash. "Jess—there you are! Where have you been? Do you know what time it is?"

Zoë stopped and turned, speaking to both Kerrie and me at once. "No. What time is it?"

I heaved a nervous breath. For all the time I'd spent trying to figure out how to do my job as a dog, I hadn't considered that Zoë might show up at the café. Wearing the same crumpled clothes I had on yesterday. Wait, was her shirt inside out? Well, she was a dog—I guess I should be grateful that she wasn't naked.

Kerrie whipped back her sleeve and displayed the watch on her wrist. "It's eight-fifteen!"

Zoë cocked her eyebrows as if this were very interesting information, indeed. "Well, I'm here now." She gave us a thousand-watt smile and winked at me.

Kerrie watched this, her forehead crumpled. "Here and weird," she said. "Um, do you want me to take this dog away? Has it got you worried? Because I can make it go if it's troubling you."

Zoë shrugged. She nodded at me. "She's fine. No worries. But we're both hungry. Are there cookies here?"

"What do you mean, are there cookies here?" Kerrie's frown grew deeper. "Did you find a sous chef? Don't you want to know if the power's on? It is, thank God. But what did Bonita say? Has anyone called in response to your flyers?"

Zoë cocked her head to one side as if she didn't understand a thing Kerrie was saying but wanted to look like she was making an effort. I had to do something. Zoë didn't have answers to Kerrie's questions—at least not real answers. I gave a quick little bark. When they turned to look at me, I barked again and wagged my tail. I had both of their attention. Maybe the best thing I could do was to get Zoë into the restaurant—at least then Kerrie wouldn't feel like she was steering the ship all alone.

I ran up behind Zoë and barked a third time, shoving my nose at the backs of her knees. Kerrie gasped, but Zoë laughed at me.

"Okay, okay," she said. As she stumbled toward the café door, she turned and looked over her shoulder. She pointed at the place where lightning struck us and mouthed, "Right there." I looked back at the spot, too. It was utterly innocuous in the sunshine, just a stretch of cobblestones under a September sky. A shiver passed through me. It was haunting to think that such a momentous, life-altering thing had happened—right there—and no one knew but Zoë and me.

If only I could turn back time—just a little—and skip that one awful moment. We could have taken a different route home. Could have walked around the square instead of through it. Would that have been enough to change things? Or would the lightning have found us anyway? Just thinking about it made me angry, so I turned my attention back to Zoë, who'd just spotted the two kids with their shaggy dog. "Hey—who's that?"

I shoved even harder.

"Geez, I'm going, I'm going. Why are you guys in such a hurry? Oh, look—a door!" In a burst of excitement, Zoë ran across the threshold, tripped, caught her balance, and bounced through, her arms up like a gymnast landing a vault. "Ta-da!"

but at least they're good at taking me places fast. The second I clear the door, my legs lead me straight to a table that's full of food—people food. At last, this is exactly what I've been looking for. The table is full of muffins and waffles and ham and eggs and canta-loupe and big cups of brown, smelly liquid.

"Hey!" says a man who's also eating from the table.

"Hey yourself," I say, my mouth full of waffle. He looks annoyed, so I offer him the muffin that's in my hand, but he squirms away like I'm giving him cat fur. You'd think the competition alone would make him eat. People are bizarre.

"What the hell," he says, thumping his fork on the table. "You're eating my food."

"If it's yours," I say, "you shouldn't leave it out here, unwatched like this. Anyone could come along and take it. You have to *guard* it."

I'm in the middle of demonstrating proper guard-ing behavior over the muffin, when the woman in the glasses hauls me away. She's rough about it, and I want to growl at her, but I don't because I hate to start a fight. It seems better to let her be the alpha for a min-ute than to get into something.

We go through a door into a new room. I look around, hopeful that this room will have more muf-fins in it, but it doesn't. So instead, I focus on eating the muffin in my hand while she talks to me. To be honest, I'd rather take my muffin outside and eat it in peace, but it looks like that won't be an option.

"What is with you? Are you drunk?" The woman in glasses leans in to sniff me, so I sniff her back. She smells minty and a little bit like pumpkin. How can she stand to smell so good? Doesn't it make her feel famished all day long? Even with my mouth full of muffin, I can't resist sniffing her more. She smells more delicious than strawberry yogurt.

When I start smelling her neck, she pushes me away. "Come off it, Jess! This is our biggest day of the year, and you show up drunk? Or stoned or . . . whatever you are?" Her neck is splotchy and red. I want to reach out and pet her, to calm her down, except I think she might bite me.

"I can't believe what you just did in there. Eating off a customer's plate? My god, Jess, you should be shot for that! Or fired at least. He's practically the only customer we have!"

Her eyes are red where they should be white. I consider asking her why the man was taking so long to eat. Isn't it obvious that he could have avoided competition over his food if he'd just gotten down to the business of eating it? I'll never understand why people dawdle over chewing. I can eat a muffin in three bites.

I finish my muffin and try biting the wrapper, but it is *not* good. The tense feelings coming off this woman are starting to affect my stomach. I shift from foot to foot, wishing she'd calm down so the knots in my belly could loosen. I hadn't expected to be so sensitive to the emotional swings of other humans. When a dog is upset, they usually have the courtesy to wander off and sit by themselves instead of putting others through their mood.

"Will you get it together?" she says, her forehead creasing. "Please? I need you today. You know I can't do all this on my own. Hell, I can't even do half of it on my own. I'm used to you doing about seventy percent."

I don't understand this at all. Somehow, she's making me feel responsible for how upset she is. Which is crazy! I haven't done anything wrong. Have I?

"Look," she says, her shoulders sagging. "If you need to have a total breakdown today, I guess it's your right. You've earned it with all you do around here. Only please don't fall apart all the way, okay? I can buck up and do more if I have to. I guess. But the least you can do is take care of the booth at the Farmer's Market. And we still need a sous chef. The Farmer's Market was your stupid idea, remember?"

She looks like she wants me to say something. Only I feel like I've already made her angry with what I said before—I don't want to make things even worse.

I lick my lips. "Um. Yeah," I say.

Her nostrils are rising in sharp little peaks. When she talks, her voice is low and growly—it makes me feel like a small dog. "Look. This is not funny. Whatever you're on, get off it. And until then, the least you can do is to get the menus up to the market stand. Don't blow it. Or I swear I will kill you myself."

She leaves me there. I expect to feel better the second she's gone, but I don't. Her bad feelings hang with me like a twist in the ribs. Even worse, I don't know what I did to make her upset. This is all so confusing—I wish I understood the rules to the people world.

I want to sit down and groom myself. Licking my paw always makes me feel better.

Only when I do, it's weird. My skin is flat and smooth. And salty, and my tongue gets dry. Yuck.

 Jessica

I walked my front paws up to the back door and batted at the knob, but it didn't budge. I couldn't get in to my own office. With a sigh, I sank down on my rear and waited, trying to figure out what to do.

A dog! How could I be a dog? I jumped up and started pacing, racking my brain for a solution, until my mind was overcome by one of those mind-altering itches, this time deep in my left ear. I scratched at it with every paw and tried rubbing it on the door, but nothing helped. The itch burned deep in my ear canal, buzzing like a tuning fork.

Just then the door swung open, revealing Zoë on the other side. I was relieved to see her in one piece (frankly, it was disconcerting to let my body out of my sight), but also concerned that she was in the Pit of Death, not in the restaurant. Had Kerrie kicked her out? Or had Zoë gone there of her own volition?

I peered at her carefully. She was upset—or so I guessed, never having seen my own face crumpled with worry before. I still couldn't get over how strange it was to look myself in the face. My eye caught on the details—the flaws in my skin, that crooked canine tooth. Earlier I'd been shocked by the glow that came from my face when it smiled. I'd never felt the contagious power of my own joy before. I missed that brightness now.

I let her hug and pet me for a minute, and in that time I tried to absorb as much of her sadness as I could. Poor Zoë. She didn't ask for this any more than I did. It must be just as scary for her as it was for me. I didn't really know what there was to miss about being a dog, but whatever there was, she was probably desperate to get back to it.

When Zoë's breathing had calmed down and she straightened up, I pushed my way inside the office. It was nice to comfort her and feel comforted in return, but I had to stay practical. We needed to get the menus and new coffee sleeves up to the Farmer's Market stand, and I needed Zoë's help—that is, *hands*—to do it.

My tidy desk held nothing but a phone, a lamp, a stack of menus, and my laptop. I stopped for a minute to stare longingly at the black screen. If only I could turn it on, I could go online and research my current situation. Who knew, maybe this had happened to someone else? Just thinking of the search strings made my paws itch—"transformation," "out-of-body experience," "woman wakes up as serious bitch."

I ached to try it, but my paw would never work on the track pad. Maybe if I could find a desktop computer with a regular mouse, I might manage that. Only where would I find one? *Not the library,* I thought, remembering how rudely I'd been kicked out of my own café. They'd never let me inside. Not an Internet café, either. My eye fell on the stack of menus and I gave myself a mental kick. I could worry about the computer later. First I had to get those menus to the Farmer's Market.

The menus were printed with a special Woofinstock variation of our logo, a dog's face looking through our usual four panes of glass. Everything on the menu had a dog-related title: the Four Paw Scramble, the Barking Leek Brioche, the Tail-Wag Terrine. Kerrie and Guy had spent weeks coming up with the special menu—now we had to pray that Naomi could produce the dishes. Assuming we drew in any customers, that is.

Nudging the stack carefully, I got a sheaf of menus into my mouth and took them to Zoë, pressing them into her hand.

"You want me to have these? But they're just paper—I was hoping for a cookie."

Honestly. She was worse than a three-year-old. I went back for the bag of coffee-cup sleeves, then paused to root around in the garbage. Kerrie and I had dumped some over-browned pumpkin cookies in there—one of those would shut her up.

I hadn't predicted, though, how much the act of sticking my head into a garbage can and pulling out a cookie would make me salivate. The second I caught a sniff of that cookie, my mind tilted. I was like a junkie—all I could think about was eating that cookie. I started to pant. My tail wagged manically. I had to have it.

Two bites and it was gone.

"Hey!" She stomped up behind me. "Did you find a cookie?"

I looked up at her, licking my lips. *Guilty.*

"You are a bad dog! You have to share, don't you know that?"

I wanted to remind her of the bread episode at breakfast, but of course I couldn't. I couldn't communicate a darned thing. Surely a cookie was the least I deserved. A cookie or two. Maybe there was another one in there?

We lunged for the garbage at the same time. She boxed me out with her hip. I tried to squeeze through her legs as she tossed napkins, paper cups, and yogurt tops out of the trash. She came up victorious.

"Aha—I found one!" Zoë held it high above my head, waving it around like a prize. She took a bite, chewing in an exaggerated way, rolling her eyes to show how good it was. I gave her a glare as I turned away, my stomach clenching. Being a dog was hungry business.

Once the cookies were gone, I was able to get back to work. Zoë carried the menus, and I took the bag of coffee-cup sleeves in my teeth. Yesterday's storm had long since moved east, and the morning was already warm and sweet-smelling. Together Zoë and I made it to the Farmer's Market at Hyak Park, a square block of grass shaded around the edges by broad-armed maple and chestnut trees. The Kittias River flowed along the eastern side of the park, slipping through Madrona as it surged on to empty into Kwemah Bay and the salt waters of Puget Sound. Next month, kids would gather here to collect shiny chestnuts and drop them in the river to watch them speed away.

Every important building in town fronted the park. A stone bridge, built in the 1950s, led from the park to the library, which had reading rooms overlooking the river. The senior center, with its long meeting hall and outbuildings for art classes and bingo, had the north side. City Hall was on the west. To the south lay the little brick post office. And next to that was Midshipman's Square, the site of our café.

As we approached the park, my anxiety peaked. There would be people here, people I knew, including the entire Woofinstock committee. How was Zoë going to manage? Would she embarrass me? Would I embarrass myself?

I was anxious, but that was nothing compared to what I felt when we stepped onto the grass. That was when I realized that the park wasn't just full of people.

It was also full of dogs.

8

Park Dog

 Jessica

The minute we entered the park, Zoë dropped all the menus and ran off. *Great,* I thought, *now what do I do?* I couldn't decide whether to leave the menus there to be stepped on or try to pick them up. My mouth was already engaged, carrying the bag of coffee-cup sleeves, so I ran a circle around the menus, then tore off for the Glimmerglass stand. Once I'd dropped off my bag of sleeves, I was free to nip one of our high school servers by the apron and drag her to the pile of menus. She laughed and pointed me out to all her friends, who thought I was hilarious. Fortunately, she stopped laughing long enough to pick up the menus. Then she patted me on the head and told me I was a clever dog—which, of course, was a profound under-statement.

I stepped away from the stand to get my bearings, blinking in the sunshine, and within seconds a pack of dogs swarmed around me. Suddenly they were every-where, tongues lolling, eyes rolling. Their breath stung my nose. Nails scratched my feet. They pushed and prodded, shoving their snouts at my belly and under my tail.

I panted, my lungs full of terror. Dogs were attacking every piece of me. I spun around, trying to shake them off, but every time I moved, I opened my tail end up to a new onslaught.

Teeth bared, I nipped at a German shepherd's face, then at a retriever's. A growl swelled in my throat and hummed past my teeth. Then I started to bark. I opened my mouth and let loose a stream of barks so loud, they hurt my own ears. Every dog that dared look at me crosswise got a lungful. A miniature Chihuahua came yipping and nipping at my paws, and I reared up like the Hulk, bellowing into its pointy face.

It all felt surreal and kind of wonderful. I'd had plenty of scary moments with dogs, but I'd never known how to communicate with them before, to tell them to give me a little space. Now when I barked, they heard me. They stepped away and went back to what they were doing. Incredible.

This was, of course, a small victory—tiny in the face of problems like being trapped in the wrong body. But still, it felt good to be understood for once. If I could only find a way to communicate to the human world that the Glimmerglass was an incredible café, we'd be all set.

This weekend wasn't just our chance at salvation—it was our chance for a fresh start. Dozens of travel writers came to Madrona over this weekend, and they all ran stories about their favorite shops and restaurants. Last year, when Leisl Adler gave the closing speech, her café, Eggs About Madrona, got a half-page story in *Woof! Magazine* and a mention in two different California papers. The *Seattle Times* took a photo of Leisl standing next to Spitz's statue, her arms crossed like a Wall Street giant, and ran it on the cover of the Life and Arts section. Eggs About Madrona serves omelets that taste like cardboard, yet they had tourists filing in all year long just because of that good press. The power of this weekend couldn't be underestimated. And my one and only job was to get the Glimmerglass's name out there.

Quite a challenge when I couldn't speak.

I looked across the green at the old-fashioned white bandstand—that was where I was supposed to make my speech on Sunday afternoon. A speech, in just thirty-two hours. How was I going to do that? With barks and whines? Using canine semaphore? One thing was sure—I wasn't about to let Zoë make it for me.

I was looking at the bandstand, racking my brain for a way to help the Glimmerglass, when my eyes spotted a familiar pair of Timberlands. As I trotted closer, my nose picked up the sharp smells of onion, peppers, and—*ah*—tomatoes. Even before I reached his stand, I knew I'd found Theodore.

I hadn't seen him in nearly a year, but he looked the same—close-cropped blond beard, close-shaved head under a corduroy cap. He still wore a kilt and his copper bracelet with BEAUTY WILL SAVE THE WORLD inscribed on it. He'd never been one for uniforms.

Theodore had been our sous chef for years, back in the Glimmerglass's halcyon days when Kerrie was head chef and Naomi ran the front of the house. Theodore might look unconventional, but he was efficient, skilled, and focused—exactly what we needed in a sous chef. With Naomi heading up the kitchen, we desperately needed someone with Theodore's skills backing her up.

Today he was busy hawking his Salish Salsa, a condiment that promised to put the "spice of the Southwest into the Northwest." It was this very salsa—or the chance to run his own home-based franchise—that had drawn him away from the Glimmerglass. He'd wanted to work at home, to set his own hours, and get away from the hot stove. Kerrie and I had understood. Theodore was everything an entrepreneur should be, and he deserved to be his own boss.

I hurried up to the table, completely forgetting that he wouldn't recognize me. He didn't even give me a second glance. Plus, he was too busy selling thirty-ounce tubs of salsa, and when I saw that, my heart sank. His business was booming. Why would he want to pitch in at the Glimmerglass when he was raking in the salsa sales?

Discouraged, I slumped down under his salsa table and put my chin on my paws. I could just picture how things were at the café. Either no more customers had come and Kerrie was working herself into a state, staring at the empty dining room, or we were swamped and Kerrie was in a state because of the backed-up orders and stress in the kitchen. No matter what, my partner was having a horrendous day, and what was I doing to help? Nothing. A big, fat nothing.

"Hey, Theo, how's it going?"

A customer in the espresso line turned to look at her. *Nice*.

I started to follow, but Kerrie slammed the door in my face, locking me outside. Me—a co-owner—shut out of my own restaurant!

Unbelievable. I paced back and forth outside the Glimmerglass, my mind filled with visions of what Zoë might be doing inside the café. How many disasters had she caused already? Had she lit any fires? Mortally offended any customers? Fired any staff?

After five minutes of nervous pacing, I gave up trying to get in through the front doors. Instead, I ran around the side of the building to the back door that led into the Pit of Death, my paws damp with anxiety. It was shut, of course. I put my ear to the door, but heard nothing. For a long moment, I stood there alone, listening to my own breathing. The more I breathed, the more anxious I became. Why hadn't I turned back into myself yet? Was this dog thing permanent—because if it was, I wanted out. Now.

I took a deep breath and told myself to just focus on the Glimmerglass. That would keep me sane. Besides, the café had to be my first priority. Otherwise, when I finally got into my body again, I'd have nothing of value left.

 Zoë

This place smells incredible. I burst through the door, wobbling on my people legs. They might be unsteady,

I sat up so fast, I almost hit my head on the underside of the table. I knew that voice—especially the way it ordered Americanos, small sized but in a large cup.

"Whattup, Max," Theodore answered. "How's life?"

There was a pause, during which I pictured Max shrugging his shoulders. I'd always loved watching him shrug his shoulders. They moved so nicely under his shirts. "You know. The usual. Hey, I was looking for your old bosses. Doesn't the café have a stand up here?"

"They usually do. Here, hold on." Theodore called to someone, a person in size-six pink high-tops who took over the salsa station for him. "Thanks, babe," Theodore said as he stepped from behind the booth. I poked my nose out from under the table to watch.

Theodore shielded his eyes with one hand and looked around. "They're usually over by the grandstand. You jonesing for a latte?"

Max did his adorable shrug again. "Something like that. How's the salsa business?"

"You know. It's work." Theodore did his own version of the shrug, which really didn't compare. "Kind of boring, if you want the truth."

Boring? My ears cocked forward.

"Yeah?" Max had his thumbs hooked in the back pockets of his jeans. "I thought you liked being your own boss."

"I did. But it's always the same, you know? I get up, I chop. I have lunch, I chop. It's all I do. The recipes are always the same, and I never stop smelling like onions." He jerked his head back toward the stand, indicating his girlfriend in the pink high-tops. "Ariel says it's getting on her nerves."

Max grinned. "You miss the Glimmerglass, eh?"

"Yeah, I guess I do. I had a lot of variety there. And they always let me try new things if I wanted."

I could barely believe my ears. This was the best news I'd heard all day. Now, how could I get Theodore to the café? Could I push him? Pull him? Without meaning to, I started creeping out from under the table, my tail wagging double time.

"Did you like your bosses?" Max asked, looking at the crowd again. Maybe he was looking for someone in particular. His girlfriend probably. Or his fiancée. I stopped wagging.

"They were awesome." Suddenly Theodore's bearded face broke into a smile. He gave Max a shove with his elbow. "Why? You interested?"

Max had to take a step to regain his balance, and as he turned, he spotted me.

"Hey, Zoë! I didn't expect to see you here. Where's your person?"

Max reached out for me, and I went straight to him. I had no pride. I just wanted to be close to him.

"What are you doing on the loose like this?" He fished a blue leash out of his pocket and snapped it on my collar. As if he needed it—I'd follow him anywhere.

"Hey man," Theodore said, angling back toward his salsa stand. "I gotta go—Ariel's getting swamped. See ya around."

"Adios." Max waved to Theodore, and, just like

that, I was separated from our once and future sous chef. That Max, he just made me forget things.

Max walked me briskly toward the bandstand as he scanned the crowd for Zoë. It dawned on me that I'd been so wrapped up in discovering Theodore, I'd forgotten to wonder what the dog in my body might be doing. What would a dog do in a crowd like this? Pee on the grass? Steal cookies out of some little kid's hand?

As Max and I crossed the square, I couldn't help but notice women's heads turn as they followed him with their eyes. I wasn't the only one with a thing for great cheekbones. I was relieved when we reached the Glimmerglass stand, where the high school students were oblivious to everything but customers and each other. They seemed to have found their rhythm, taking orders and pumping out drinks as fast as the espresso machine could make them.

"Hmm, not here." Max crouched down beside me. "Where do you think she went?"

Your guess is a good as mine, I thought. *Though I'd give a lot to know.*

Max moved his hand to my ear, and I shifted closer to him. I'd had no idea my ear itched so badly, but his touch sent shock waves through my skin. The harder he rubbed, the more I leaned in. A rush of joy filled me—this was better than molten chocolate cake. Still, the ecstasy was tempered by the unsettling feeling that I would never be able to get enough. No matter how long he rubbed, the itch would still be there, like a lasting regret. Besides, this wasn't really what I was after. I wanted to be in my human body, feeling Max's skin on mine the way I had when we shook hands yesterday. Why couldn't we repeat that moment again and again?

"There she is," Max said, standing abruptly. I wanted to look, but the ear rubbing had me in a stupor. All I could do was look lazily across the crowd, where I saw nothing but fleece vests and jackets. And Guy, our ex-chef, leaning in close for a tête-à-tête with Leisl at the Eggs About Madrona stand. Was he hitting on her? Angling for a new job? Leisl didn't strike me as the kind of person who would shark someone else's employee, even one who'd recently quit.

"Let's take you to Jessica," Max said, leading me forward. "And remind her that you shouldn't be wandering around by yourself. If you get in trouble, how am I going to ask Jessica out?"

Ask her out? Ask me *out? Seriously?* I nearly stumbled. Had I heard him correctly? Max Nakamura—Hot Max—wanted to ask me out? I picked up my pace and gave him a closer look. Sure enough, he was craning his neck to see Zoë through the crowd. *How incredible. How wonderful!*

This took me by complete surprise. Could a man like him—the town's beloved vet—really like someone with my dog-hating background? Was he the one and only person in town, aside from Kerrie, who saw beyond all that?

As I floated along beside him, I thought back to the way he'd rubbed my ears. He was so gentle. So considerate. Did that mean he'd be a gentle man to live with? Was there any correlation between the way a man interacted with dogs and the way he was in life? Would Max be a considerate lover because of the way he'd massaged my ear?

This was starting to feel very wrong.

Zoë

This is the most incredible day I've ever had. Never, ever, have I seen and done and been so many things in such a short time. Ordinarily, it would be amazing enough just to have had bread for breakfast plus a muffin (even without the wrapper). But now I'm at a park that's completely packed with dogs of all types— tall dogs and short dogs, Frisbee dogs, ball dogs—and I'm different from all of them.

When I arrive, a bulldog comes up to me. "Hi," I say, eager to sniff his nose in greeting. But I'm so tall, I can hardly say hello. Even squatting down, my body is all wrong—hips up high, head even higher. The bulldog sniffs my pant leg and turns away, clearly unimpressed. As if I don't smell good. As if he doesn't even *care* what I had for breakfast.

I try the Newfies, but they just roll their eyes at me and drool. The chocolate Lab skips away. I race after the Aussies and almost touch one of their tails, but they don't seem to notice. When I cut to the side and run off in a new direction, no one follows.

Now my chest feels heavy, like I just swallowed some gooey, wet sea creature. I know what that feels like because of the time I ate a jellyfish right off the beach. After that I threw up five times. I've always thought that if I came across another jellyfish on the beach, I would *not* eat it—that's how terrible I felt. The truth is, though, that I probably would. I just can't help myself with things like that. The stronger a thing smells, the more I feel compelled to devour it. Even if it'll make me sick afterward. I wonder why that is?

Now my insides feel sea-creature queasy as I watch the dogs romping around the lawn, ignoring me. I'm whining silently, to myself.

But wait. *Wait.* I see him before I smell him. My dad! My very own dad, standing near the car. He came for me!

I race over at top speed and lunge at him, licking his face. We fall on the grass. He shrieks like a little girl and tries to push me off, but I have to prove my sub-mission, so I keep licking. My tongue is super dry, but I keep on licking. He has to know how sorry I am for getting lost. He has to see how much I respect him.

Dad pushes me off and stands up, brushing grass off his pants.

"What the hell are you doing? Are you deranged? Is this some kind of stunt?"

"No." I'm panting after all the running and licking. "No. No stunt. Don't you recognize me? Didn't you miss me?"

"Who the hell are you?" Dad's wiping off his face. "Are you on drugs?"

"I'm Z—" I start to say. But I stop myself just in time. Of course he doesn't recognize me. I'm in the wrong body. Suddenly I get a flash of how I must look, acting like my usual doggy self, but in a human body. I've never seen a person lick another person before. My face gets hot as I realize that this probably isn't the way people behave.

Is it too late to act correctly? Dad's eyes look wild. I've frightened him. I duck my head so I look like less of a threat.

"I have your dog," I say, standing very straight and speaking carefully. "Your dog, Zoë. The one who got lost, but she's very sorry and will never do it again. Ever. She wants to go home, so much. Will you take her home now? Please?" *And me too,* I wanted to say, but I didn't. I wasn't sure how to get him to take me, too. Being in the wrong body suddenly felt incredibly confusing. If only I were still a dog, I'd know just what to do to make him and Mom love me more. I'd be extremely quiet and careful—Mom was always telling me not to ruin her beautiful house. She likes pretty things.

Dad is squinting around, but I see Jessica first, coming our way with Dr. Max. I love Dr. Max, but I don't run over to him. I want to go home with my dad, so I stay where I am. Instead I use my new finger to point.

"There she is. See? Zoë." I lean toward him. "Isn't she beautiful?"

Dad gives me a look I don't understand. His eyes look sad, almost like he's misbehaved, but his eyebrows are angry.

"We don't have a dog," he says in a sharp voice. He brushes at his pants again and climbs in the car.

"Wait—she's right here," I yell. I run up to the car and hit the windows with my hands, but he doesn't look at me or at Jessica. He just drives away.

Jessica

We were too late. By the time we reached Zoë, she was already deep into some kind of drama, running after this poor man as he tried to get away in his car. He looked nice enough, though his suit and tie were awfully formal for a day in the park. In a town that felt most comfortable in jeans, he didn't really look like a fit.

This sounds paranoid, I know, but I could have sworn he gave me a strange look as he drove away. A haunted look. Then he swung his eyes back to the road and pulled away.

Max went straight to Zoë. "Are you okay?"

Zoë's face was a study in hurt and confusion, but she didn't tell us what was bothering her. Instead, her eyes were fixed on the bandstand, which was all set up for the Pet-and-Person Beauty Contest. A cluster of cameras from local news stations perched in front of the stage, and a crowd of kids sat on the grass, waiting for the show to start. From where we stood, I could see Leisl and her purebred standard poodle, Foxy, primping for the contest. Our emcee's voice came over the loudspeaker:

"Is your dog the most beautiful in the world? Then step right up to the bandstand and choose a costume from our costume wall. We're on a quest to find the most beautiful dog in all of Woofinstock, and we need your help. We'll give prizes for most congenial, best smile, best hair, and a grand prize for the most handsome pet and owner. Come on, folks, let's get started with the sixth-annual Pet-and-Person Beauty Contest!"

Before I could blink, Zoë had me by the leash. "The most beautiful dog, that's us. Come on, *doggie,*" she said to me, "we have to win that contest." She glanced in the direction the car had gone and mumbled something under her breath. "We can show him how perfect we are. Let's go."

I stumbled after her, flailing with my four paws. She was still shaky on two legs, but through sheer force of will she seemed to get everywhere she was going. I wanted to object, to dig in my heels and say that nothing at the Pet-and-Person Beauty Contest was going to get us back to normal, so who cared?

But, apparently, Zoë did. She hauled me with the strength of two dozen sled dogs. Within seconds, I found myself next to her at the registration table, standing across from Malia Jackson and Alexa Hinkey.

"I have the most beautiful dog in the whole world right here," Zoë blurted. "Is it too late to enter in the contest?"

"Aww, isn't that sweet!" Alexa leaned across the table. "How's our little lost friend doing? She's so much more trusting than yesterday." She held out her hand, and I dutifully pretended to sniff it. "Are you feeling better after a good breakfast?"

She was asking me, but Zoë answered.

"Yes, I am," she said proudly. She turned to me and mouthed "Muf-fin."

Malia might have seen—she gave Zoë a strange look over the top of her reading glasses. "If you win the beauty contest, you get to take home that big basket of treats from the Clover Leaf Bakery." She tipped her head in the direction of a wicker basket mounded with pancake-sized molasses cookies, snickerdoodles, and chocolate-mint crinkles. As soon as I saw it, I started to salivate. One second later, my rational brain pointed out that if I let Zoë eat that whole thing, my body would be twenty pounds heavier when I got back into it. *If* I ever got back into it. I kept a close eye on Zoë. If she set my leash down for even a second, I was set to bolt.

Malia handed Zoë a packet of brochures and flyers. "I know you know all about this weekend, but I have to give you this." She turned to me with a wink. "Don't forget to call on the Lost Dog Committee if you need us. Our number's right on the front of the Madrona map."

"Now head on over and find a costume for your doggie," Alexa told Zoë. Together, they walked me up to the wall of outfits. "And then get up there and make Madrona eat their words. Show everyone what a special bond you and this beautiful girl have. If you can take the crown from Leisl and Foxy, no one will ever accuse you of being a dog hater again. You mark my words." She crouched down in front of me, and suddenly her casual clothes seemed right to me. Comfortable. Approachable. "My goodness but you are a gorgeous doggie. You go strut your stuff and show them what a winner you are. Everyone in town is going to be watching. Represent the Glimmerglass!"

That caught me cold. The Glimmerglass . . . everyone in town watching . . . of course! Why hadn't I realized that this was a way to get the Glimmerglass's name in front of throngs of people? Suddenly, I was all nerves. Now I really did want to win, for the café's sake. If we could draw in just thirty extra covers for lunch and dinner, we could keep Naomi paid for another month. That was worth entering any kind of contest.

Still, when I saw the costumes, I almost backed out. Ahead of us, a woman was squeezing her pug into a bee suit with spring-loaded antennae that bounced around his eyes like little bobble heads. In front of them, waiting to go on stage, I saw a boxer wearing a Princess Leia wig and a dress that hung from its neck, complete with fake plush arms and a black blaster-belt. Heaven help me. These dogs had no idea how humiliated they should feel. They were so clueless they'd get up on stage with their puppy-dog grins on, not caring if the audience roared at their expense. Well, not me. I might be canine on the outside, but on the inside I still remembered how to be self-conscious. I'd wear the costume—not that I had much choice—but no one could make me like it.

Zoë dove into the costumes and started pawing through them, ignoring the neat order they'd been arranged in. I pried my gaze away from Princess Leia and looked up at the wall of outfits. What instrument of torture would Zoë force me into? The crab suit? The princess wig—the one with the golden curls and pointy headdress? Or the hat that looked like a giant Scooby Doo head?

I was surprised when she came back with a Wonder Woman costume.

"I like this color," she said, fingering the red bodice. "I wish I had a costume. You're very lucky."

Me, lucky? I chewed on that thought while a volunteer dressed me, closing the outfit in the back with Velcro tabs. Zoë guided the headband around my ears, then she and the volunteer stepped back and sucked in a collective breath of admiration.

"You put Lynda Carter to shame," said the volunteer.

"Beautiful!" Zoë clapped her hands.

I couldn't help it. I broke into a grin and started to pant.

9

Crowning Glory

 Jessica

As we waited to go on stage, I started to feel nervous all over again. This was so not me. I never did this kind of thing—I didn't even dress up for Halloween. It had been years since I last wore a costume.

"Okay, we're here for a purpose," Zoë said as she crouched beside me. "And don't even pretend you aren't listening. I know you understand." She looked up and down the line of teams waiting beside us. "We have to win this. We're the prettiest dog here, and we have to show it. Also, we need the cookies. To do it, we have to beat them."

I followed her gaze to the team on the stage. Foxy, dressed in a sequined bolero and flamenco pom-pom hat, followed Leisl around and around in a circle, doing a version of a Mexican hat dance. Every time the music paused, Foxy held up his paw for a high five. Leisl winked at the audience before clapping her palm against Foxy's paw. "Good boy!"

The crowd ate it up.

"We have to do something like that," Zoë said. "Something together, as a team."

In that instant, three truths collided in my brain. First, it dawned on me that this contest included a talent show. And I had no talent. I didn't sing, didn't dance. I couldn't do anything worth watching.

Second, Hot Max was sitting in the front row. When I looked again and realized that he was a judge, a knot gathered on top of the knots that were already making a mess of my stomach.

And third, Zoë was dragging me on stage.

Zoë

It doesn't matter how many times I say "cookies" and "good dog," she fights me every step. I know all her tricks because I've tried them, too—rear end on the ground, nails dug in, head jerking back and forth. But I'm too smart for her. And too strong.

We get on stage and the sun shines right on us. A loud voice says, "Please welcome Glimmerglass Café owner Jessica Sheldon and her dog Zoë," and people clap. Then everything is quiet. Beyond the stage, I can see people watching us. I wave, and they wave back.

Then I point at Dr. Max with my new pointing finger. When I was a dog, I never knew why people were always sticking their fingers out. It never made sense. Was there something stuck on it? Did they want me to lick it? But now I know that it's for things that are too far away to touch or lick. I hate to think how many good snacks people have pointed out to me that I missed because I didn't know.

Dr. Max waves back at me. The people are waiting for me to do something, and I wonder if I should sit. Or stay. Or both.

It's completely silent.

Jessica is whining beside me, like she has to pee, only I don't think she does. She reminds me of a dog I saw at a kennel once that whined whenever people left the room. I look at her and say, "Don't be scared. They love us. We can make them laugh. See?" I wave at the crowd again and people laugh and cough and squirm in their chairs.

I think she believes me, because she grabs her end of the leash in her mouth and starts trotting across the stage. I follow after her and people laugh. I give them a big smile. Jessica isn't smiling, though—she looks serious, like she's on the verge of a growl. She takes me close to a chair and gives a sharp bark. I'm not sure what to do, so I sit down. The crowd ripples with laughter.

Now I see what Jessica is up to, and it is a great joke, but it feels a little wasted on this audience. If people find it funny to see a dog directing a human around, imagine how much a crowd of dogs would like it.

Jessica barks two times, so I fall onto the floor and play dead. The next time she barks, I lie on my belly, staying, like a herding dog, waiting for orders. My eyebrows are up, legs ready. Jessica backs up slowly, her eyes locked on me. Then she sits down, waits, and barks.

I race over to her, like a good dog. She smiles and

licks my face. Then, making sure everyone can see, she holds out her paw, like she's giving me a treat. I bend down and pretend to take it. I pretend to chew, too. Mmm. Everybody laughs, and it's such a warm feeling, it's like being rubbed dry with a towel.

We both stand up, and it's all over. The loud voice announces the next pair (an English bulldog who smells funny and tap dances) and we go off the other side of the stage. As we walk off, I look at the crowd and see a man in a baseball hat. My dad wears baseball hats—maybe that's him?

I charge off the stage and push my way through the crowd. Everyone is watching me, and they reach out to touch me because I was so hilarious in our act, but I keep my eyes on Dad. There he is—I see him. I'm close enough to leap on him, but that didn't go well the last time, so I resist the urge. I get right up close to him, though, and that's when I see that it isn't him at all.

He smells wrong. And looks wrong. I stop and pretend that I'm looking at someone else, far behind him.

I miss home and it hurts.

☕ Jessica

When we left the stage, adrenaline rushed through me with such force, I felt like I could fly. We did it! We went up on stage and represented the Glimmerglass without embarrassing ourselves. I was impressed that Zoë had caught on to my idea so quickly. She was no fool.

A Woofinstock volunteer came to take off my costume, and I was so busy lifting my paws and holding still that at first I didn't notice when Zoë dove headlong into the crowd. Everyone turned to stare, even the bulldog that was tap dancing on stage. I opened my mouth to yell, but all that came out was a mangled growl-bark. What was she doing?

Zoë plowed through the audience with a pointer's focus, then suddenly stopped. She stooped to examine her arm, like she was brushing off a speck of dirt, then turned and looked for me, her face painted in disappointment. My heart lunged in sympathy. Seeing my own face twisted in such sorrow made me want to weep.

Just then, Leisl's polished shoes appeared next to my paws. "I should have known she couldn't take care of a dog. Not even for one day," she muttered, picking up my leash. Her blond hair tickled my nose. Leisl turned to Foxy. "Foxy, sit! Stay!" Foxy's rump dropped to the ground. He shifted on his paws and sat ramrod straight in his costume. I hoped I hadn't looked as silly in my Wonder Woman outfit as Foxy did in his bolero.

When Zoë arrived, Leisl held out my leash with a look of reprobation. Though how she could chastise someone whose shoulders slumped that woefully, I don't know.

"You can't just leave your dog like that. What if she'd run off and been hit by a car?"

Zoë stared at the leash for a minute, then lifted her perplexed face to Leisl. "Why would she get hit by a car?" She turned to me and said, "That man wasn't who I thought he was. Weird! I really thought I was sure . . ."

"Didn't you hear anything I said?" Leisl asked.

Zoë shrugged. "Don't worry. I have the leash now." She waggled it in proof. "Now we're attached to one another. That makes everything okay, right?" Zoë gave me a wink, but Leisl didn't hear the joke in her voice.

Leisl frowned. "You have to be the one in control. At all times. If you let her think she's the boss, she'll run all over you."

An amused look played over Zoë's face as she gazed at Leisl, then glanced down at Foxy. "No bossing allowed for you, huh? Sorry, buddy."

As we walked away, I had to snicker. Leisl had been my toughest critic on the Woofinstock committee, and I'd gone home many nights praying that she would just disappear. She bred standard poodles as a sideline and considered herself to be the supreme expert on all things canine. I enjoyed the irony of seeing an actual dog laugh right in her face.

Until, that is, Zoë turned to me and said, "Come on, let's go. I'm going to mark around the edge of this place, so everyone knows we were here today." Swinging the leash between us like we were little girls at the park, she turned to go.

Aghast, I lunged for the leash, chomped down on it, and gave a yank back in my direction. No way would I let her pee in Hyak Park. Never.

"Hey!" she cried. "Bad dog!"

Those words made the crowd turn to look at us, even though the bulldog was reaching his big finale.

Hot Max craned his neck to see us from the judge's table, and humiliation boiled up inside me. The last thing I wanted was to have an altercation right in front of everyone. I growled softly. Zoë crouched down in front of me and bared her teeth, right in my face.

For an instant, I was so taken aback that I froze in place. What to do? Should I be a good dog and obey, even if it meant letting my human companion humiliate herself? And what about the fact that *she* was actually *me*—or at least looked like me to everyone in town. Didn't that double my responsibility for her reputation?

I took a breath and tried to focus on my priorities. My number-one job was to help the Glimmerglass, and to do that I needed to make Jessica Sheldon, Glimmerglass owner, appear as dog friendly as possible. So I dropped my ears and followed her, my hair bristling with the knowledge that people (Max included) might still be watching. The last thing I needed him to think was that he'd fostered a dog with a woman who peed on grass in public.

As I trotted after Zoë, my stomach churned. How had I gotten into the mess? None of this was meant to be—I shouldn't be here, stuck in a dog's body, trying to make my human body behave. I should be focused on important things, like saving my café. Zoë should be off peeing wherever she wanted, and I should be working. Why, *why* was this happening? *Please, world, can't I just be human again?* Was it really so much to ask?

When Zoë got to the edge of the grass surrounding the bandstand, she bent her knees and started to crouch. I tensed my muscles, surprised at the power I felt in my hindquarters. Pushing off as hard as I could, I flew at her. My paws struck her on the shoulder. She shrieked as she went down, and I flew over her, landing with a stumble on the grass.

She rolled around on the grass a few times, then popped up. "Hey—I have to pee here. How are they gonna find me if I don't leave my scent?"

They? Who were they? Sometimes she made no sense. I panted at her, confused. She slapped an open palm on the ground.

"You wanna wrestle? Is that it?" I glanced over at the beauty contest crowd, relieved to see that they'd lost interest in us. Zoë waggled her arms around like she was working invisible nunchakus. "Better look out. I have the longest arms in the world. And don't forget, I have thumbs!"

Zoë tackled me, arms around my neck, and we both went sprawling. I bounced up, and she pushed me back down. It was surprising to feel how big she was—as a human, I'd never thought of myself as someone who outweighed a dog. She tried to pin me on my back, but I flailed with my paws, punching her squarely in the face. As she recoiled, one of my back paws scraped across her knee.

"Ow!" She stopped instantly, plopped on the grass, and inspected her wound. "That *hurt*." Looking closely at her knee, she drew in a shocked breath. "Blood—there's red blood on my leg." She showed it to me, her eyes wide. A long gash crossed her kneecap, and a small trickle of blood ran from one end. Holding her leg still with both hands, she bent down, sniffed the cut, and then licked it. And licked it. And licked it again.

When it was cleaned to her standards, she looked up at me with resentment in her eyes. "You hurt me. I was playing, and you hurt me."

I wanted to apologize and to remind her that she'd started it, but I had no vocal cords. I was mute—and frustrated. My head was full of questions and thoughts and I couldn't convey a single one. With a sigh, I nuzzled my head underneath her hand by way of an apology. She stroked me softly.

Now, I thought. *I should take advantage of this situation and bolt right now.* Zoë had let the leash fall slack in her hand—with one good bound I could break free and run back to the Glimmerglass. Yet somehow that just felt wrong. I couldn't take advantage of her injury and this quiet moment between us. I didn't have a code of ethics for behavior as a dog, but I decided on one right then. I wouldn't run away from someone who needed comfort, not when I was in a position to give it.

We sat there quietly, each feeling like a fish out of water, as I sniffed the air. My nose brought in all kinds of scents, some of which I recognized, and some I wasn't sure about. Strangely, a few of the scents made my mind pop with pictures. Near the fire hydrant, I'd had a mental flash of a large, healthy, male dog. When we were near the stage, I'd sniffed the steps and had an eerie feeling that a female puppy had come that way minutes before. Where were these images coming from?

Now, as I sniffed the breeze, my mind bombarded

me with pictures of Foxy. I stood and wandered after the scent, heading through the grass, nose down. Behind me, Zoë jumped up.

"Hey, are you smelling someone? Who is it? Who?" She slumped back down on the grass. "I can't smell anything."

I barely heard her, I was so wrapped up in Foxy's scent. My brain kept firing off pictures to match the different notes of scent in his pee: oats and carrots, and the pumpkin dog cookies we sell at the Glimmerglass. It was Foxy and . . . something more. A feeling. What was it? Fear? Worry? Yes, that was it. Where the puppy on the stage had smelled exuberant, Foxy's scent had a trace of anxiety, like he was worried about something. He smelled healthy, but not happy. I followed my nose, wishing for more details, but the smell trailed off. I raised my head and realized that someone was talking with Zoë.

It was Guy, our former chef. What was he doing here? And why was he talking to me—or, I meant, to Zoë?

"I thought I'd give you the chance to invite me back," he was saying, standing with one leg out, fingers hooked in the waistband of his shorts. He wore a bright yellow tank top that said BORN TO BE WILD across the front. "The Glimmerglass must have lost—what—a few thousand dollars by now? I bet you're wishing you never let me go." He jutted his chin at Zoë in a challenging way.

I desperately wanted to jump in between them, but Zoë didn't give me the chance. She snatched up my leash and, with an exaggerated limp on her injured leg, approached Guy until her face was inches from his. Twitching her nose to one side, she sniffed, then sniffed again.

"I know what you're up to," she said in a low voice. "You don't have to be that obvious. You're looking for a fight."

He took a step back. "Fight? What do you mean?"

"You know what I mean. It's written all over you. You want to throw down, right here. Okay, come on. Let's do it."

"What—are you insane? No, I don't want to fight."

"I know you do. I can smell it."

A look of revulsion crossed his face. "Whoa. And I used to think you were hot," he said with wonderment in his voice.

"Come on—I know you came here to fight me. What are you waiting for?" Behind us, the loudspeaker started to blare. "Afraid you might lose in front of all these people? Afraid you don't have what it takes? Well, you're right. You don't. You're small and you don't seem very bright. I give you two seconds before you land on your ass."

Guy looked like he didn't know which way to run. The person on the loudspeaker cleared their throat. "It's time to announce the winner of the Pet-and-Person Beauty Contest. Our runners up are Leisl Adler and Foxy—" Zoë's head cocked to the side, listening, "—and our winning team is Jessica Sheldon and Zoë!"

"Zoë—that's *me*!" With a gleeful bound, her injury

forgotten, Zoë raced away from Guy toward the band-stand, dragging me along behind her.

 Zoë

I'm the winner! I leap onto the stage, full of smiles, and everybody smiles with me. Except Jessica—she still has her growly look on. I think she liked it when I tried to fight the short man, though. He reminds me of those garden gnomes people put on their lawns for dogs to pee on.

Everyone claps for me because I'm the big winner. Everyone, that is, except Foxy's mom. She's too busy scowling at Foxy.

I clap for the people in the crowd, and they like that. Dr. Max comes on the stage with two shiny winner's hats in his hand. When he comes up to me, my urge is to lick his face, but I don't do it. I've noticed that people shake hands instead. I put out my hand and Dr. Max shakes it. And then I remember my hurt leg, so I stand on the other one. I want to lick my wound again, but I don't do that either because Dr. Max is putting one of the shiny winner's hats on my head. It feels funny, like someone's holding my skull with their hands. I like it.

Dr. Max has me sit in a fancy chair that's draped in red. Red reminds me of my wound, so I barely use that leg as I go to the chair. Dr. Max puts the other winner's hat on Jessica's head, and she wags her tail at him.

When Jessica has her hat on, Dr. Max has her sit

beside me in the big chair. She jumps up and puts her front paws across me, like I'm her doggie bed. Her hat sparkles with silver. Jessica leans in close to me and opens her mouth in a big smile while a man comes up and takes our picture.

Jessica and I stay where we are while Dr. Max gives Foxy and his mom different hats. I like our hats better, but I don't say so. I just enjoy snuggling with Jessica in our special chair. As I pet her, dog fur floats up in a cloud. I've never seen the top of my own head before. My ears are pretty cute.

It lightens my heart to see her being happy like this. Maybe she's starting to enjoy being a dog? I hope so—she deserves a little time off from her worries.

While we're sitting there, I see the man in the baseball hat again. This time I don't run after him, though. The sight of him makes my insides hurt the way my knee does. I think of my mom and dad, and their voices, and their shoes, and the way their clothes smell in the hamper.

Is it so much to ask, to get to go home?

When people start leaving their chairs, we get up, too. Dr. Max is coming to see us, but I can't talk. I have to get home. I wave at him and run away down the stairs, making Jessica hurry to keep up with me on her end of the leash. I jog back to where I almost fought with the garden gnome, but he isn't there anymore. I look around and see him standing by a red car.

See how lucky I am? The man has a car—perfect! And it's red. I trot up to him, Jessica at my side.

When I get there, I'm not sure what to do. How can I convince him to give me a ride?

"Whaddya want?" He doesn't seem happy to see me.

I don't touch him or suggest a fight—not this time. Instead I try to look pleasant. "I want a ride in your car."

His eyes get small when I say this. I say it again.

"In your car. Will you take me for a ride?" I wonder if there's some special way I should put a request like this?

"What is this," he asks, "some kind of cryptic invitation to your place? Are you asking me over?"

"Sure," I say, glad he's giving me some help in our conversation. "In your car."

He shrugs. Then he opens the door, and I jump in. This is the best—I love cars. Maybe he'll even let me drive. Once I'm settled, Jessica jumps into my lap. She's whining, but I don't know why. I ignore her.

"Your place, huh?"

I nod, and he starts to drive. Through the window, I see Dr. Max standing on the grass, watching us, so I roll it down to say "hey," but I'm too late—he's turned away. His face looked strange, which makes me think he probably didn't want to talk anyway.

I'm excited, and my skin tingles all over. As the garden gnome turns the key, I have visions of all the things that could happen once we start driving. I could go home; I could become a dog again; I could get ice cream from a drive-thru. My top choice would be to go home, of course, and this seems highly likely. When I was a dog, whenever I went away, I always went back home in a car.

The garden gnome drives, and I put my head out to feel the wind blowing on my cheeks until a bug flies into my eye. Jessica leans out and pants. I try to sniff the wind, but it's empty, like glass. No smells. Just wind and plenty of bugs.

Instead of going to my house, we arrive at Jessica's— the little place where we slept last night. The gnome turns the car off and leans back in his seat. His hand touches my shoulder. He rubs it.

"So," he says, and his voice sounds smooth and lilty. "Do you wanna invite me in?"

Jessica starts to growl. I hush her because I have an idea. Maybe I have to prove my dominance over the man before he'll take me home. That makes sense. Why would he do what a beta dog wants? He wouldn't. No, I have to beat him at wrestling first, then he'll take me where I want to go. It's a relief that I'm starting to understand the way these humans operate. I'll take him inside and wrestle the snot out of him.

I get out of the car, and he follows me to the door.

10

Canine Seduction

 Jessica

This was a disaster. Frantically, I raced across the grass between Guy and Zoë, trying to frighten Guy off. I nipped at his ankles and leaped at him, pushing as hard as I could with my paws.

"What's with your dog?" he asked Zoë, kicking out at me. "Is she mental or something?"

"She just thinks she's a person," Zoë said, taking me by the collar. "And sometimes she's *very bad*."

I didn't care what she called me, but I didn't like being hauled by the collar. It made me gag. Of course, I didn't like Guy's bedroom eyes or the way he kept touching Zoë's shoulder either. The thought of my body entwining itself with Guy's—naked—was so repulsive, I was willing to undergo plenty of pain to keep it from happening.

How had he known where my apartment was?

Zoë led him—and hauled me—in through the sliding glass doors, which still stood open from the morning. She let go of my collar, and I gasped a full breath of air, looking around my impersonal little apartment. Without the ability to see reds or oranges, it looked even drabber than I'd remembered. I couldn't help but view the place with new eyes, as if I were visiting someone else's home. There were no photos on the walls, no childhood mementos. No boyfriend's jacket graced the backs of my bar stools. I had books lined up in alphabetical order as if daring anyone to touch them.

Kerrie always accused me of not putting down roots, but the truth was that I wanted roots desperately—I just couldn't get them started. The only thing in the room that made my heart jump was Kerrie's grandmother's cookbook, the one she'd lent me after she stepped down as chef at the Glimmerglass. I loved looking through the old recipes, imagining unknown grandmothers rolling out dough in sunny kitchens, twisting special shapes for their grandchildren. If it were possible to dream up a family, I would have thousands of grandmothers by now.

I ran my eyes over the room and spotted a heap of mail on the floor under the slot in the front door. Lying on top, slightly askew, was a large lavender envelope. Even from here I could see the handwriting, the same writing I'd stared at a million times before dropping other envelopes into the recycle bin. With a purposeful motion, I turned my back on it.

Zoë said something I couldn't catch, and I turned to see her facing off with Guy, standing in the middle of my tiny living room. Thank goodness they hadn't discovered the bedroom. Nothing repulsed me like the idea of Guy-the-sparkplug naked. What about him could possibly attract Zoë? She wasn't really going to have sex with him—was she?

She turned to Guy with a sashay of the hips.

A lugubrious leer spread across his face, giving me the shivers. I ran around behind him and started to growl.

"Uh," he said, looking over his shoulder at me while he scooted toward Zoë. "I think your dog hates me."

Zoë gave a little shrug, went right up to Guy, and set her chin on his shoulder.

His leer spread. "I always knew you had the hots for me. You know how I've wanted to get my hands on that fine body of yours. I was sure you were just playing with me. All those nights I followed you home—you knew I was there all along, didn't you? Just playing hard to get."

Playing with him—*followed me home!* I felt the fur on my back rising 'til it bushed out like a porcupine's. That's how Guy had known where my apartment was. The creep snake was stalking me. My growl escalated. Guy moved to run his hands across Zoë's bottom, but she flinched away. When he angled toward her, his shoulder turned and her chin dropped off it. Without hesitation, she stepped in closer and replaced her chin. When he turned again, she whipped her face around and pranced away, shaking her head back and forth in a taunting motion. I was mystified, the growl stalled in my throat.

"What are you doing?" Guy asked, backing away. Zoë continued to prance around the room, bending her body in a "come and get me" stance. Suddenly, she stopped, every muscle still. With a twitch, she sprang back to action. Her eyes gleamed as she ran over, dropped her chin on his other shoulder, and growled softly in his ear.

"Who's the dominant one now, huh? Think you need to reconsider our hierarchy?" She gave him a shove with her shoulder. "Wanna wrestle?"

"Um, okay." Guy looked decidedly unsure. Still, he positioned himself on the sofa, arms and legs spread wide. I started to growl again and placed myself behind the arm of the couch, where I could bite him if things got sexy. What would Max think if he could see this? My human body was acting in ways even S&M practitioners would find perverted. If I could have blushed, I'd be pink to my toenails.

Zoë stood across from Guy and snarled.

"Like it rough, do you?" he said, shifting deeper into the couch. "I should have guessed. Playing it tough at the café, firing me like you didn't care. I always thought you'd be rowdy in the sack."

My teeth were inches away from his hand. I couldn't get a clean bite, I decided, not with his hand splayed on the sofa, but I could make him scream. Just then, Zoë launched herself at him, landing with her knee squarely in his crotch. Ignoring his squeal of pain and the way he snapped shut like a cell phone, Zoë hammered her left shoulder into his right. She caught both of his hands and pressed them out, spread-eagle. Then she barred her teeth in his face.

"I'm the toughest you've ever seen, aren't I? A real alpha. You might think you can beat me, but you're totally wrong. I can beat anybody, any day."

Inside, I snickered. Zoë might be unpredictable, but

I had to hand it to her—she had self-confidence dripping out her ears. No one was going to make her do anything. I wish I had half her chutzpah.

Guy's purple face withered with pain. With a sudden burst of strength, he threw Zoë off him, heaved off the couch, and waddled away, fumbling at doors until he found the bathroom. I heard the click of a lock. My ex-chef was locked in my bathroom, and Zoë and I stood in the front room alone.

She stared at the bathroom door, a blank look on her face. "Huh. I guess he didn't think he could beat me. Well, that's good, then. I wouldn't want to humiliate him—then he wouldn't drive me anywhere."

I was so relieved I flopped down on the floor. This had been a near miss. If Guy had been willing to fight with Zoë, would she have mated with him, as his reward? Was that what she was after? This led to a frightening idea. If I couldn't get back into my own body, I'd have to endure this same torture again and again and again. All the more reason to get us switched back—quickly, before I actually had to bite someone. But how?

Zoë shook me out of my thoughts by walking up to the bathroom door. "Hey, man! Why don't you come out? We don't have to wrestle—if you're okay with being the beta, that's no problem. Let's go for a ride."

I heard a muffled *no,* and the sound of someone double-checking the lock. Zoë shrugged and came over to me. She bent low and scratched my chin.

"Doggie friend," she said, her voice honey-sweet, "will you help me? I need to make a picture."

For a minute, my mind was so overwhelmed with the way her fingers soothed my itches that I couldn't hear. Then she stopped. Our eyes met, and I had the disturbing experience of locking gazes with myself. My eyes were actually rather pretty—shot through with a thousand shades of brown, honey overlapping with coffee and oak, almost swirling under the light. Looking into them, I sensed a compassionate being behind the irises. Was that Zoë, or some residual part of me?

I certainly felt like I had all of my bits and pieces with me in the dog body—my faculties, my brain, my soul, if you wanted to call it that. But there were other things as well. Along with my sense of smell, I seemed to have a vast encyclopedia of images connected to different scents. That, surely, was part of Zoë. And look at her—she could speak English. She could walk and feed herself, things it took a human child years to learn. Clearly, part of my skill set had stayed with my body. Like it or not, we were both part dog, part human. I remembered how the smells in the park had distracted me, overpowering my senses. The dog part was in there all right—and it was strong.

Zoë tipped her head to one side as if she were trying to cock an ear. "Help me make a picture? *I'll scraaatch yoooou.*"

The mere mention of scratches made my tail thump. Before I knew it, I found myself in front of my desk, nudging the drawer with my nose. Of course it didn't open. Zoë bent down, examined the drawer, and splayed her hand open like a scout with a new Swiss army knife, selecting the right tool for the job. She settled on her forefinger and gave the drawer a poke. Nothing happened. She poked it again.

With a sigh, I stuck out my tongue and nudged the drawer handle toward me. Zoë, watching me carefully, got down on her knees and gave the drawer a lick, just like I had. Stifling a laugh, I caught her hand in my teeth and led it gently to the handle.

This time Zoë got it. She slid the door open. "Ohhh." She pushed it closed, then opened it again. "Huh! All that stuff, hidden inside. Amazing." She slid the drawer in and out a few more times, then tipped her head so she could watch the runners slide back and forth.

Sitting right in the middle of the drawer was the paper she wanted, plus a tidy array of pens and pencils, organized by color. Or, at least, they were usually in a rainbow array. Right now they looked like varying shades of gray.

I left Zoë to her own devices and went back to my top priority, the Glimmerglass. The poor, poor Glimmerglass. How on earth could I get more customers in the door?

Oh, who was I kidding. Even as a person, I'd have had a hard time convincing people to go to our café. Food was a whimsical choice for most people. If they weren't motivated by convenience and price, their decision to pick one restaurant over another could be based on the smallest thing. The color of the awnings; the font of the menu. A sudden craving for guacamole. It was tiny touches, like a special Woofinstock menu, that drew people in the door—not any sales pitch from me. And here I was, a dog, utterly unable to give a sales pitch even if I'd wanted to. A dog with no vocal cords. No thumbs. I was just a big, white, long-legged dog that most of the town thought was adorable.

Hmm. Adorable.

What would happen if an adorable dog suggested the café to customers? Ordinary people might not listen, but would dog people? Might a tip from a dog be just the kind of little touch that would send people into the Glimmerglass?

I bounded to my room. Pawing open the sliding door of my closet, I went to the stack of neatly folded T-shirts and nosed through them until I found what I was looking for. A shirt with bright squares on the front, shaped like four panes of glass. I knew that it was sky blue, even though it looked dove gray at the moment. Across the top ran the words GLIMMER-GLASS CAFÉ.

Working as fast as I could, I used my teeth to spread the shirt out on the floor, front-side up. Then I went to the bottom and shoved my nose inside. It took me eleven tries to get my head into the shirt, but once I did, I was in business. I crawled forward, working my paws alongside my face, until my front paws popped out the armholes and my head burst through the neck.

Panting with exertion, I pushed my bedroom door shut to look at myself in the tall mirror on the back. Amazing. I looked stunning, all white fur and gray shirt with the logo like a blaze on my back. I turned this way and that, admiring my new outfit. *Zoë has to see this*, I thought. *She's the only one who'll understand how terrific this is.*

I hurried back to the front room, ready to catch her attention, when something tiny zoomed in front of my eyes. Zip, zip. There it went again.

I whipped my head around, but it was gone. One

second later, I spotted it, straight overhead. My heart thumped like a subwoofer. Whatever that thing was, I had to have it. All thoughts of cafés and T-shirts vanished. Before I could register a single cogent thought, I felt my feet moving, my mouth gaping, my ears flicking back and forth.

The thing—a fly—looped through the air above the sofa. I clambered onto the cushions, nimble as a mountain goat. With four feet perched on the back of the sofa, I launched up and out, mouth wide open. As I flew through the air, the fly collided with the roof of my mouth. I clamped down, satisfaction surging through me. I had it—I'd caught it! I chomped, excited to the tips of my one-million-plus hairs. The fly was mine!

The instant my feet hit the floor, I remembered why people don't eat flies. It buzzed against my teeth, more unnerving than a dentist's drill. Revulsion swirled uneasily in my stomach. I opened my mouth and the fly looped away, but the disgust stayed with me. I'd just tried to eat a fly. I'd caught it in my mouth, for pity's sake. I was part dog now, like it or not.

That thought made my heart sink. I went into the kitchen, nosed around until I found that shriveled cherry tomato, and ate it.

Zoë

The gnome stays in the bathroom a long time. I'm glad, because pens turn out to be hard to use. None of them work. They feel like metal and slide around the paper. There's probably a trick with them, like there was with the drawer, but I don't have time to discover what it is. I find a wooden pencil that works better. I chomp it a few times to mark it as mine, then I start working.

I bite my tongue with my teeth while I draw a picture of my house. If I were working with dogs, I'd try to describe my house by smell, but that won't work with people. Already I've learned that people need to see a thing to believe it. Smells seem to mean nothing to them, shocking as that is.

When I'm done, I go to the bathroom door.

"Come out, short man!" I say in a loud, commanding alpha voice. "Hey, you! Come out!"

The door opens a paw's width. Behind the door, the man looks nervous.

"Don't jump me again," he says, all low and growly. "I'm a green belt. I could whoop your ass." He has his hands in front of his face, balled up like a cat's.

I back up, arms at my sides. Now that I'm the established alpha, it's my job to be kind and reassuring. "No jumping. See? I'm not jumping." Silly man. There's no need to fight him now, not after he ran away and hid the last time. My position is solid. "Can we go for that ride now?"

He steps out of the bathroom and laughs. "What ride? Where?"

Ah-ha! I have my picture ready. I hold it out, using my fingers and my thumb. My breath is hot.

He looks at my paper and snorts. My eyes get big. If he snorts, is that a sign that he's ready to get going?

I can hardly stop my feet from prancing. I watch the gnome carefully.

"What is this?" he says.

"My house. That's where I want to go. Can you take me? Right now?"

"Oh, c'mon—you just busted my balls and now you want a ride?"

"Yes!" What a relief that he understands. Jessica is in the kitchen, licking the tile floor. I hope she'll come when I call, because I want her to get the car ride, too. There's nothing dogs love like a ride in the car. Especially a car ride home.

I think of Mom patting my head and a warm, oozy feeling rumbles in my chest. Dad used to put me in my crate at night. When I lay down on my bed, I could hear them walking upstairs with soft, muted footsteps. I heard that sound and my tongue would hum, quiet and happy, because everyone was home together at the same time. I breathed long through my nose. And then I would sleep.

I have to get home. I look at the man and my heart feels huge, like a ball I can't fit in my mouth. It makes my ribs ache.

He laughs, and I'm sure this is it. I'm ready to get in the car. My mouth is dry.

"I can't drive you here," he says. "This isn't a map—it's a picture of a house. Any old house. It could be any house in Madrona. A roof, a door, a dog in front. What the hell is this?"

He throws my paper on the floor. My insides tumble from warm to cold. I lick my lips.

The man turns to go, and then spins back around. I

stare at him, wondering where I went wrong. Am I standing too close? Smiling too wide? Did I frighten him too much? I take a step back and close my mouth. A coldness settles over me, while heat creeps up my neck.

"I used to think you were hot, Jessica, with that great body and everything, but you have turned total freak. I'm glad I'm done with your stupid café. It's lucky you didn't ask me back because I'd have turned you down flat. I don't care how sexy you are—Guy is outta here."

He walks away. All the way through the door. I run after him and stand on the grass, but he doesn't stop. He doesn't open the car door and call for me. I don't get in the car. I don't go home.

11

Woofinstock Crush

 Zoë

I sit down on the couch and concentrate in silence. Jessica is near the door, staring down at a purple envelope so hard, for a minute I think it might grow whiskers and start meowing. But it doesn't. She's wearing a new costume, a blue shirt that's tight at the neck and baggy at the waist. Curious. Still, I push her out of my thoughts and buckle down. I made a mistake with the garden gnome, I feel sure of it. A mistake I can't afford to make again, not if I want people to help me get home.

I must have offended him somehow or made myself seem unworthy of help. Was it what I said? Or the way I held my face? I've noticed that some people do a lot of smiling while others hardly smile at all. Which one is right?

The garden gnome said he couldn't find my house with the picture I made. Clearly, I have to come up with a new way of getting back home. I've already become half of the prettiest dog-and-person team in town, but that didn't bring my people back to me. I need a fresh idea. Mom and Dad are both people, and it seems like my new understanding of humans should be able to help me track them down. I close my eyes and concentrate on what it means to be a person.

I really don't understand the way humans deal with food. At the café this morning, why did that man let me take his food? Why was he eating it so slowly? It wasn't that he didn't care about it—if that were the case, he wouldn't have minded if I'd stolen a hundred muffins off his plate. He did mind—he even got mad. No, people definitely care about food. They're just . . . picky. And awfully slow to defend their share.

When I think of food, a million smells pour into my brain. I remember the times I've smelled my mom and dad's clothes when they came home—they smelled just like the café where I had the pumpkin cookies. Like oily and salty things, and strong cleanser, and coffee. They smelled amazing.

Hmm. The café. Maybe that's where they go when they leave home? My eyebrows twitch with the power of this new idea. It all locks together perfectly—that's where I need to go to find them.

"Hey," I say to her. "Are you hungry?"

She looks up with famished eyes. Her tail wags like crazy.

"Ha—I knew you would be! My tummy says it's lunchtime. Let's go to that place we went this morning, the place by the metal dog." She wags even harder and starts to jump up and down. I'm pleased with myself and my excellent new plan.

Before we leave, I put on my shiny winner's hat.

When we see my mom and dad, they'll notice me and then they'll see the dog I'm with. Who knows—maybe they'll take both Jessica and me home together. "I like your new blue shirt," I say, proud that I can see the color so well. "You have your costume, and I have mine. Let's go."

 Jessica

I couldn't run to Midshipman's Square fast enough. Between that stupid fly and the old tomato in the kitchen, I was having some shocking lapses of memory. Looking back, I realized that I'd gone hours without thinking of Woofinstock or finding a sous chef. I'd been too wrapped up in grotesque dog things, like eating old food off the floor. Maybe I was becoming even more doggish as time went by. Well, if that were so, I had to fight against it. I couldn't let Kerrie and the café down.

Now that we were headed that way, I was determined to make up for my absenteeism. To begin with, I had a new theory about how to get back into my right body. Maybe, I thought, if Zoë and I went back to the scene of the lightning strike, we might be put back to normal. Hope made me agitated, so I ran circles around Zoë the whole way there. The noon sun heated the T-shirt on my back, but I didn't let that slow me down.

The closer we got to town, the more anxious I felt. Still, the world kept intruding, wiping away my mental to-do list. First it was the smell of a barbecue down near the beach, then a squirrel that darted across the road. Zoë actually had to grab my leash to keep me from racing into traffic. How humiliating. Deep in my gut, I had to acknowledge that the longer I stayed in this body, the more doglike I would become. All the more reason to reach Spitz's statue right away.

We arrived and found the square mobbed with an early afternoon crowd of people and dogs. Smells bombarded me. Sweat and fur blended into an amazing perfume. People from all walks of life swarmed together, their pressed-linen shirts mixing with cargo shorts and tank tops. I noticed this, but for once I also noted the wide variety of dogs—the tiny, shivering papillons mixed in with panting Newfoundlands and wary-eyed Australian shepherds. The hairs on my neck rose. My tail brushed the air tentatively. I'd held my own with the dogs at Hyak Park that morning (had it only been that morning?), but I'd never walked into a pack like this.

I was hoping Zoë would skirt the worst of the crowd, but no. With that dorky crown perched on her head, she plunged into the fray, vibrating with energy, her hunger forgotten. Once again, I marveled at her ease. She seemed to have an insatiable capacity for in-the-moment happiness. How did she do that? Was this why people loved dogs—because nothing ever got them down?

I looked at the sea of lolling tongues and panting mouths around me. The dogs all looked so . . . happy.

Dogs certainly did have that free and easy spirit down pat. And the people around me seemed to know that and appreciate it. Every time I saw a person looking down at their dog, their faces brightened and gentled with love.

As I pushed toward Spitz, dog after dog turned to sniff me. I passed by them all, the swirl of scents jumbling in my brain. I only stopped once, when I caught a scent I recognized. There was no name I could attach to it, no words to describe it, but it felt instantly familiar and strangely compelling. I pulled Zoë ten feet across the square, following it, before I ran smack into Foxy and Leisl Adler.

"Oh, hi," Leisl said to Zoë. She flicked a disapproving look at Zoë's crown, then bent down and offered me her fist—to smell, apparently. I couldn't help it. I cringed away. "Not very social, is she?"

Zoë looked at me as if such a thought had never occurred to her. "She's absolutely perfect," she said staunchly. I glowed a little. For the first time, it occurred to me to feel lucky that it was Zoë I had switched places with. If I had to be trapped in this furry frame, at least it was nice to be appreciated. Imagine if I'd been paired up with Leisl.

Foxy, who'd been sitting, came to meet me, the sunlight casting a golden sheen over his curly head. Leisl jerked back on his leash.

"Foxy, heel," she snapped. With an anxious upward glance, Foxy sprang back into position. Again, I felt grateful for lax Zoë. No matter how many dogs swirled around us, she never tensed up. Her mood stayed as loose as the leash that hung between us. I couldn't remember ever feeling that mellow.

Zoë and I both decided to move on at the same time. "Bye," Zoë said and waved, more to Foxy than to Leisl, though it was Leisl who returned the gesture. I was glad to escape them, but as we walked away Zoë said something that surprised me. "She's tough," Zoë whispered with a note of admiration in her voice. We wove through the crowd. I struggled to keep from getting tangled with the other leashes. "She must be an alpha. If I were Foxy, I'd do everything she says. People must follow her everywhere."

Uh, not exactly. For all her experience with dogs, Leisl was hardly the most popular person on the Woofinstock team. I'd even heard Malia Jackson call her bossy, and that was saying something.

At last we reached Spitz. In the midday sun, his copper body shone too brightly to look at. A pair of kids in swimsuits perched on top of his doghouse, riding it like an extra-wide horse, while tourists snapped pictures of their dogs next to the hero of Madrona. I held back, unsure what to do. Should we touch him at the same time? Say some kind of incantation? Or did we need lightning? I looked up at the sky and—for the first time—cursed the perfect day. We got few enough of them in the Northwest. Where were the clouds when I wanted them?

While I hesitated, considering, Zoë sauntered right up to Spitz.

"This dog had me so confused at first," she said, speaking just loud enough for me to hear. She ran her hand over his copper head. "From a distance, he looks completely real. No scent whatsoever, though. Now I can see how he is. Metal, through and through."

Watching her, my heart drooped queasily. This felt all wrong. The sunshine, the crush of people—none of it felt like last night. All the same, I moved close to Spitz and set my paw on his at the same time Zoë touched his head. Nothing. The sky didn't even darken. I gave a sigh that was so ragged Zoë peered at me.

"Oh, right, you're hungry, huh? Yeah, me too. Lunchtime!"

Zoë

As we head to the café, people keep turning to look at Jessica. She's so pretty—she turns heads wherever she goes, even in that shirt that fits her so badly. I go right up to the café door and start to go inside, but Jessica hangs back.

"What, you want to stay out here? I thought you were hungry."

She leans back against the leash, so I drop it. "Okay, you can stay here if that's what you really want. But I won't promise to save you anything. If I find any muffins in there, I'm eating them."

Her mouth pops open in a pant, but she stays where she is. Who knows what's going on in that fuzzy head of hers. She definitely has no idea how to get muffins.

The second I enter the café, I know I'm in the right place. It has the perfect mix of smells, plus some I didn't remember before but that feel just right. Cinnamonybeefy-basil smells. *Yes*. This must be the place—Mom and Dad love this kind of food.

The people inside—the ones wearing black and white—look happy to see me. I check the big room for my mom and dad, but I don't see them. Yet. It's crowded inside, but everyone's cheery. Until, that is, the lady with the red glasses comes in from the back. She aims right for me, almost scaring me with how quickly she approaches.

"Jeez, Jess—where have you been? I don't think I can take this! I've been going crazy here without a sous chef, the house packed, and no help from you. I've tried your cell phone fifty times. What the hell is going on?" Her face is squashed like a broken chew toy.

Hmmm. Not sure what to say. "Here I am," I say, hoping I'm doing this right. "Sorry about the cell phone."

"Yeah, well, you should be. What's the point of a cell if you don't answer it? I need you here—things are getting desperate. Have you found a sous chef yet?"

I think of the man from the bathroom. Didn't he say the word "chef"? But this lady scares me, and I don't want to answer the wrong way. Her head might pop.

I say, "Maybe." Then I smile and say, "Don't worry. I can fix this."

"You can?" Her face softens, like a mean dog's when it's falling asleep. "Really? You found us a chef? Oh, that's terrific." She droops against the wall. Her glasses are red and sparkly. "I'm sorry I went ballistic," she says. "I should have known you'd fix it. You always do." She points at two doors that have little windows in the top. "The sooner they can get in there, the better. Naomi's barely keeping up."

I start to go to the doors, and she touches my arm. "And Jess? Thank you. Thank you."

I give her my big grin, and she goes away. Even after she leaves, I can't stop smiling. Because I'm going in the room that has all the good food smells. I push on the doors and enter the kitchen.

 Jessica

I sat in front of the café and blinked a few times, gathering my thoughts. I wanted to help the Glimmerglass, but I wasn't sure how—I just knew that I couldn't be of much use inside the building. Whatever I was going to do, it would be here, in the crowd where the people were. Still, I had a hard time keeping my mind on task, and the overpowering smell of dog wasn't helping.

"Hey, Mom, look at that," a little girl's voice said behind me. "That dog's staring at that restaurant."

My ears flicked around, but I didn't turn my head. A second later an adult answered, "Weirder than that even. See what the dog's shirt says?"

Seconds later, someone was taking my picture. "She's like Spitz, only alive!" the little girl exclaimed. My mouth popped open and I panted, keeping my gaze fixed on the café door. Another family spotted me and wandered over, the kids looking at my T-shirt while the dad read the Glimmerglass's menu in the window. My heart picked up its pace. *Come on, shirt, work your magic!*

I sat stone-still while couples and families paraded by me, all chuckling over the idea of a spokesdog staring at a restaurant. Everyone had their own joke to make. "That dog sure is hungry!" or "How many dog bones do you think they paid her to do this?" I smiled at everyone and stayed where I was. As long as the magic was working, I wasn't going to mess with it.

Until, that is, my nose picked up a distinctive smell. It was onions and peppers, and just the right number of tomatoes, plus some secret ingredient that I couldn't name. Garlic? Chipotle? I snapped my head around and spotted a woman carrying a thirty-ounce container of Salish Salsa. She was still chewing, as if someone had offered her a free chip to dip in a sample bowl.

I did a quick calculation. I could stay where I was, enticing family after family into the café, or I could leave my post and try to persuade the most talented sous chef in Madrona to join us again. The debate took about a half second.

In a flash, I was at the Glimmerglass door. Luck was on my side—a family was heading in at the very same time and I tagged along, keeping a low profile. Once inside, I ignored the lunchtime buzz in the dining room, hung a quick right, and slipped to the back room, praying I wouldn't run into Kerrie. Or Zoë.

The Pit of Death was silent. I trotted to my desk, heaved up on two paws, and took in the new pile of bills and junk mail. Another lavender envelope stuck out of the heap. *Well, she was persistent, I had to give her that.* My nose started to twitch, and before I realized it, I was sniffing the envelope from corner to corner. It smelled like cigarette smoke trapped in old carpet. Cheap perfume. Grape jelly. I sneezed, and the movement shocked me back to my mission. Before I could get distracted again, I grabbed a couple flyers in my mouth and bounded to the door.

Getting back outside was easy—I pushed the door open myself. But once I was in the square, I couldn't figure out which way to go. I plunged into the crowd and instantly regretted it. The mass of legs and feet became a wall around me. It was hard to breathe with the papers in my mouth, and the ink on them smelled awful. Before I knew it, I found myself at Spitz's statue with no idea where to go next.

I sat down, watching feet pass me by—happy feet that all knew where they were going. Just as I was thinking that I might as well go back to the Glimmerglass and try to draw in customers, I spotted a pair of pink high-tops through the crowd. I bolted toward them, darting in and out of people's paths. The high-tops led me to the edge of the square, to a table set in a shady area in front of the health food store. And the familiar smell of Salish Salsa.

When I spotted Theodore's Timberlands I almost wept with relief. He was helping a tank-topped customer, but as soon as she walked off with her thirty-ounce tub, I ran behind the table and shoved my nose at Theodore's hands.

"What the? Oh, man, you're a big dog." He pulled

his hand back, but I waited, then leaned in again, praying he wouldn't be afraid. "Check this out," he called to his girlfriend, Ariel, the one in the pink high-tops. "This dog's all over me."

"What's she got?" Ariel reached forward and took the flyers out of my mouth.

I will love you forever for doing that, I thought as I panted in her direction. Together, she and Theodore unfolded one of the flyers on their table.

"Oh, look," she said, "the Glimmerglass is hiring again."

"Yeah," Theodore said, nodding. "Jessica left me a voice mail. Said they're desperate for a sous chef."

The two of them exchanged looks. "You wanna do it?" Ariel asked. "You always loved it there."

"What about the stand?" he said. "I admit, I was intrigued when I heard Jess's message, but I didn't want to leave you high and dry with all the salsa work."

"I can handle it," Ariel said. She seemed confident in her pink Converse. Like she could sell salsa in her sleep. I felt the tide turning in my direction, so even though I had a horrible case of cotton mouth from the flyers, I let out a loud bark. They looked at me and laughed.

"Weird," Theodore said, stroking his beard. "That dog brought those. Like, on purpose. Like she knows who I am. But I've never seen her before—have you?"

"Nope," Ariel said, straightening up. "But animals know things we don't. Spiritual things. They pick up on energy waves and chakras. I think you'd better go and do this. It's like fate or something."

"You sure?" Theodore already had his white apron off. My tail was wagging so hard I felt a breeze on my butt.

" 'Course. Go. Have fun. Create something."

And just like that, Theodore and I set off across the square. *When I turn into my human self again,* I vowed, *Ariel's going to get all her coffee drinks free. For life.*

I tailed Theodore all the way to the Glimmerglass's front door and tried to trot inside with him, but Sahara blocked me and shut the door in my face. "No dogs today," she said in a way that seemed unnecessarily cold. Especially for a dog in a Glimmerglass T-shirt.

I sat outside and tried to look happy, like the cheeriest café mascot in the world. Smells wafted off the crowd, overwhelming me with the scent of wet dog hair, hot dogs, and coffee. A muddy dog walked by and I nearly followed it just to get a better whiff of that dank dampness.

"Hey, Zoë," said a voice behind me. I hopped up, my tail already wagging. Max bent over me, snapping a green leash onto my collar. I felt his breath on my ear and shivered inside. "You're out here alone, eh?" He shook his head and winked at me, as if the two of us were in on the same secret. I lifted my head to sniff his chest—he smelled amazing, like wind and weather, and that incredible mint soap they sold at the Farmer's Market. He smiled at me and his cheekbones danced in the shadows. "I'll have to talk to Jessica about that," he said. "I know she's new to this dog-ownership thing, but you'd think she would at least leash you up to something, huh?"

Actually, she'd probably think that was cruel and unusual punishment.

"Let's get you some water," he said, leading me across the square.

I followed along, walking right beside him. I couldn't help feeling self-conscious, knowing that Max could stare down at me without my being aware. Of course, I reminded myself that he wasn't staring—why would he? He thought I was Zoë. Just a dog named Zoë. Nothing more.

We walked to the edge of the square, where Max led me to a communal doggie water bowl. We had to wait in line while a slobbery bulldog lapped and slurped, splashing half the water onto the cobblestones. When it was our turn, I gave the water a cautious sniff. It smelled decently clean—like water that had come through pipes, not from a cesspool.

I didn't want to drink it, but I was so thirsty I gave it a few laps. Then a few more. I couldn't afford to get dehydrated, not now. I read once that by the time you feel thirsty, your brain is already so dehydrated that you perform worse on standardized tests. With the way smells and sounds were distracting me, I needed all the mental power I could get.

For instance, I repeatedly had to force my mind off Max and onto one of the problems at hand, like helping the Glimmerglass. Not that it was easy, since Max had those amazing cheekbones. I could spend all day just watching him smile and talk and stare off into space. And I liked watching him use his hands. He had such confidence in his movements, and a quiet kind of grace. When he cupped his hand to smooth down his hair, I imagined that same hand sliding down a woman's back, and it gave me shivers.

But again and again I wrestled my mind back to the restaurant. I was relieved that, when we left the water bowl, Max led me back to the front of the café, where anyone passing by could see the Glimmerglass logo emblazoned on my back.

"You know," said Max, speaking in that undertone people use with dogs, "you're one lucky puppy, getting teamed up with Jessica. If you play your cards right, you just might get to stay."

Oh, no—I sure hope not. Please, don't let me stay like this forever. Still, it was nice to hear Max say I was lucky. I leaned in closer and hoped for more—more petting and more talk of luckiness. Also, I just liked listening to his voice.

"I know she isn't sure about dogs, but I think it's just because she's never had one. And who knows, maybe she had a bad experience when she was a kid or something. A lot of people are scared of dogs because something bad once happened to them."

My mind flashed on that mystery scar on my arm—on Zoë's arm now. I had no idea how I got it. Was it dog related? Or from something totally different, like a burn or a car accident? It had been there as long as I could remember. None of my foster parents knew how I got it—I supposed only one person in the world might know. And I wasn't feeling up to asking her.

I swallowed hard, my throat tight and small, and thought of those lavender envelopes. They'd been arriving for two months now. One every few days. Did they all say the same thing inside, I wondered, or did she mix up her message? Did she really think she could explain herself on a 5×7-inch piece of paper?

As Max ran his right hand around under my chin, I felt myself relax despite my tense thoughts. The ecstasy was so great the world turned bright and overexposed—too bright for me to see or hear or smell anything. My entire existence was wrapped up in the feeling of his fingers in my fur. Max really had the touch. I could get used to this.

Just then Max's hand stopped moving—he seemed lost in his own thoughts. I flicked my eyes open again and caught a glimpse of Kerrie through the window, her copper earrings swinging as she directed a family to their table for afternoon milkshakes and cookies. Seeing her there made my heart sink. Kerrie's talents were wasted in the dining room. Sure, she was good with customers, but considering how good she was with food, it seemed like a tragedy.

When we'd first opened the Glimmerglass, Kerrie made unbelievable creations. Spicy edamame-cilantro spreads on airy little puffed crackers. Lemon ice-cream sandwiches with gingersnap cookies, dotted with crystallized ginger. Chicken glazed with her own sweet-tangy sauce (the secret was minced, pickled pearl onions). Kerrie had the touch. People brought their out-of-town friends to the Glimmerglass just to prove that Madrona had its own haute cuisine. Fridays and Saturdays, the dining room was full. With a waiting list.

And then disaster struck. Kerrie's good friends, the Meyers, had brought their nine-year-old daughter Hannah in for a birthday dinner. She ordered Kerrie's famous tortellini and our special kid's salad, vegetables sliced in fun shapes with our secret dipping sauce. Hannah was delighted, and the whole staff went all-out to deliver her birthday angel food cake with chocolate sauce. Everyone in the restaurant sang. Hannah blew out nine candles and looked like the luckiest girl on earth.

We had no idea what happened or why, but later that night, Hannah got sick. Sick enough to go to the local all-night clinic. Sick enough to be airlifted to the Harborview Trauma Center. Very dangerously sick. It was touch and go all night. When Kerrie found out about it, she took the last ferry to Seattle and spent the night pacing the emergency room floor with the Meyers, praying for the best.

Hannah recovered, but Kerrie never did. There was no way of knowing if her meal had been contaminated, but Kerrie couldn't stop thinking about it. She spent hours trying to figure it out. Were the ingredients tainted? Had something gone wrong in the kitchen? Was it something a server did? A dishwasher? A flaw at the farm that grew our produce?

The Meyers never blamed Kerrie or the Glimmerglass. They were sure the explanation was simple, like an allergic reaction, and when they had her tested, it turned out that Hannah did have a pine nut allergy they hadn't known anything about. Even so, Kerrie couldn't shake the thought that the danger might have come from her kitchen.

We changed all of our suppliers, overhauled the systems in the kitchen, but Kerrie still wasn't satisfied. The idea that Hannah could have died that night haunted her. She grew nervous, pulling dishes back at the last second and insisting on refiring them, or dropping so many utensils on the floor we had to buy extra spoons and spatulas just so we'd have enough clean ones to get through the night.

In the end, Kerrie quit the kitchen. She hung up her apron and refused to cook for anyone but her own family. I had to scramble to find Guy, and when I did, we considered ourselves lucky. The Glimmerglass rebounded, more or less, and was doing fine until I had my infamous dog incident. But Kerrie never came back to the kitchen. Even now, years later, she didn't like to talk about what had happened that day. I knew it wasn't her fault—wasn't anyone's fault—but when I told her that, she didn't hear me. All she could see were her friends' faces in the hospital as they waited for news about their daughter.

Max stretched his arms overhead, breaking my train of thought. "Can you wait for me to get a coffee?" he asked, tying my leash to a bench near the café door. He disappeared inside, and I counted the seconds, deciding that the longer he was gone, the longer the line inside the café must be. I'd tallied up ten minutes by the time he popped back out, a steaming cup in his hand. *That was good.* Maybe my shirt was working.

Max came back to me and sat on the bench. I sat

on the ground, trying not to think about what my back end might be in contact with. I could be sitting in gum, or pee for all I knew. How unfair that I couldn't have a decent seat in a chair like everyone else. I sniffed around, but the air was so full of smells I couldn't be sure which belonged to the ground and which were sprayed on the bench legs behind me.

If there was one thing I was learning, it was that dogs didn't have much say about anything in this world. They couldn't go where they wanted, couldn't sit where they wanted, couldn't eat what they wanted. They couldn't even speak up for themselves.

Dogs are the lowest creatures on the totem pole. For all that the Woofinstock team loved their pets, even they didn't let their dogs make many decisions for themselves. Dogs were treated like children that no one bothered to train for a grown-up life. It had never occurred to me to feel sorry for them before. They always seemed so happy I figured their lives were perfect. As I was coming to see, that wasn't the case at all. Dogs were just pros at making lemonade from lemons.

I looked around the square at the multitude of dogs and was amazed by the sheer number of wagging tails and happy faces. These dogs' lives hadn't been perfect, but none of them held a grudge. No matter how long they'd been left home alone or made to wait in the car, they forgave instantly and completely. And instead of feeling superior because of their ability to forgive, they were just happy to let the past disappear from memory.

If only I could do that. *If I could let the past go*, I thought, *I would be so free*. All of my childhood injuries would evaporate. I wouldn't be angry at Guy anymore. And those lavender envelopes would turn into what they were—pieces of paper.

12

Canine in the Kitchen

 Zoë

The doors swing shut, and I walk into dog heaven. I'm in a shiny room that's full of food. I see bins full of chopped carrots, racks of eggs, and a cart piled up with more bread than I've ever seen. All I can think about is eating.

There's a woman here in a white coat and hat who smiles at me over her shoulder. Her face is sweating and her hands are moving like flashes of light. A tag on her coat says her name is Naomi. I can read it! The jumbly letters people are always staring at suddenly make sense in my brain. I look around and read a few more words (EXIT, EMPLOYEES ONLY). Amazing—I'm turning into a real person!

I turn to the woman and say with great pride, "Hi, Naomi."

She says, "Hi," without turning around. The door I came through swings open, smacking me in the butt. A man dressed all in black rushes in, sticks a piece of paper on a high metal strip that's covered with other papers, and dashes out. Naomi glances at the slip, then goes back to her work, shaking her head.

"Can you tell me something?" I say, nice and loud so she can hear me over the noise of frying things. Naomi looks back at me. I give her what I imagine is a hopeful-human look. "Why is she—" I tilt my head toward the swinging doors to let her know I mean the woman with the red glasses. "—upset? Everything here is great except for her."

Naomi shrugs. "Kerrie? Oh, I don't know," she says, slapping a piece of chicken into her frying pan. "Maybe because we've been slammed and have no sous chef to prep anything. Maybe it's because you promised to get us a sous chef last night, and when you showed up here, you didn't even seem sorry about letting everyone down."

I frown. I feel very small, but I'm not sure why. This is a happy place, a place that's *full* of food. What's there to be upset about?

If that woman were a dog, I'd offer to rub her stomach—that would calm her down. But of course I don't. Dad didn't like it when I pounced on him in the park, so I have to be careful. Besides, I've noticed that even though people all have hands, they never spend time rubbing each others' bellies. I don't understand it, but that's the way it is.

"Well, it's not like anyone's dying," I say. Maybe these people are just hungry. Of course—everyone snarls when they're hungry. If I make everyone something really tasty, I bet they'll be happy. Who doesn't like to eat?

Naomi has turned back to her stove, so I decide to

leave her alone. She seems wrapped up with her own project. When the man in all black comes in again, I stop him. "Can you help me?" I say. "I need to find the good food."

"The good food?"

"Yeah, you know. The meat." Duh.

He gives me a crooked look. "Um, it's in the walk-in, where it always is. Are you looking for something in particular?"

"Nope. Just meat."

I go into this "walk-in" place, which is icy cold, and find enough meat to feed fifty dogs. There are little pink cutlets and round hamburger patties, cubes of stew meat, and pink chicken breasts. I'm desperate to eat it all, immediately, but instead I turn around and close my eyes. The red-glasses woman—Kerrie—was angry enough before. I wouldn't want her to find me gnawing on the lamb shanks. I take a deep breath, turn around, grab the first meat I see, and run back into the kitchen.

Steak! I got steak! I'm excited, and I start to shimmy before I remember that I don't have a tail. I set my steak on a counter, find a bowl, and start mixing up a wondrous creation that will put a smile on Kerrie's face.

I throw one good thing after another into a bowl and work them with my fingers. They blend together and release a warm cloud of smells, like a rotten thing on the beach. I mix peanut butter and eggs and cheese and honey, then I smear my creation on both sides of the steak. Then I find a bag of shattery things called potato chips, and I dump these on top.

My steak looks so incredible I almost cry. Any dog alive would give its canine teeth to have just one bite of this steak. I have to keep reminding myself that I can't taste it, can't even lick it. This is a gift.

I make a noise in my throat to get Naomi's attention. She turns and sees my steak, but she doesn't smile the way I expected. She's quiet for a long time while her chicken sizzles, probably out of respect for my cooking prowess. Naomi has a face like a boxer's, and it twitches when she looks at my cooking. In the middle of twitching, she lifts one eyebrow, the way a dog would cock its ear when something confusing happens. "Um, did Kerrie really send you in to cook? What about finding us that new sous chef?"

I shrug. "Do we really need a new chef? You're here and you're cooking. I'm here and I'm the best cook I've ever seen. Look at this steak!"

She doesn't seem to be getting it, so I point to myself and then at my steak, using my pointing finger.

"Jessica, I love you," she says. "I'm trying to be patient here. But that looks disgusting."

She gives my cooking a sad look. I look at it sadly, too. I guess I should have gone outside and looked for a dead bird to put on top, like I thought about doing. Only, the truth is, I think it looks pretty perfect right now. I like Naomi, but I don't think she should be in charge of cooking. Her idea of tasty is all wrong.

I decide I don't care what she thinks. I sniff a thing called "ketchup" and pour it on top of my steak. My gift is utter perfection. I'm ready to give it, and I'm pleased when Naomi pushes on the moving doors and says something to Kerrie.

She comes in and looks at my cooking. Then she yells. And yells. And yells.

 Jessica

Max must have been the most popular veterinarian in town. He'd just finished giving me a complete rubdown, from my ears to that insane spot just above my tail, and I was ready to follow him around the world. I turned and gave him a huge, dopey grin.

"Like that, do you? Ear rubs?" He massaged my ear in a slow circle. A groan escaped me, and I gave a guilty start. It was a strangely sensual experience. In my euphoric haze, I could barely piece two thoughts together, but I did realize that I felt differently about this than a real dog would. After all, as I'd seen from Zoë's attempts at seducing Guy, dog sex operated on a different level than human intimacy. Caresses didn't play a part. I was probably the only dog in all of Madrona who enjoyed the sensuality of getting her ears rubbed by a man with such sensitive hands.

This is the one thing I'll miss when I change back. Should I be that fortunate.

Just then a pair of young women in very high-heeled sandals and short skirts walked by. "Hi, Max," they both cooed, ignoring the way my hackles rose. They waved coquettishly and one of them giggled.

I felt Max shift on the bench beside me. "Hi," he said. His hand dropped back onto my head. As the women walked away, my hopes shriveled. I could never compete with women like them. Never in a million years. They were beautiful, confident, flirtatious. A man's fantasy.

"Boy, not my type," he murmured under his breath. I glanced up at him, amazed. "Really. Too overdone, too fake. But I'll tell you, Jessica sure is beautiful."

I gasped. Me, beautiful? *Me?* Had he really just said that?

"She has the prettiest face. I think she's the prettiest woman in this whole town. She has the whole package. A great body, those big eyes, a perfect mouth. I mean, her mouth is absolutely perfect."

I gulped. My mind flashed to what I'd seen of myself lately. Zoë did have a love-of-the-moment confidence that put a sheen on my features. When she grinned, an enticing melody played on her face. It was a pretty enough face, I guessed, but I was too close to judge. What really mattered was what Max thought, and he'd used the word *beautiful*.

"She has more than just physical beauty, though," he went on, speaking too softly for anyone to hear but me. "I've seen her working—she's always calm and powerful at the same time. And content. Like she's happy to be living here. Like there's nowhere else on earth she'd rather be."

I felt sure that I must be glowing—that everyone could see the thousand twinkle lights that lit up in my chest. Was this really happening? Did Hot Max really think I was the prettiest woman in town? I wanted to pinch myself. Or run in circles and chase my own tail.

I thought back to all the mornings I'd watched him come in for his Americanos and gave myself a mental kick. Why hadn't I spoken to him months ago? Since when was I such a chicken? *It was this whole dog thing,* I thought with a groan. It had me all twisted up inside. Just because he was a vet who loved dogs, I'd assumed he wouldn't give me the time of day. *I have a problem,* I thought. *I have a really big problem.*

"You know, Becky was never really happy here," he said.

Becky? Becky? Who was Becky?

"Even before she took that job in New York, she never felt right in Madrona. It's too small, I guess. She didn't like the way clients recognized me at Madrona Market. Nothing to do here, she said." Out of the corner of my eye, I saw his hand wave around to indicate the hubbub in the square. "Like this isn't plenty going on? It's plenty enough for me, that's for sure." I felt his knees move as he shook his head and leaned back against the bench. "New York would grind me up and spit me out. I don't know why she ever thought I would go."

Now I felt guilty for listening in on his private affairs. Not that I missed a single word. Poor Max with his girlfriend (*ex-girlfriend?*) Becky, who had moved to New York. I'd broken up with a boyfriend that way—I knew how easy it was to question your decision to stay behind. When my last boyfriend moved to L.A., he'd made it clear that I was welcome to go along. Granted, it wasn't the most sweeping-off-my-feet invitation I'd ever received, but still, he had offered. And I'd declined. And spent the next four months wondering if I regretted it.

"I don't regret it, though," Max said, jumping up

and coiling the end of my leash around his hand. He led us to a patch of trees planted around the edge of the square. I guessed that we'd come here for me, because he thought I'd like to sniff the bushes, so I pretended to while I kept my ears alert. "I couldn't live there. Not when I *want* to live here. I grew up here—I don't want to leave. Why would I? I love that people recognize me. I love it when they ask me dog-care questions in the grocery store."

I had to sit down. Max's sudden confession had me befuddled with emotions, including shame at having overheard something that was only meant for a dog's ears. I didn't know people confessed such private things to dogs. This must be another reason people kept them around—they could hear a thousand secrets and never blab. That really was a gift.

Of course, what rocked me about this revelation wasn't the depths of the secrets; it was hearing how he felt about me. I desperately wanted to hear more.

My insides squirmed and I realized that I wasn't being wholly accurate. I wanted to be a *person* hearing this tender confession. I wanted Max to take my hand and look into my human eyes—not feel his hand absently stroking the top of my head.

Aargh.

 Zoë

The woman in the red glasses has a red face. She doesn't stop yelling, even when it hurts my ears. Even when Naomi tells her, "Easy, Kerrie," and puts a hand on her arm. Red Glasses picks up a wooden spoon and holds it in front of my face.

"Are you purposefully trying to sabotage us? Jessica, this is our restaurant! How could you kill the one thing you love? Is this some early midlife implosion or something?"

She shakes her head and all the color leaves it. "I just don't get it. I can't fathom why you'd try to ruin our café. What were you thinking?"

I lick my lips because I'm nervous. "I thought you might be hungry. Everyone feels better when they eat something."

Her eyebrows drop over her eyes. She looks mean. "And I thought you had a sous chef," she whispers. "We both know you can't cook."

I look at my creation. It looks incredibly good to me. What's the matter with this woman? Maybe she isn't right in the head. Maybe that's why people leave food on their plates without eating it—because they aren't very smart. I sigh.

"You know, this isn't as sad as you think," I say. "No one got hit by a car. No one's sick or about to die. We're here surrounded by all this food—we should be happy."

"Happy? Happy? We're on the verge of bankruptcy and you want me to flutter around being happy?"

She glares at my steak like it's full of worms. I want to say the right thing, but I definitely don't want to make her angrier. People are confusing—their faces say one thing and their words say another. I don't know what will make her calm down. She's so mad already, any answer will probably only make things worse. "I don't know," I mumble.

Her nostrils flare. Her eyes get narrow. I think I gave the wrong answer. Quick as a lick, she grabs my arm and walks me out the swinging doors, into the restaurant, and we crash into a man with a shaved head, a beard, and a lot of tattoos.

Right away, Kerrie starts talking to the man instead of to me, which is a huge relief. Their conversation is quick and intense, and they whisper so I can only hear little bits like "this weekend," "sous chef," and "big white dog."

Big white dog! I think of Jessica and my heart swells with pride. She's so gorgeous in my body.

I start to relax, but when the man disappears into the kitchen, I get worried again. Kerrie turns back to me, and I can see that her face is still red.

"That was your doing, I suppose? Somehow or other?"

I glance around the room, looking for some clue to what she's talking about. I don't know whether I should take credit or not, so I shrug and look at my shoes.

She sighs and puts her hands on her hips. Then she surprises me with a sugar-smelling hug. People are just too weird.

"Come here," she says. "There's something I want to talk to you about."

She leads me into the back room, the place where Jessica and I ate cookies before, and picks up a square purple envelope exactly like what Jessica was staring at in her apartment.

Kerrie's voice is soft. How she could go from being so mad to so sweet is a real puzzle. "We've gotten about thirty of these by now. Think you might be ready to tell me what they're about?"

I use my shrug again. "I don't know," I say, because that's the truth.

She points to the writing in the corner. "Debra Sheldon? Do you have a long-lost sister I don't know anything about?"

Do I? That seems fun. "Not sure," I say.

Kerrie puts a hand on my arm. I like it when she's being nice like this. "Haven't you opened any of these envelopes?"

I shake my head. Something in the way she says it makes me so sad that water collects in my eyes.

☕ Jessica

I looked shyly up at Max, hoping he didn't notice how heavily I was breathing. What more would he tell me? About his first crush? His feelings on marriage? Or—my ego fluttered—more about me?

Max gave me a few more minutes at the bush I was pretending to smell, then turned back toward the Glimmerglass. A cluster of people in sailing clothes passed us, clearly off for an afternoon cruise. "C'mon, Z," Max said. The nickname made me stand a few inches taller. I trotted behind him. "Let's go see if Jessica's done in there. Maybe she wants to get dinner in a couple hours."

Dinner—the very word had me drooling. I'd forgotten how hungry I was. That pumpkin cookie had been hours ago, and Zoë and I never had found any lunch. I found myself wondering what had happened to the basket of cookies we won at the pageant. Apparently Zoë had forgotten to pick it up.

As if reading my mind, Max dipped his hand into his coat pocket and fished out a bone-shaped cookie. "Sit," he instructed.

Oh, I sat. I even wagged. And hoped to hell that dog cookies tasted like cannoli.

Max offered the cookie, and I took it as daintily as I could. I ate it all in one bite—with no hands, I didn't really have a choice. The biscuit was dry as dust and slightly salty. In other words, it was heaven. I looked adoringly up at him in lieu of a thank you and was rewarded with another biscuit. Max really did seem to understand dogs.

We wandered back to the café and paused outside while Max looked in through the glass doors. The thought that he was looking for Zoë delighted me, but it also made me squeamish. I pictured myself, blissfully back in my human body, heading out on dates with Max, walks with Max, to dinner with Max. It looked wonderful. It looked fun and sexy and exciting. But it also looked too good to last.

At some point he'd learn the awful truth, that I was completely alone in Madrona, except for Kerrie. I didn't have a Mom-and-Dad's-house, a hometown, anything. All I had were some flimsy purple envelopes that smelled like stale cigarette smoke. And the Glimmerglass. Which was almost bankrupt.

Fifteen feet away, the café door swung open. Kerrie

and Zoë came out, heads close together. "You sure you're okay to get back out there? Don't get me wrong—we need you to. Our crowd's been good this morning, but it's going to take a lot more promo to keep us full for the dinner service and tomorrow. But if you need a minute to collect yourself—"

Zoë shook her head, wiping a hand across her face, a lavender envelope clutched tightly in her hand.

13

A Woman's Best Friend

 Jessica

Was Zoë crying? Why did she have a lavender envelope? I nearly choked in panic. What had Zoë done? What had she told Kerrie? I strained at the leash, trying to tug Max closer—quickly, before the earth fell away beneath me.

Kerrie gave Zoë a quick shoulder hug, then turned back to the café saying, "Go get 'em, then, tiger. Keep up the good work. And we can talk about that—" she indicated the purple envelope "—whenever you feel ready."

As I watched the door shut behind Kerrie, my heart shivered. I wasn't ready for Kerrie to know about those envelopes—I just wanted them to stop coming. Not that I didn't trust Kerrie. I did. But I wasn't ready to dive into that whole issue. Not with anyone.

Still, I tried to calm myself down by remembering that Kerrie was the most trustworthy person I knew. I could still remember the day we met. We were taking the same restaurant management class in Seattle, and,

on the very first day, the instructor paired us up together on a homework project because we both lived
in Madrona. I'd already noticed Kerrie because of the
confident way she wore her dangly earrings and multi-
colored glasses. I, in my black pants and camel-colored
turtleneck, was dressed to blend with the walls. I
longed to have even a Dixie-cup's worth of Kerrie's
flair.

Our assignment was to pick a local restaurant and
analyze how well its marketing fit its clientele. Within
seconds, it was clear that Kerrie and I appreciated the
same things in restaurant decor—warmth, modern so-
phistication, and plenty of polished wood. Logos, we
both knew, had to be an outer reflection of what the
restaurant offered on the inside. For our project, Kerrie and I picked the Salt Cellar, which had a kitschy
and cartoonish logo that was wrong, wrong, wrong
for its twenty-nine-dollar entrees and page-long wine
list.

By the following year, the Salt Cellar was ancient
history, and Kerrie and I were business partners.
Every evening when I got home from my day job, I
would head over to Kerrie's house to plan. In her dining room, we passed baby JJ back and forth while
Kerrie's husband Paul whipped up dinner. From the
moment Kerrie first sketched our logo on the back of
an envelope, all the details fell into place. I would be the
business half of the partnership, handling the lease,
the ordering, payroll, the budgets. Kerrie was our
creative genius, the one who woke up in the middle
of the night, her head bursting with visions of lemon
flan and rosemary-roasted pears. Paul bravely looked

on, nervous over the terms of our small business loan, but also filled with faith in his talented wife.

For me, these moments were like stepping inside a Hollywood movie. As a couple, Kerrie and Paul were in a different stratosphere from any of my foster parents. They joked like best pals and seemed to communicate whole paragraphs with just a few words. Life in foster care had always been tense, especially at home, but Paul and Kerrie's house was a happy oasis. I watched them like they were teachers in a master class on family life.

I stayed on my best behavior when I was with Kerrie. This family feeling was so new to me I kept waiting for the day it would all disappear—or Kerrie would disappear. So I cleared the table, did the dishes, and laughed at all their jokes. All of my paperwork was filed on time. I took notes about what they wanted for their birthdays and gave them excellent gifts. I tried to be perfect.

Amazingly, Kerrie kept with me. Ever so slowly, I began to trust her with my secrets. After one year, I told her about my foster families. After two, I told her about the worst one, the place where the dad was an alcoholic. I was sure she'd start slipping away, but she didn't. Instead, she watched over me, as if she could replace the mother I never had. She subjected every potential boyfriend to her patented "mom look," a hawklike glare that she swore could spot treachery a mile away.

Eventually Kerrie even learned about my fear of dogs. She and Paul had a goofy yellow Lab named Jane Eyre, and Kerrie quickly realized that the dog

and I couldn't be in the same room without me having a panic attack. I don't think Kerrie ever understood my fear, but she accepted it. As she used to say,
"We all have quirks, Jess. Paul is a little OCD, and I
can only sleep on my left side. Your deal is dogs, and
that's just the way it is."

The trouble was, I had more secrets than the ones
I'd already shared. They all centered around those stupid purple envelopes, so when I saw Kerrie and Zoë
talking about them—with Zoë in tears—I had reason
to worry. The second Kerrie went back into the café, I
put all my energy into hauling Max toward Zoë. We
were about twenty feet away when a man with no
shirt on came up to Zoë and said something. She put a
hand on the man's arm. Beside me, Max bristled,
yanked on the leash, and we skidded to a halt.

Zoë, who still hadn't seen us, smiled up at the man
like a sunflower watching the sun. My skin crawled.
*What was she up to now? Please, no more seductions—
please. I don't care if he does have a car, or even a
plane.*

Next to me, Max exhaled noisily. He looked down
at me, and we locked eyes with a force that made me
swallow. He made a wry face.

"Not my lucky day, huh? Guess she's out of my
league."

What? *No,* I wanted to scream, *no—she isn't! She's
absolutely, squarely in the middle of your league.
She's not into that guy. She just wants to ride in his
car!*

Max stiffened his spine, wrapped my leash around
his hand one more turn, and led me up to Zoë. I

caught a whiff of the shirtless man and inhaled a lungful of cheap cologne.

"Here she is, safe and sound," Max said to Zoë, his voice tight. He held out my leash. "I'll see you around."

Zoë gave him a glittering smile. "Dr. Max! You brought her! You're a good man. *Such* a good man."

She lifted her hand as if she wanted to pat him on the head, but Max leaned away.

"Uh . . . thanks. I guess. I've gotta run. See you." He bent down to run his hand along my cheek and under my chin. Disappointment vibrated through his fingertips. "Thanks for the walk, sweet girl."

Oh, Max! I was swooning inside. How could it be that I'd just found out my perfect guy liked me back, and there was nothing I could do about it?

On top of everything else, he'd gotten the wrong impression about this shirtless guy, whoever he was. I opened my mouth, desperate to communicate with Max. I wanted to tell him everything—that I wasn't Zoë, I was Jessica, trapped in the wrong body. That I didn't give a rip about this guy. And that I really, really wanted to see what a date with him would be like.

Of course, all that came out was a long howl. Max turned and chuckled, but as his eye caught Zoë's, his face fell.

She waved enthusiastically at him as he walked out of the square. I could have wept.

When Max was out of sight, Zoë swung back to the shirtless man. "You said you would take me for a ride in your car?"

"Sugar, I'll take you anywhere you wanna go."

Oh, that is just enough. I might have been a dog—
unable to speak or open things or drive a car—but I
had the right to exert myself, especially where my real
body was concerned. No way was Zoë going to sleep
with some skanky man just to get a ride in a car.

Some forms of communication are universal. I edged
close to the man, trying to avoid the sharp scent of his
cologne. With one back foot on either side of his size-
twelve Converse, I huddled down and peed.

14

The Agile Dog

Zoë looked at me like I'd just shot the president.

"Why did you do that?"

I put on a blank face and pretended to smell my foot. The man vanished without a word.

"Don't look like that." Zoë had her hands on her hips. "I *know* you're listening. And I know you were bad, too. Really bad! That man was going to help me. Why did you pee on him?"

Yeah right. Help her how? As far as I could tell, Zoë was having a ball in my body. What could she possibly need help with? She was the one who'd just shared my most prized secret. And probably made a mess of things in the café. She could waltz through life just as easily on two legs as on four. It wasn't as if she had a restaurant to promote.

"Listen, I'm the person around here," she said. "I'm the one who needs help. You're the dog, you're supposed to *help* me. That's what dogs do."

I snorted out my nose.

That made Zoë get red in the face, which, I have to say, is not the way my face looks best.

"Ahem, Miss People-Don't-Need-Help," said Zoë, jutting her jaw like a sassy little sister. "You are utterly wrong. I was helping you after we'd only known each other one day. I helped you talk to Dr. Max and walk home in the storm. I let you hug me when you were scared. I even helped you deal with the man who came in the white van. You were nervous about talking to him, I could tell." She shook her head. "I let you see that you could just smile and have fun. I've been showing people that all my life, but they never really learn it for themselves. People just don't understand things."

That set me back on my tail. Was Zoë really trying to say that *she'd* been helping *me* in our encounter with animal control? That was beyond laughable. Could she truly believe that?

"You poor people," she said. She was staring at me, her hands at her sides, with a look of overwhelming compassion. "You're all the same. Like puppies. Squirmy and always in trouble, right? And then you get scared and sad and come running to us for comfort. It's a good thing people are as good as they are at giving ear rubs. And driving cars. And building sofas."

Suddenly Zoë broke into a smile, her anger forgotten. She trotted over and smacked me playfully on the hip. "Know what I can see because I'm taller than you? Tents! Big party tents!" She pointed toward the green, where vendors had their give-away booths. I'd forgotten all about the vendors. I hoped the high schoolers had the Glimmerglass stand all in order. "There might be *food* there!"

 Zoë

Jessica perks right up when I say "food." I knew she would. Her dog instincts must be kicking in.

We run all the way to the big patch of grass where the tents are. Every tent has a table with a person behind it. Before we get to the first one, I can smell cheese and sausage and I'm suddenly famished. I eat five sausage cookies before the lady says I can only have one. Like I'm supposed to count while I'm busy eating? The people world is weighing me down with all of its rules. Talk about boring.

We eat as many cookies as we can. Sometimes people tell me that the treats are for dogs, and then they look at me funny when I eat one. I look around to make sure no one is watching and then I put two more in my pocket. If they're for dogs, then I know I'll like them.

Besides, people food is hard to eat. Dog food is easy. Crunch and go.

Still, sometimes the people are irritated when they say it. *That's for dogs!*—like I've done something wrong. They have a way of saying things that makes me feel alone even when I'm standing in a group, as if I'm not part of a pack anymore. It's exhausting trying to fit in with people, struggling to understand the dos and don'ts. Sometimes it makes me feel sick to my stomach. I try to cuddle next to Jessica, but she's busy eating cookies. I think of my family, but that doesn't make me feel better—I feel worse. I've tried so many things, but nothing has worked. No one wants to take me home. Mom and Dad haven't found me yet, and I miss them so much my heart hurts.

Maybe the town hasn't heard yet what a perfect dog-and-person team we are?

I'm eating a chicken-liver treat that's shaped like a cat when I hear it. A big, fake-sounding voice says, "Calling all canine athletes! If your dog loves to run and jump, three o'clock is the time to enter in the fourth-annual all-comers Woofinstock Agility Competition!"

I turn to Jessica, my mouth gaping open.

"Fragility competition?"

She chokes on her cookie, so I know I must have heard right. I need to enter that contest. If we can win, Mom and Dad are sure to hear about it. If they will only come up to Jessica, I can get another chance to talk to them. I'm sure I can do it without scaring anyone away this time. All I have to do is smile and nod—and not get too close.

I tell Jessica to follow me to the contest area, and at first I think she's refusing because she runs over to a booth that smells like coffee and doesn't have a single dog treat to hand out. She grabs a huge stack of folded papers in her mouth, even though the boy and girl working the stand say, "Hey, what's that dog doing? She's stealing our menus!"

She's faster than they are. In a flash, she's at my

side. I take the papers out of her mouth, since I know how hard it is to breathe when you're carrying something with your teeth. Then we set off.

Jessica

As Zoë and I walked to the Agility Competition sign-up area, we passed family after family. I poked Zoë's hand with my nose, and she opened it up, displaying the menus like a fistful of treasure. Then I barked, which caught a family's attention.

"Hi!" Zoë said brightly. They saw her open hand and dutifully took a menu, taking a look at it as they walked on. We repeated this game until every last menu was gone. Half the people noticed my shirt and commented on how cool I was. A few kids even asked their parents if they could have Glimmerglass T-shirts, so they could dress up "just like that dog."

I was so tickled by how well this worked I decided to let Zoë enter me in whatever contest she wanted. Plus, with my shirt on, I was a walking billboard. So I tried not to care when Zoë regaled everyone with stories of how fragile she was. And I pretended not to notice that Zoë was still wearing her crown from the beauty contest. Amazingly, a few people who'd seen our act stepped out of line to tell Zoë how much they'd enjoyed it. We were becoming minor Woofinstock celebrities.

As Zoë signed us in, I sniffed the air, noticing the faint salt smell that blew up from the beach. I felt a sudden longing to be there, running along the sand, but I made myself turn instead to focus on the sunlit agility course. Leisl and Foxy were warming up on the equipment, and the second I saw them, I felt a burst of competitive fire. Sure, competing in my T-shirt would help the Glimmerglass no matter what. But it would help the Glimmerglass *more* if Zoë and I could do well. I was suddenly determined to do my very best, and since Zoë and I had never done this before, I could hardly count on her to lead me through it. I needed to memorize the route and lock it in my brain.

The course had five sections. First, the dogs jumped over a series of hurdles and through a hanging tire. That seemed straightforward enough. Then they came to a line of poles in the ground that they had to zig-zag through. Again, not too challenging if I could get the rhythm down. After that, the dogs went through a tunnel, then up and down each side of a teeter-totter, after which they ran a few more hurdles to the finish line. The teeter-totter, I figured, was where I could make up some ground. Most of the dogs, even the most experienced ones, hesitated at the top off the teeter-totter. Some jumped off early and were disqual-ified. I understood this kind of mental challenge—I could sail through the teeter-totter section.

The judges let us out onto the course to practice, but of course Zoë had no idea how to run me around the obstacles, so I worked on my own. I moved away from the others and practiced jumping over a few hurdles, backing well up in order to get a good run at it. As it turned out, I was quite the leaper. This was great! My legs felt rock solid as I sprang off the ground, soaring over the hurdles in one graceful leap. Suddenly, I had the ballet skills I'd always dreamed of. For the space of a full breath, I *flew*. It reminded me of gliding underwater—weightless and exhilarating.

I felt better about the contest after jumping the hurdles. If my body—um, Zoë's body—could do the tricks, I could handle the rest. I hung behind a border collie and watched it work the zigzag poles. When it was my turn, I charged right in and started swishing my front paws from side to side, but I got all tangled up and turned around. Suddenly I felt very warm in my T-shirt. I was dizzy and didn't know which way was forward and which way was back. I had to quit and try it a second time, going more slowly, not looking at the poles this time. I was going too fast to see them before I reacted. Plus, my body was bigger than some of the contestants' and it was hard work to dart side to side quickly enough to catch each pole. I had to get the rhythm and the pace set beforehand and then do it like a dance.

Next I moved to the tunnel. I have to admit that I almost gave up the whole enterprise right there. Looking down that tunnel was like peering into a well—it brought up strange shades of memory, of being trapped in a dark place. Inside, the air was blue and foreboding. When I peered in, every inch of my body cringed. Since when was I scared of small spaces? Was this a real memory I was feeling, or some kind of dog instinct? I tried to shake it off, but the feeling was stubborn—it stayed even as I summoned my nerve and ran through, headlong.

After that, I stepped off the course, my confidence shaken. Apparently understanding the course in the abstract was completely different from *doing* it as a dog. I couldn't trust my human insight to get me through. I'd have to learn the course like every other dog—with my paws.

The teeter-totter was popular. Every handler wanted to run their dog over it a few times, and that caused an ugly jam around the ramp. By the time I got up the guts to try it, everyone was watching me. I stumbled at the top—making the switch from going uphill to going downhill was a lot harder than it looked. I nearly fell off and had to claw my way frantically back into balance. Of course I missed the mark I had to hit on the downhill side.

Suddenly, I wasn't feeling very good about the race.

Still, my name was on the list—I couldn't back out now. I watched an Australian shepherd streak through the course and felt my heart sink.

When I found Zoë on the sidelines, she was wedged between Leisl and Foxy.

"What," Leisl was saying, loud enough for everyone nearby to hear, "weren't there any 'dog hater' T-shirts available?"

Zoë glanced down at her own inside-out shirt and then at mine, perplexed. She looked back up with a wrinkled brow and said, "What do you mean? Why would I wear a shirt like that? I don't hate dogs."

"Oh, yeah, the way you didn't hate them when you screamed bloody murder at them in your café last year?" A row of people behind Leisl laughed. "Threatened to boot them all the way to China . . ."

I crept up next to Zoë and cringed. It looked like Leisl was still bitter about losing the Pet-and-Person Beauty Contest.

Zoë's chin jutted out staunchly. "I don't hate dogs." She looked around at the snickering crowd.

Poor Zoë. I had to hand it to her—she was more earnest in my defense than I ever could have been. Of course, it helped that she truly did love dogs.

The loudspeaker announced the first contestant and the crowd turned away from us. Zoë crouched down, her face miserable. "How can she say that? That's mean." She stroked my head absentmindedly. "Why would anyone hate dogs? She sounded like she really meant it, though. Like she knows something I don't." She looked foggily at me until her gaze sharpened with realization. "You! You hate dogs!"

No, no—really. . . . I froze, unsure what to do. Above all else, I wanted Zoë to know the truth. She was becoming a strange sort of sister to me, another piece of my own being. I didn't want to hold back, even if the truth made me ugly. But what was true?

I shifted uncomfortably from paw to paw. I didn't know why I was afraid of dogs. An ironic thought occurred to me that I might have been a happier kid if I'd had my own dog. Then I would have known truly constant love. I gave a little snort that caused Zoë to give me a sharp look.

"You don't really hate dogs, do you?"

No, I concluded. No, I didn't. Dogs might be scary, but I didn't hate them. Not anymore. At certain moments, I was even starting to like them.

I leaned in toward Zoë and licked her cheek.

Her face blossomed with smiles. "I knew you didn't. You like me, don't you? You *love* me!"

I licked her again. What a nut. I really was growing fond of her.

🦴 Zoë

The dog race is exciting, and it makes my heart beat faster. The dogs fly back and forth in a blur, jumping over yellow and blue and red obstacles. The ones on the sideline bark, and I want to bark, too. Instead, I yell, "Hey!"

Everybody's yelling, and I fit right in. I can yell as loud as I want. Even Jessica doesn't give me any funny looks.

"Hey!"

This is such a thrill. The dogs are completely focused. I try to wave my arms at a collie while it's racing, but it doesn't flinch—that's pure talent.

The people are very funny about this, parading around with important looks on their faces as if the contest is all about them. How ridiculous. Obviously the dogs are the stars of this show, not the people. Maybe the dogs should be the ones holding the leashes, leading the people around by the neck.

Foxy goes into the ring with his pink lady, and they do a nice job. Foxy's smart—he looks at his person before every move. I think of Jessica looking at me like that, and the idea makes me laugh and laugh. I'm still laughing when they call our names. I bound into the ring, and Jessica bounds out, too, ready to go.

For a minute, I feel a powerful urge to climb on the yellow and blue and red toys. I hold myself back and remember that everyone's watching. Since this is a people game, there are rules to obey. I follow Jessica behind a white chalk line. She's bent down, ready to spring. I stand like that, too. Everyone's silent while we wait (*for what?*).

I can hear my heart go bump, bump, bump.

"Go!" yells a woman in a white hat. Jessica jets over the line and runs immediately to three yellow hurdles, which she leaps with style. I run behind her and jump them, too. What fun! She jumps through a tire, but I don't do that. I don't trust these shoes I have on my feet—they're too bulky, and they'd probably catch on the tire and make me fall. Don't people know that feet are meant to touch the ground?

Jessica runs through a row of sticks and makes them swish. I swish through behind her and people laugh. I wave at them and they laugh even more.

Next she runs to a tunnel and dives right in. I'm impressed—if I were her, I'd be shy of a tunnel that flapped in the wind like that.

The people get louder when she runs to the big red ramp. Jessica scampers up one side, pauses for only a second at the top, and breezes down the other side. Her paws hit a white stripe on the ramp and everyone yells. I yell, too, though I'm so excited I have no idea what I'm saying.

Jessica looks pretty in my white, furry body. She stops and turns better than the collie did. If my mom and dad are watching, they'll know for sure that we're the best dog-and-person team in the world. No one could doubt it now. Jessica flies over the last yellow hurdles. She runs across another white line, and I run there, too. A man in a white hat holds up his arm and shouts, "Fifty-eight seconds!"

Everyone cheers, but I'm not all that impressed. It's not that hard to hold up your arm and yell something. I could hold up my arm and yell "hey"—it's not as hard as running through a blue tunnel or making it over that ramp. People are impressed by the strangest things.

I give Jessica my best-in-the-world smile, and she smiles back. For a minute, I'm too happy to remember my missing family.

☕ Jessica

Thank goodness, I was too focused on the course to see what Zoë was doing. From time to time I caught the blur of her shirt or the wink of her crown, but I didn't see her until the race was over.

The instant the judge announced my time, the crowd exploded. My heart swelled and excitement filled me until I had to move. Suddenly, I realized what dancers must feel when their emotions tingle through their bodies, making them leap and shimmy. I felt like I could run a marathon.

Zoë danced in the crowd, arms in the air, her crown glinting. I pranced toward her and reared up on two feet, wobbling precariously. For a minute, I wavered, sure I'd have to drop to the ground. Then Zoë caught my paws.

I balanced against her, grinning, and we danced up and down through the crowd. She met my gaze, filling me with a hearts-and-bubbles kind of feeling. There we were, my human body dancing like a fool with me inside a giant white dog—and I'd never felt so pleased.

Even when I caught a glimpse of Alexa and Malia weaving through the crowd, I didn't let embarrassment overtake me. I went with the moment. And I danced.

15

The Feline Persuasion

 Jessica

Zoë and I came in second. Foxy bested me by one point (apparently I touched one of the hurdles during a jump), and with his great time, he was the winner. Leisl looked like the proudest parent on earth when the judge draped the gold medal around Foxy's neck. I have to confess that I was just as happy with my silver—and Zoë was thrilled that hers matched her crown.

"I'm really proud of us—everyone can tell we're the big winners in our sparkly hats," she murmured to me before popping up to shake another hand and accept more congratulations. It was strange to be with someone who joined the Woofinstock festivities with such glee. I would never have entered any of these contests on my own, not in a million years. But here Zoë was, leaping into everything without blinking. She was only interested in having fun, and her joyous vibe attracted people.

"You own the Glimmerglass, right?" said a man

with three children as he shook Zoë's hand. "My kids are dying to meet your dog."

Before I knew it, three small pairs of arms wrapped around my middle. A little girl who smelled of peanut butter and jelly smooched my ear while her brothers rubbed the T-shirt up and down on my back. I wagged madly. The attention was heavenly; it made the sun shine brighter for an instant.

The family caught Zoë's attention, saying something about an early dinner and hot dogs. Before I knew it, I was sitting on the grass near the Agility Competition grounds, eating two hot dogs of my very own. Zoë also had two (no ketchup, no mustard). She'd watched how the parents of the family paid for theirs, and when she found a ten-dollar bill in her pocket, she marched right up to the stand, held it out, and asked for "Two for her and two for me." Thank goodness. I had no idea how hungry I was until I took the first bite.

When the family moved away (off to the Glimmerglass for sundaes), I felt exhausted and a little bereft. It was only midafternoon, but it had already been such a long day. What I wanted most was to stretch out on the grass and take a nap. But, of course, Zoë had other ideas.

As people moved on to other activities, the crowd thinned, giving Zoë a clear view of a table on the far side of the field. She stood, shaded her eyes for a second, and made for it like a fish after a worm. I followed behind, nervous as usual about where we were headed and what Zoë would do when we got there. Without really daring to hope, I looked up at the sky and scanned it. It was empty. Only a few white clouds lingered around the edges, enough to obscure Mt. Rainier in one direction and the Olympic Mountains in another, but not enough to produce any lightning. How could a land that's notorious for rain be cursed with such beautiful weather? And how would I ever get back into my rightful body without a little lightning? I thought of Hot Max and longed for a storm.

Zoë came to a halt in front of a long table that was dominated by Malia, Alexa, Mayor Park, and the rest of the Lost Dog Committee. Nearby sat a cluster of beige pet carriers, stacked two high like units in a mini apartment block. From one of the carriers came a cautious meow. A furry black paw poked between the bars of the smallest carrier. A strange feeling cramped in the pit of my stomach. My nose began to twitch of its own accord as every nerve in my body turned its attention to the carriers. I knew what was in there—obviously, the Lost Dog team was hosting some kind of cat adoption day. All the same, my body felt compelled to do more than know—I had to see, smell, touch. Taste, if possible.

Without even considering whether it was a good idea, I trotted up to the little metal fence that ringed the collection of carriers and pressed my nose against the bars. Inside was grass, about ten feet square, and the block of carriers. A blanket and a few throw pillows sat in the corner. There were four—no, *five*—cats sitting inside the stacked containers, some of them sprawled on plush kitty beds. I caught a whiff that was decidedly feline. Saliva filled my mouth. Every part of me quivered. My eyes were so intent on soaking in every detail about the cats before me I thought they might pop straight out of my head.

"Hi, there. Can I help you?"

I jumped. My paws went damp with relief when I saw that Malia was talking to Zoë, not to me. Zoë's eyes were also fixed on the cat carriers.

"I wanted to see the cats," she said, dragging her gaze away from the cats and toward the humans for a half second. At the far end of the table, I heard Alexa going over the rules of adoption in a serious voice with two potential cat parents. They would have to sign a contract, she said, that stated that they would provide food, a clean litter box, and good medical care for the cat's lifetime. The cats were already spayed and neutered. I wondered if there was a clause forbidding people to fight over whose turn it was to empty that litter box.

"Well," Malia said, standing and opening the gate for Zoë. "Why don't you come on in? That way, you can actually *pet* one."

Zoë

I think I might faint. My legs shake as I follow the woman inside the gate. Are they actually going to *help* me touch a cat? Can it be that easy?

Jessica wants to follow us, but I give her a big grin and a shake of the head. "Not for dogs, sweetie," I say. Ha! I drop the loop-end of her leash over a fence picket and follow after my leader.

I adore cats. Of course I do! But they're fickle. You

never know what a cat is going to do, even a cat you've lived with for months. One minute they're cuddly and sweet, and the next they're slicing away with those claws. You can't trust a cat.

When the woman opens one of the boxes and pulls out a droopy cat, I take a step back. She tries to hand it to me, but I cross my arms and stay where I am, so she flops it over her own shoulder instead.

"This is Smoke Jumper," the woman says. "We call her Smokey for short." Smokey twists her head to look up at me. "Rrrow?"

My heart flips over as I panic. What does Smokey want? Does she know I'm a dog? Can she see all the way inside me? I wouldn't put it past her. Cats have their own magic.

Smokey is growling like a Berner with a piece of bacon.

"She purrs like a champion, doesn't she?" the woman says. "She's a real lovebug. We fostered her at our house for a while, and I can say she's great with kids and dogs."

Really? I narrow my eyes at Smokey. I used to trust a cat that lived next door. I even slept near him a couple of times under the maple tree . . . until I woke up with a bleeding nose. That was when I learned that the safest way to play with cats is to bark at them. Humans, however, seem to have an entirely different relationship with felines.

"Do you want to pet her?" the woman asks.

What, with my *hand*?

Smokey's golden eyes blink like an alien's. Fur sticks

out all over her head. She yawns, showing a mouth full of razor-sharp teeth.

"Um, I don't know," I say. I want to touch the cat, sure, but I don't want to lose any skin. And what I really want isn't to pet the cat—it's to get a good smell of her and then chase her all the way across town.

"She isn't going to hurt you," the woman said. "Haven't you ever had a cat before?"

"No."

"Well, they like gentle affection. Just stroke softly along her back."

I take a deep breath. Jessica is watching me, and her envy makes me feel brave. I put out two fingers toward the cat. When I touch her, she's soft, but I jerk away.

"Try it again," the woman says.

I lick my lips. It hadn't gone that badly the last time. Holding my breath, I touch Smokey again, more slowly this time. I am incredibly brave. Jessica must be wild with jealousy. The cat looks up as if she likes it. That rumbling sound comes out of her belly, like she's eaten a car engine.

Smokey head-butts my hand, so I reach under her ear and scratch.

"Does your ear itch?" I ask. "I know how that is." Honestly, being able to scratch my own body—anytime—is the best benefit of turning into a human.

"She really likes you," the woman says, smiling.

I give Smokey a skeptical look. Her eyes are closed in little slits, and she's holding out her chin for more rubbing. I angle my hand to rub her ear canal, and she leans in, pressing against my fingers. Petting her gives me a funny feeling, like I've turned all liquidy inside. It feels nice. I wonder if all people enjoy petting animals this much. If they do, then why don't they spend more time petting dogs?

 Jessica

Zoë's cat moment was more than I could take. Watching her stroke that furry little body, I felt such desperation, I thought I might explode. I wanted to beat down the fence, race inside, and ... what? What would I do if I got close to a cat? I had no idea. But I was incredibly anxious to find out. My longing for that cat was the most unnatural thing I've felt since I was a kid and had a passion for those giant marshmallow peanuts.

It took all my willpower to turn away, to grab the loop-end of my leash with my teeth and slide it up and off the picket. Once I did, once I got away from the smell of cats, the chemicals in my brain fluttered back to their normal level. Or, at least, their normal dog level.

I padded across the grass with my leash in my mouth, putting distance between myself and the cats. The strength of my desire for them was terrifying. And it wasn't as if my thoughts had been pure. Oh, no. I wanted three things—to chase, to sniff, and to use my mouth to get a good sampling of cat. Ideally in that order, though I wasn't picky. If I had to lick the cat and then chase it, that was fine.

This is ridiculous. I gave my head a rigorous shake to clear my thoughts. I liked cats. I'd always considered myself a cat person. What the hell was I thinking with all this chasing and sniffing?

I was about fifteen feet away from the cats when it occurred to me—I was on my own. I had my own leash in my own mouth, and Zoë was occupied for at least the next twenty minutes. This was a perfect time to check in on the Glimmerglass. I could check on the preparations for dinner service, see how Theodore was settling in, and make sure Kerrie was okay. I set off at a run.

The square was packed with people and dogs. As I neared the café, my heart did a double backflip. There was a line—an actual line—snaking out the front door.

I rushed up to the door and slipped through, using a stroller as a foil. Once inside, I rushed toward the back, planning to head into the kitchen, but I came to a halt when I heard the sound of sobs from the back office. The noises were muffled, and I had to creep all the way up to the door and place my nose down at the crack to hear.

"I can't believe I did this!" That wailing sound was Naomi's voice. "Today of all days—and it was all going so well. Right before dinner service!"

"Shh," said Kerrie. "Try to keep calm. This is a really nasty burn, and you might be in shock. My husband's on his way right now to take you to the emergency room. Just try to keep quiet and don't worry."

"Don't worry—but this is the make-or-break weekend! And it was my first day being head chef."

Kerrie made a few soft mama-hen noises. I heard a

bustle behind me and ducked into the open supply closet just as Kerrie's husband Paul dashed in, his face pale. He pushed the door open.

"I called ahead—they're expecting us. Ready to go, Naomi?"

I heard the sounds of people standing up, then Paul and Naomi walked swiftly past me down the hall, Naomi holding a loose towel around her arm. I shuddered. Burns were a part of kitchen life, but every restaurant owner worried about "the big one." We had to take care of Naomi—she was part of the family. But could we afford to give her paid leave? I desperately wished we could—she deserved that and more. In a place where her job was hanging in the balance, though, it seemed unlikely.

At least I knew our health insurance premiums were all paid up. That was one thing Kerrie and I had agreed on up front. We would always take care of our employees' health, even if it meant paying those bills out of our own pockets.

Taking a deep breath, I pushed the door open wider and padded into the office. Kerrie sat at my desk, her head in her hands. I nosed under her elbow until she sat up enough for me to squeeze my head onto her lap.

She dropped her hand on top of my head automatically. We sat like that for a full minute, until she looked down, almost surprised to see me there.

"Oh, you're the dog from this morning, aren't you?" She stroked my brow. "I'm sorry I couldn't let you in before, but I was afraid my partner would freak if she saw you here. It's fine that you're here now—Jessica's off somewhere. Drumming up business that we aren't going to be able to handle. Not now." Kerrie drew a ragged breath and rooted around in my desk drawer for a Kleenex. "It's ironic, isn't it? She's actually doing a great job of bringing us business, she got Theodore back for us, and then this happens. Bam." She blew her nose emphatically.

"Of course, I'm acting like I'm not royally pissed off at her because of all the hard work she's been do-ing, but between you and me, she's had some kind of power outage in the brain department. I was so mad at her when she was in the kitchen before." I lifted my ears halfway, both curious to know what Zoë had done and terrified to hear.

"She was cooking. And it was really gross. I mean, *nasty*. I would have said she was trying to make a joke or something, but she doesn't joke like that, ever. And she was really odd about it. Earnest. Like she thought what she was making was terrific. Can you imagine?" Kerrie looked down at me and made a face. I shud-dered inside, imagining what Zoë would want to cook. Probably liver-stuffed hot dogs with puréed ham on top. Poor Kerrie.

"I'm really worried about her." Kerrie sighed. "There's a lot she keeps hidden inside. It's hard to know what's going on in her head." She reached out and pulled a lavender envelope from my in-box. "These things keep coming, but she won't tell me who they're from. And I don't think she even opens them—isn't that weird? I didn't think she had any family, but they're from somebody named Sheldon. Debra Shel-don. I would have thought she'd be so anxious to get to know any family member, she'd rip it open right away." Kerrie blew her nose again. "I thought we were close. That I knew her pretty well—better than anyone else. But I just don't see why she wouldn't tell me about this. I thought she trusted me."

The breath caught in my throat. I wanted to howl—I do trust you! I do! It hadn't occurred to me that Kerrie might feel this way. I hadn't told her about Debra because I wasn't ready to think about those envelopes, let alone speak about them. It had nothing to do with keeping anything from Kerrie. I just didn't know what I was supposed to do with all the feelings that bubbled up every time I saw one of those purple cards. How should I act toward the woman who abandoned me? If I had told Kerrie about it, would she have helped me figure it out?

I was groaning in silence. How could I have missed my chance to share this with Kerrie? It would have helped me so much, even if I hadn't known how to react to the envelopes—I saw now that telling her about it would have been a huge relief. Why hadn't I seen that earlier? Why did I always think that holding things inside was the safest thing to do?

"Jess is such a wonderful friend," Kerrie went on, still holding the purple envelope. "Honestly—I've said this to Paul a thousand times—I don't see why she isn't married. I'd marry her, if I were a guy. I think she's perfect." She looked down at me. "Well, a little reserved. Quiet, sure. But a stellar person." A tear slipped over the rim of her eye and ran down her cheek. "I wish she were here to tell me what to do. She's always so good at making a plan. And she might be off-her-rocker weird right now, but she *is* doing her part. We have plenty of customers, just no chef to cook for them. I'll be so depressed if our café dies."

And that's exactly why it can't happen. I let Kerrie pet my head one more time, then I took a purposeful backward step away from her. She turned to me. "Where are you going? Are you quitting on me, too?"

I moved forward, caught her skirt in my teeth, and pulled back gently. She stood, just as I'd hoped, and followed me as I backed out the door.

"Wait, are you the white dog that got Theodore to come back? He told me all about it, how you brought him a flyer and looked so cute and enticing. His girlfriend thinks you're a demigod or—what was it?—a guardian angel."

Sure. I'll be whatever you want me to be. I kept backing up. When we got to the door, I let go of her skirt and walked slowly toward the kitchen, praying she would follow me.

I almost lost her near the dining room, when the sound of the crowd pulled her off course, but I grabbed her skirt again and pulled.

"You are persuasive, aren't you? Oh, all right. I guess I have to break the news about Naomi's burn to Theodore anyway. He isn't going to be happy. He always made it clear that being head chef is not what he's about. Responsibility isn't his bag."

Sure, I thought, *talk to Theodore. Talk to your navel. Talk to anyone. Just do this one thing and follow me into the kitchen.*

Kerrie followed. The kitchen smelled like paradise. Four pans bubbled on the stove, but Theodore was nowhere to be seen. The room was empty. Kerrie, ever curious, walked over to the stove to see what was cooking. My tail wagged, cautiously optimistic.

"Hmm, nice risotto. And those mushrooms look great. Oh," she said, picking up a spoon, "I'd better give Naomi's béchamel sauce a stir."

After a stir here and a whisk there, she seemed to remember herself and stepped back. Then she glanced over at the prep counter, filled with containers of freshly chopped vegetables, and then at the rack of waiting tickets.

"Wow, that's a lot of orders. Where is Theodore? He's really got to stay on top of this stuff, especially with Naomi gone."

She looked around behind her. *Now,* I thought. *This is the moment.*

In a quick motion, I hoisted my front paws up on the counter, bit the spoon by the handle, and pushed it at Kerrie's hand. She looked down at it and shook her head. "Oh, no, doggy. I was just giving a little stir before—I'm not a chef. Not anymore."

I pushed again. Harder.

"No, I really mean it. I don't do that now."

I heard someone come out of the walk-in behind us, so quietly Kerrie didn't notice. The faint scent of Theodore's lemon soap tickled my nose, just strong enough to let me know he was there. I re-gripped the spoon handle and pressed it on Kerrie one more time.

"Look," she said, turning to me, "I don't know if you are some kind of magical dog or what, but I don't see why you have to push me like this. Cooking just isn't a thing I do anymore. Not professionally, anyway. Why can't everyone just accept that?"

Her eyes were warped with pain. The dent in her forehead was deeper than ever. *I shouldn't be forcing her,* I thought. *I should be nice and let her do what she wants. Like I always have.*

But then my mind took a dangerous turn. *What would Zoë do if she were here,* I wondered. Would she let Kerrie stay in her safe zone, seating customers at the front of house? Not a chance.

I ran around to Kerrie's other side and nudged the spoon at her hand. She was about to say something— "no," most likely—when Sahara burst in through the swinging doors, more tickets in her hand.

"Table six is wondering where their risotto is and there's a really unhappy man at three who ordered mushrooms and is sure they're getting slimy by now." She looked at Kerrie, then spotted Theodore and shifted her glance his way. *No, don't look at him! If Kerrie sees him there, she'll hand over the spoon and go, and that'll be that. Case closed.* I gave my noisiest bark, bringing all eyes back to me. One more time, I nosed Kerrie's hand, then pressed the spoon at her.

"Well," she said softly. "I guess I can plate a few mushrooms. And dish up the risotto. Even I can't get that wrong, can I? It *is* an emergency."

I gave her my most gleeful bark, my tail wagging like a victory flag. She turned to the stove and began to plate.

"One risotto, one mushroom," she called to Sahara, lining the dishes up on the counter like the pro she was. Then she looked up at the ticket rack with her old practiced glance. I could almost see her calculating how long each of those dishes would take and which she needed to start first. Pans began to rattle. I heard spoons scraping against ceramic bowls. A second later, aromas popped through the air as fresh peppers and onions slid into hot pans.

Kerrie's hands moved this way and that as she mixed and measured. My tail couldn't wag hard enough. Theodore crept up beside me and started plating salads at the station farthest away from Kerrie as if he didn't want to disturb her flow.

"You are one groovy dog," he whispered to me. We both watched as Kerrie slid calzones into the oven with one hand, tied on an apron, and started sautéing Brussels sprouts, all in one fluid motion. The queen was back. Long live the queen.

I got back to the cat adoption stand just in time. Zoë had stepped away from the cats and was searching for me in a panic, her face strained. She raced up, dropped to her knees, and breathed hard in my ear. "There you are! I've been looking everywhere," she gasped. "Let's get out of here. They want us to take home a *cat*!"

I looked over to where Malia Jackson stood, adoption papers in hand, staring after Zoë with a quizzical expression. Zoë noticed it, too, and she quickly busied herself with collecting the end of my leash. "I thought I was just going to touch one. Now they say we have to keep it." She shook her head, her face as strained as if they'd asked her to do the fox-trot with an alligator. "You can't trust cats," she said. "I don't care what she says about them purring and cuddling. You just can't trust them. A cat is the last thing we need."

She looked back at Malia and gave her a wave, then pointed to me as if we were in the middle of some kind of doggie-pee emergency. My fur puffed out with pride that I was able to save our team from this awkward moment.

Besides, I had to agree with her—a cat was the last thing we needed. As Zoë speed-walked me away from the cat adoption area, I looked back over my shoulder at the people circling the cat carriers. There were moms and daughters squealing over the kittens, young couples with their heads together, picking out their first joint pet. Normal families doing normal things. My heart gave a dry little gasp of longing. Then Zoë said, "Ooh, look over there!" and reminded me to look forward at what was coming instead of looking back.

16

Love, Honor, and Obey

 Zoë

I see a group of dogs ahead and I'm drawn toward them. If I had my own way (and if no one were watching), I would run straight to them, but Jessica is lolly-gagging, slowing us down. Her nose is glued to the ground, probably picking up all kinds of juicy smells.

"Look, dogs! Let's go," I say, trying to put all my excitement into my voice so she'll hurry up. At last we get to another big square of grass marked off with a white fence. People with dogs are standing along the side; people without dogs are sitting in white folding chairs. Near the fence, there's a table with important-looking people sitting at it, frowning at clipboards. I want to tell them how ridiculous they look, frowning like that, but I don't. Instead I take Jessica up to the table and talk to the person who smiles at me first.

"Hi!" he says. He has a big, sloppy grin, like a Saint Bernard. "The Obedience Trials start at five-thirty. They're the last contests of the day. Do you want to sign up?"

I don't know what to say, so I raise my eyebrows and tip my head to the side. He pushes a paper across the table at me and points at it. "If you haven't done it before, the novice level is probably the best. Your dog just has to heel on a leash, sit and stay for thirty seconds, and come when you call it."

"*Her*," I correct him. I give him a hard look. There must be something wrong with him if he can't tell that Jessica's a girl. People are a bit slow sometimes. "Are all these dogs novices?"

He shakes his head. "No, about a third of our group is in the open class. That's more advanced. These are the tasks they have to perform. Off leash." He turns the paper over and points to a much longer list.

I look down at Jessica, glad to see that she's paying attention to all this. I really want to win an obedience medal. Mom was always saying that I never listened, never obeyed. Sometimes I heard her talking with Dad about taking me to an obedience class. I don't know why they never did it, but they didn't—they just complained about how bad I was. This is my big chance to show that I know obedience inside and out.

I want to win, and I don't want to just be a novice. Getting a novice medal is like being called the best puppy because you only pee a *little bit* on everybody's feet. Jessica and I have an edge here, since she can understand everything people say. But I don't want us to aim too high. Then we'll never win.

The sloppy-grin man is waiting. I crouch down beside Jessica. "You decide, girl," I say. I know everyone's listening, so I put on that cute voice people use when they're talking to dogs. "Should we go for novice?"

I catch her eye and give my head a shake. "Or open class?"

She barks. I reward her with my best smile and stand back up. "Open class, please. She's Zoë the dog. And I'm Jessica. The person."

Jessica

I'd been nervous about the Agility Competition, but I walked into the obedience area with my head held high. If I couldn't breeze through this, I didn't deserve to ever be a human again. The only downside to the whole endeavor was that it wasn't likely to change us back into our rightful bodies—unless the magical secret lay in working together with Zoë. Which it could be. It could be hopping on one foot for all I knew. What would it hurt to follow Zoë's lead and enter one more of these crazy contests—one that we just might win?

Besides, I needed to get my T-shirt in front of more people. Now that Kerrie was cooking, the Glimmerglass had a rare opportunity to gain a serious following, but we had to strike while the iron was hot. Ha, ha. New customers would bring in funds for Naomi's paid leave, the electricity, and next month's rent—and they'd also keep Kerrie distracted long enough to get her cooking feet underneath her again.

As we headed to the space near the fence where contestants waited, I scanned the crowd for Max, but didn't see him anywhere. Where was he? It had only been a few hours since I'd seen him last, but it felt like a week. Maybe he was at the clinic, saving some poor dog's life. Or at home, doing his laundry. Washing his sheets and spreading them, nice and clean, on his bed. I bet he had the warmest bed in the world. Warm and seductive ... A rush of R-rated images flooded my brain, and I lingered on them until a barking dog snapped me back to reality.

I didn't see Max as I reviewed the faces outside the ring, but I did see Leisl and Foxy, heads lowered in concentration, and half a dozen people I recognized from either the café or the Woofinstock committee. A few of them waved at Zoë, and she waved back. Just seeing them gave me a curious sense of rightness, as if I were exactly where I belonged. It was a *Cheers* feeling, I supposed—Madrona was becoming a place where people actually knew our names.

As we waited for the first round to start, the loud-speaker blared with "Louie Louie," Washington's un-official state song. Zoë immediately started to dance, waving her arms over her head. Little kids standing near us saw her and started dancing, too. I hid behind her legs.

"Oh, come on," she said, scooting to the side. "Don't be like that. Let loose for once!" She shimmied and shook her hips. Really, she wasn't half bad. Could I dance as well as that when I was in my human body? I'd never tried.

I kept my four feet on the ground. It was all very well for Zoë to dance—at heart she *was* a dog—but I had more serious things to think about.

"You can do it, you know," she said. "You *can* have fun. I've seen you. We danced at fragility, and that was great. I loved it! You did, too."

Sure. True. But I'd been flying high on adrenaline. Now I was stone cold and about to be faced with a new test. We had to pay attention and prepare. I wasn't nervous, but I wasn't in a dancing mood either.

Still, I had to admit, Zoë did have a knack for starting things. Half the people around her were dancing in place. The song switched to "Good Vibrations" and more of the crowd took up the beat. People sang along. Dogs' tails wagged in time. A few younger dogs jumped up and down, barking. Even I started to feel the zing of their energy.

"Hey!" A strident voice sliced through the joy. Leisl stood in front of us, her hands clenching Foxy's leash like he was a Bengal tiger with man-eating tendencies. "Will you settle down? The dogs need to focus— you can't ask them to do obedience after getting all hyped up like this."

Everyone around me stopped dancing. The dogs stopped wagging their tails. The Beach Boys sang, "Good, good, *good*!" to an uncaring audience.

"That's ridiculous."

I jumped when I heard Zoë's voice above my head. "Relax," she said to Leisl. "Dogs need fun. It's absurd to think they can't do serious work after they've been dancing. Dogs aren't stupid—you shouldn't treat them like they are."

Leisl stared at Zoë, her face frozen. Foxy's ears twitched as he tried to follow what was going on. "Well," Leisl said at last, "my dog needs quiet to concentrate. And since he's the reigning champion, I think I might know a little something about getting ready for Obedience Trials." Before Zoë could respond, Leisl cinched up Foxy's leash and strode away.

Zoë, face flushed, crouched down beside me and pretended to play with my collar. "That's nuts. Why are we here, if it isn't to have fun?"

If I could have spoken, I would have told her that Leisl wasn't in this for the good times—as a breeder, she needed Foxy to win and make his offspring more valuable. I wondered what Zoë would think of that, of a person making her living from her dog. Probably, she wouldn't care as long as the dog had plenty of fun—which Foxy didn't.

As I considered Leisl and Foxy's situation, I felt my attitude pivot 180 degrees. Something I'd noticed about Zoë was that she didn't waste time second-guessing herself. She was who she was, with no apologies. And, just as incredibly, she seemed to actually like me—the real me, not any of the people I tried to be. She would probably even have liked me during the dog-hating incident—she was just accepting that way. Maybe I needed to take a page from her book and learn to accept myself, too.

I let my mouth pop open in a smile and instantly felt better. My tail swayed back and forth. I took a few in-place steps in time with the music, which had switched to "Foxy Lady." Zoë looked down, saw what I was doing, and gave her booty a little shake. She winked at me.

Just then, a voice on the loudspeaker announced the first dog-and-person pair, and everyone's attention swung to the ring. A collie heeled next to its owner as they walked in a stiff figure eight. The owner didn't have a leash—this was all up to the dog. Then the collie was told to sit and stay while the man walked to the other side of the ring. He called the collie, who bounded toward him. When she was about halfway, he barked out an order and she skidded to a stop, then dropped onto the grass, panting. I watched, amazed. Zoë slowly sank to her knees beside me.

"Wow, this is really tough. How will I remember what to have you do?"

Ah, now who's wishing they'd prepared? Well, surely I could focus and have a good time, all at once. The two weren't mutually exclusive. I let my tail wag as I nudged Zoë's arm until she lowered the instruction sheet so we could read it together

By the time I'd read the list through and looked up again, the collie was in a "long sit," panting as she sat on the grass, looking at the crowd. Her owner was nowhere in sight. The long sit went on. And on. A baby cried in the audience, but the collie didn't budge. Somewhere, a dog whined. The collie's ears twitched, but she stayed put.

"She's really talented," Zoë whispered, nodding at the collie. "She only made one mistake, when she had to fetch the little stick he threw. I think she was supposed to bring it right back, but she squeaked it a few times first. I saw them—" she indicated the judges "—do a lot of writing after that."

Zoë's voice sounded tight. She chewed her lip as she watched the collie's owner return, call his dog, and celebrate the end of the trial.

A few seconds later, the loudspeaker announced a

new pair, a blue heeler and its white-haired owner. As they went through the maneuvers, Zoë's shoulders inched higher and higher. She plucked at the grass around her knees, shredding the blades into tiny bits.

I tried giving her a playful shove with my hip, but she glared at me. Then I licked her face. That earned me a half smile that melted away the second she turned back to the ring. When she reached down for a new blade of grass, I put my paw on top of her hand.

She turned to me, and our eyes met. I let my face break into a smile-pant, working with all my might to let my eyes show what I wanted to convey. *Let's just have fun.* As she looked at me, a range of emotions played over her face, none of which I could read. At last she said, "I just really want to win. I need us to be the best at this."

There was something in her voice that made my heart clench. Why did Zoë feel such a strong urge to win this? It was clear from her tone that this wasn't just about getting another silver necklace. Whatever was worrying her was keeping her from having a good time—it had to be pretty important.

My thoughts were interrupted by a Woofinstock volunteer with a clipboard, calling for "Jessica and Zoë" to get in position. I trotted behind a tense Zoë as she made her way to the gate near the judges' table. A bichon frise had just ruined its long stay by hopping up halfway through—it smiled at us as it left the ring. We stayed in place while the next contestants, a boy with an Irish wolfhound, went through their program.

I tried to relax and enjoy myself, but Zoë's rushed

breathing distracted me. She was staring out at the course with blank eyes, like a cat peering into the middle distance. I shifted from paw to paw. My tail thumped the ground. I yawned audibly. Nothing caught her attention. Zoë knotted her fingers together and gnawed one side of her lip, oblivious to everything but her own stress.

How was that for irony? Now that I'd come around to Zoë's way of thinking, that a little lighthearted fun might just make life more enjoyable, Zoë turned into a first-class worrywart. I glanced up at her. Her whole face was pulled into a scowl, as if someone had pinched the front of a rubber mask. Her shoulders hunched, her lips twisted with worry. I sighed. *She's acting like me. And it isn't particularly attractive.*

The wolfhound and its boy came trotting out of the ring, and Zoë straightened up. She looked anxiously down at me, then, as our names were called, walked stiffly into the middle of the ring.

I trotted in, tail flying high. This was my third contest of the day, and I knew what was coming—applause, marvelous applause! I did a little spin so everyone could see my grinning face, wondering if they could read my Glimmerglass shirt from the stands. Zoë was right—this *was* fun. Except that she didn't seem to be enjoying any of it, not even the cheering.

We stood side by side in the middle of the ring. I looked up at Zoë, waiting for her to start, but she didn't budge. She bit her lip instead. I waited. Behind their table, the judges also waited. The timer was waiting. The crowd was waiting.

Zoë didn't move.

What's wrong with her? I couldn't do the first move without her—the whole point was that I was supposed to follow her lead. That was how I demonstrated obedience, by waiting for her cue before I did anything.

The applause had long since died away. Everyone was watching, waiting for some kind of movement from Zoë. I sidled closer and leaned into her leg to remind her that she wasn't alone.

"What do I do?" Her terse whisper made my hackles rise. Carefully balancing on three feet, I traced a small figure eight on the ground with my paw.

"Right! Loops!" Zoë strode off, and I had to jump to stay alongside her. We made a figure eight that was so tight, figure skaters would have envied us. When we arrived back at our starting place, Zoë stopped cold. This time I froze, too. If she couldn't remember what to do again, we were sunk. We'd stand out there, immobile as zombies, until we either ran out of time or got laughed out of the ring. My paws felt like ice. I was officially not having fun.

Zoë

I just *can't* remember. I close my eyes, but all I can see are the black letters from the instruction sheet, jumbled up like kibble in a bowl. I try to think back to the wolfhound—what did he do after the loops? My brain plays picture after picture of a dog and a boy walking out of the ring, but nothing from this part of the routine.

When I open my eyes, the crowd is a big blur of colors—too many colors. The world feels like a thousand bees, attacking me with colors and noises and people's eyes watching. I want to hide. Or run away. I glance at Jessica, but she can't help me now. Hers are just one more set of eyes, staring and waiting for me to do something.

Why did I do all that dancing when I should have been learning what to do?

Someone makes a throat-clearing noise on the side of the ring. It's Foxy's person, the lady in pink who was snarly before. She leans forward with her hands on the fence. "Drop on recall," she whispers, just loud enough for me to hear.

Drop on recall! Right! I give her a grateful smile. What a surprise—wasn't that nice of her? She was like one of those growly dogs at the park who act tough and then come up and lick your ear.

I open my mouth, all ready to go. But, wait, what does "drop on recall" mean? I look at Jessica, but she's just smiling like she doesn't have a thought in her head. Then, in a flash, I see a vision. I see the collie sitting and waiting, then running and stopping short, almost in midair. It's one of the craziest things I've ever seen a dog do—how could I forget?

"Sit, Zoë," I tell Jessica. My heart jumping, I scurry to the other side of the ring, then stop and face her. "Come," I say. When she's halfway to me, I bellow "down!" as loud as I can. Jessica belly flops onto the grass.

We did it! I'm sweating with relief. After that, it gets easier. I see the bone-shaped chewy toy lying on the grass and pick it up. Jessica sits—I can tell she remembers what this is about. When I throw it, she's supposed to run, get it, and bring it back, without any chewing or squeaking. She does it perfectly without even one chomp. I'm envious as I watch her bring it back, but I don't bend down and put it in my mouth for a quick gnaw. Nope. I leave it on the ground. Lying there, like an ice-cream cone that's just waiting to be licked. Like a luscious, squeaky, deflatable, bone-shaped ice-cream cone.

Sigh.

Jessica's whimper reminds me that we have more work to do. I definitely know what's next—the sit-and-stay that goes on forever. Talk about boring. Thank goodness she has to do it, not me. I take her to the far edge of the ring and tell her to sit, which she does. Then I turn around and walk all the way across the grass, out the little gate, past the judges' table. We must have won this. Nobody could possibly look as good as we did.

17

Party Animal

 Jessica

There was no way we'd scored well enough for the top three, let alone first place. Zoë had taken such a long time figuring out the drop on recall, I felt sure we were nearly out of time. I plunked down for the long sit, knowing that it was futile. Although, I had to admit, we had done one thing. We'd shown Leisl that even rambunctious, dance-crazy dogs could perform in the obedience ring.

I was stunned that she'd been the one to help Zoë. Without that prompt, we would have stood there forever, looking like imbeciles. With it we only looked like first-timers who really didn't belong in open class. And that wasn't such a bad thing. Plenty of earlier contestants had been the same. Like the bichon frise who got up to sniff the grass during her long sit. Or the German shorthair who tripped his person right in the middle of their figure eight.

The late-day sun was warm, and I had to blink to keep myself from falling asleep. It surprised me that

Zoë had gotten so worked up before the competition. Sure, the whole town was here, watching, but these were all dog people—they knew better than to stake the reputation of a person on what their dog could or couldn't do. No one cared if a dog wandered off during its sit-and-stay. They were like parents that way. Everyone's kid was going to misbehave at the playground someday—there was no point in taking it personally.

That was a new realization for me, and it added to my sweet, melted feeling. For years I'd seen the people of Madrona as members of an elite softball team that I wasn't being asked to join. Today I saw them as a pack of kindly lifeguards—relaxed, but ready to jump into the water at the first sign of trouble. Everyone looked out for dogs here. And they looked out for dog owners, too. These weren't the mean streets of Chicago— this was a town whose only fault was sometimes caring too much for its canine friends. Now that I was one of those friends, I had to admit that I felt the love. And appreciated it.

I was lost in these thoughts, admiring the way the lowering sun cast fluttering shadows on the grass, when a familiar, sparkplug-shaped head caught my eye. Guy was standing outside the fence, pointing at me. As I watched, he turned to his companions—a group of T-shirt-clad Madrona citizens—and said something that must have been funny, based on the way they all laughed. Then he craned his stumpy neck, spotted Zoë, and pointed her out with even more explanation. Followed by more laughter.

My warm glow vanished. Anger churned in my belly,

stinging my nose. I stared at Guy, willing him to stop, but he kept on pointing and snickering. Clearly, he was telling his friends all about his weird sexcapade at my apartment. That ass.

Every muscle in my body tensed, until the act of sitting caused me physical pain. I readjusted my feet, calculating how quickly I could snap his neck with my big canine teeth. A growl escaped me. I caught myself snarling, my muzzle curled up like the skin on a shar-pei's back.

I knew it would disqualify us. I knew it would blow Zoë's chances at getting another sparkly necklace to add to her collection. But when I saw the judge open his mouth and lift his hand, about to call us for time, I lunged.

The ground flew by beneath me. I stretched out my stride, pushing my four powerful paws against the ground. I wasn't sure if I could leap the fence, but the Agility Contest had given me confidence in my jumping skills. With a massive shove, I pressed my upper body off the ground and kicked with my back feet. The fence just brushed my belly hairs as I sailed over.

I landed on top of Guy. We went down in a heap, my front legs collapsing under the weight of the rest of my body. I felt the air rush out of him. Then I rolled to the side, landing on top of shoes and toes. I lay on my back, looking up at a ring of surprised faces, half of which wore green Woofinstock T-shirts. Two dogs raced up and immediately started smelling my crotch.

I heard a shout of anger. Then a shadow crossed my eye. Something bony struck the side of my head,

making my vision turn white on that side. I whim-
pered, squirming to get up, and felt a hand grab the
scruff of my neck. It shook me hard, like a wolf with
a hare.

A blow on the side of the ribs made me double over.
I stumbled and fell. There was yelling, but I couldn't
make sense of it. All I could focus on was the pain.

*T*he next thing I knew, I was lying in a woman's
arms while she cooed to me and stroked my head. I
moaned and readjusted my chin. She clucked her
tongue and said, "Quiet now. You're all right—just
rest there."

Ah. It was Zoë. I snuggled in a little closer.

"Are you okay? You seem okay. I sure hope you are."

The feel of her fingertips, gliding up my long nose,
onto my forehead, and down to my neck, acted as a
kind of mantra, distracting my brain while my body
relaxed. Pain moved like a snake down my spine,
pulsing in my shoulders, my back, my hips, and finally
my tail.

"Did you get bored during the long sit? It did go
on forever. I understand. But why did you knock over
the little gnome man? I don't think he's interested in
playing with us. He was pretty mean to you."

I opened an eye and looked at Zoë.

She gestured with her chin toward the judges' table, the site of some kind of commotion. With great
care, I pushed up on my front paws until I was sitting
and gazed across the grass. A group of people stood

like a wall with their backs to us and the rest of the crowd. Beyond them stood Guy, looking defensive and red in the face, backing toward his car. I heard one of the judges say, "There's *never* a reason to treat a dog like that. We all saw what happened—your re-action was way out of bounds. I don't care if you do know that dog, there was no reason to hit her. Or kick her."

Guy said something I couldn't hear. Then Mayor Park took a step closer to him. "As a citizen and the mayor of this town, I can tell you that Madrona does not accept that kind of behavior. It's in direct viola-tion of our animal welfare statute. I suggest you go before we call the authorities."

Guy stomped off, and I lay back down. I didn't feel altogether good about the way Guy had just been run out of town. Of course I didn't want him to keep spreading ugly rumors about Zoë and me, but I also felt bad. If I hadn't knocked him down, he never would have hit me.

And I really shouldn't háve done that in my Glim-merglass T-shirt. Had anyone noticed? Would it make any difference when people decided where to have dinner?

Still, the judge was right—Guy didn't have to kick me. There was no call for doing that to a dog. Ever. If there was one thing I'd learned from this switch, it was that dogs wanted to please. Beating one because you were angry was like taking a sledgehammer to your computer because you didn't know how to turn the thing on.

"Well." Zoë's voice broke through my thoughts. "I

guess we didn't win." She looked disappointed, and again I wondered why she cared about this contest. It wasn't as if Max had been there to see us.

"Let's get moving. What do you think?" I panted in agreement. I was feeling worn and pummeled. Frankly, I was ready to get out of this body and back into mine so I could take a three-day nap.

That, however, wasn't what Zoë had in mind.

"That sounds like a party going on, right over there," she said, turning one ear toward the beach. Sure enough, dance music rumbled toward us from the fancy beach houses that faced Kwemah Bay. As we walked away from the Obedience Trials, I turned my paws toward home, but Zoë didn't follow. She was facing the beach. "Let's go!"

I stopped, torn. It was about seven o'clock, and the sun would set soon. My habits all told me to go in one direction—directly home. But a part of me had always wanted to go to one of those beach house parties. They were notorious in Madrona for being open to all, yet I'd never been to one. I was too shy, that was what Kerrie always said. Too scared was more like it.

If I was ever going to go, why not do it now while I could hide behind my fur? This was my big chance to slip inside, to pretend like I was part of Madrona's in-crowd. *And,* I had to remind myself, *all this adventure must be getting me closer to a solution than sitting at home would.* What did I have to lose?

Together, Zoë and I wandered downhill toward the shore. The sky glowed gray and orange overhead, and the September evening had a cooling-off feel. We followed the music to a well-lit white brick palace with tennis courts and a long curving drive. Beyond the lawn, I saw the tan beach stretch out to the water. Giant potted conifers and scarlet fuchsias flanked the house's front door.

"Ooh, red," Zoë said approvingly, touching the front door (which looked gray to me). Without the least hesitation, she walked right up to the door, turned the knob, and went inside.

The floors smelled like lemon and wax, plus dirt from outside and something from the beach—seaweed? Legs and feet were everywhere. The noise pounded on my eardrums. I heard other dogs, a baby crying, someone dancing in high heels.

Behind me, Zoë worked the crowd like a pro. This was something I never expected to see—my face and body shaking hands with strangers, striking up conversations. She made the sailing teacher laugh and bumped hips with the postmaster. The president of the college brought her a beer. Zoë was the life of the party. She was everything I'd always wanted to be and more.

The sight of her grand success made me shrivel inside. Why couldn't I have ever had the nerve to come to a party like this? To make friends with these people I'd always wanted to know? It wasn't as if Zoë was smarter or funnier or cooler than I was. Well, maybe cooler, but not smarter.

I crept away to a quieter corner of the house and was overjoyed to find Max sitting on a couch, leafing through a magazine. Had I just caught Hot Max hiding from all the single women in the other room? He looked content, sitting alone, his hair wet from a late afternoon shower. He'd changed since the morning—now he wore a soccer shirt that said HOLLAND TOTAAL-VOETBAL. I felt a sudden urge to climb into his lap.

He smiled when he heard me trot into the room.

"Z-dog! What brings you here? I didn't think this was Jessica's scene."

When he mentioned my name, a shade passed over his face. *Oh, Zoë,* I thought. *If only you knew how badly you've hurt him. If only you realized that Max probably has a car, too.* I sidled up next to the couch, presenting my ears, which he promptly began to rub. With a tremendous sigh, I sank into the feeling, letting the noise and crowds fall away. The more he rubbed, the more insistent my desire became. Itches I didn't know I had floated to the surface, were sated, and were replaced by new, deeper ones. Without intending to, I moaned, then licked my lips to cover my embarrassment. Two seconds later, my eyes fell shut. All that mattered was Max's hand on my ear.

Suddenly, an overwhelming urge to tell Max everything—about Zoë, about me, about how much I liked him—clouded my brain. I panted and tried to catch his eye. He looked at me and our eyes met, but then he looked away.

I whined softly, and he looked back. For a breathtaking second, our gazes locked together. I peered deep into his pure-black irises, deeper, deeper, until I felt positive I was seeing his true soul. My heart clenched. I felt a world of understanding open between us. Max must have felt this; he must have seen who I really was. I couldn't breathe. My heart stopped beating.

Then Max ruined it with a smile that lit those beautiful cheekbones.

"Who's a good dog?" he said lightly. "Who's the best dog in the universe?"

I sat back, crushed. He'd looked, but he hadn't seen. So much for nonverbal communication. If I wanted to tell him about the switch, I'd have to use a blunter tool.

Max sighed softly and leaned back in his seat. "Here I am at a party full of women, and I'm sitting in the back, petting you."

I thought of all the sundresses and tube tops on the dance floor and my spirits dropped. "The thing is," he went on, "I just don't want to meet someone new. I want to be with Jessica." His hand dropped onto the top of my head. "But she's not interested. I guess I just need a little time before I plunge into that scene again."

This was almost too much to bear. More than ever, I longed to find a way to tell him the truth, but just then pandemonium launched through the door in the form of five rowdy dogs. They smelled like the beach, and wind, and each other's urine. There was a time, I realized with a start, when the arrival of this many dogs would have sent me into apoplectic shock. It was nice, now, to hear them coming and feel assured instead of afraid. I could bark as loudly as any dog. I could hold my own with this herd.

Max laughed when he saw them and extended his other arm. Like a five-headed monster, they nosed and licked his hand. A shepherd mix ignored my warning glare and sat on Max's other side. Envy and hatred filled me. I stood and tried to shoulder it out of the way, but when I did a Jack Russell—female—snuck behind me and leaped onto Max's lap.

I whirled on her with my teeth bared. Max gave a quiet chuckle. "Now, Zoë. Don't be jealous. The other dogs deserve attention, too."

I shrank back, appalled. Was I acting jealous? Had I really just tried to chase another dog away from Max—because I was envious? I'd never done anything like that before.

You have no business being jealous, I told myself. *Max isn't yours. And you aren't his. Get over it already.*

Zoë

This is the greatest party ever. Everyone is cheering as I walk in wearing my fabulous winner's hat and necklace. Finally, I'm coming to enjoy life in a human body. I give the crowd a wave, and someone hands me a yellow bubbly drink that looks suspiciously like pee. But when I sniff it, it's sweet, like apples. I drink it and it sends bubbles down my throat.

People are dancing, and I dance, too—like a show dog, on two legs. I talk to everyone and they say curious things like, "Jess, we've never seen you at one of these gigs before. Glad you could make it." I say, "Oh, yeah—I love a party!" and everyone nods with approval.

Loud music is coming from big black boxes. I shiver a little because the music reminds me of home, with my mom and dad, in our house. They used to play music sometimes. Loud, happy music. When it was on, they would lock me in the spare bedroom, which I didn't like. Even after the music ended and the guests went home, they sometimes forgot to let me out, and then I'd get in trouble for peeing on the floor. Once they forgot to feed me dinner. I was so hungry I ate a pillow and got in an awful lot of trouble. I never made that mistake again.

My drink is empty. I look around and head toward a long counter with a man behind it, making more drinks. There are people standing around the front of the counter, but they're just talking, so I push my way to the front and get my own glass of bubbles.

"Hey," says a woman in a peanut butter–colored dress. "Hey, you can't cut the line like that."

I look around, but I don't see any lines. Plus, how would I cut one? I try giving the woman a cheery smile, but that just makes her face look pinched.

"Try using a little common courtesy," she says in a voice that made me feel ashamed. "You know—wait your turn. Say please and thank you."

My mouth is dry. A lot of people are watching us now and they aren't looking too happy with me. I want—desperately—to be a good person, not a bad one. I open my mouth and say, "All right—whatever you want. Please *and* thank you."

That makes the woman's face pinch up even more. "You have to say it like you mean it, dearie." She rolls her eyes and turns away.

I bite my lip. My face feels burning hot, and no one will meet my eyes. I hear someone grumble, "Who invited *her*?" Now those bubbles aren't sitting quite right in my stomach.

A woman walks by and bumps my shoulder. She smells like my mom, and suddenly my eyes fill up with water. I miss home. I miss Gobbler and his funny cat noises. I miss the way Dad would say, "In you go, Zoë," whenever he put me in my crate. Any time I did too much running or jumping, he would take me by the collar and put me in my crate, and then I knew I had to settle down. It was nice when he did it—I could feel his fingers under my collar, touching my neck.

The water drips out of my eyes and runs down my face.

☕ *Jessica*

I wandered through the front room and caught a glimpse of gregarious Zoë, surrounded by Madrona's movers and shakers. Desire made the pads of my feet itch. I wanted that life, I wanted Max, I wanted to be a human again. I couldn't stand it anymore. Keeping as quiet as I could, I left the front room and headed down a hall toward what I guessed were bedrooms. One by one I nudged open doors and peered inside rooms until I found what I was looking for. In a back bedroom, far from the noise of the party, a desktop computer sat on a card table. I pushed the rolling chair away, rose up on my back feet, and pawed at the mouse. Wonder of wonders, the screen lit up.

My heart started to pound, and it wasn't just from

the effort of standing on two feet. Answers, I felt, were very close. I opened my mouth and started panting as I pushed the mouse to the Internet browser icon.

It took me five minutes to successfully double click the mouse. The card table wobbled precariously under my weight, and my heart doubled its pace. At last the browser opened, and the power of the Internet was mine—almost. I just had to type in that search box and all would be revealed.

Except that typing was nearly impossible. Every time I hit the keyboard with my paw, I typed four letters at once. My nose was no better. I tried my tongue, but it wasn't strong enough to push the key. Frustration made me whine. The table rocked beneath me as I smacked, licked, nosed, and nudged the computer. Nothing worked!

I spied a mug full of pens and pencils to the left of the computer and lunged for it—if I could get a pen in my mouth, maybe I could use it to push the keys. Only when I pushed my body forward to reach the pens, the card table leaned away from me, its spindly legs tipping like grass blowing in the wind. *Oh, no.* I held my breath as the table swayed in slow motion.

"Zoë, is that you? What are you doing in here?"

The voice made me jump, especially when I recognized it as Max's. *Not him—not now!* When I jumped, even more of my weight pushed against the table. I fumbled with my paws, trying to back off the table, but I couldn't get any traction. I slipped on everything. My paws skidded off the keyboard and flew across the table, causing my chest to ram the table's edge.

The table fell in one clean motion. I cringed, not

daring to watch. The crash reverberated in the room for a full five seconds. When I finally got up the nerve to look, all I could see was the upended table shrouding the pile of toppled hardware.

"Oh, that's bad." Max's voice made me hang my head. He came up beside me and peered over the table. Then he looked ruefully at me. "Bummer."

My head dropped even lower. I wanted to sink into the carpet, but I settled for slinking toward the door instead. I was almost there when Max stopped me.

"Hey, Z-dog, it's all right. You're okay."

Okay? Several thousand dollars' worth of computer equipment lay in a heap on the floor and he was telling me it was all right? Was he crazy?

"You're a dog—these things happen. You're not in trouble. What did they expect, leaving their doors open when they knew their house would be full of dogs?"

That's right, I thought, *I am a dog! What a great excuse!* For the first time, I felt relieved to be in a furry body. And grateful to Max. Plenty of people would have been angry—some might have hit a dog in a situation like this. Max was made of cooler stuff.

"Come on," he said, leading the way toward the door. "Let's go back to the party. I'll figure out a way to break this to the owners." In the doorway, he hesitated and turned back to me. "What's weird is that you looked like you were up there typing. Nuts, huh?" He tousled my head and I gave him a pant-smile. *How I wish I could tell you the truth.*

Max crouched down and put his hands on either side of my face. My heart beat uncomfortably in my chest, even more loudly than it had when the computer fell. His face was close enough that I could see the freckle above his left eyebrow and the twitch of the muscle in his cheek. His lips looked unbelievably soft. Dark lashes flicked across his eyes when he blinked. I swallowed.

Then I licked him.

"Hey, that's sweet." He laughed. "Funny Zoë. You're no average dog, are you?"

18

A Dog in the Moonlight

 Zoë

This party has made me miserable. I've done a little crying, quietly to myself, and now I'm sitting on a sofa, watching people dance without really seeing them.

I feel horribly alone, like I did at home when I used to sit in my crate. Only I'm not in a crate now, I'm at a party, where I can do anything I want—run or jump or dance—but I'm still miserable. I don't like this new life very much. People are always saying things to me and expecting me to say the right thing back. But how do I know what's right? I don't. I just say things and then they look at me like I'm the dog that pees on everyone.

Being a person is so much more than having thumbs and being tall and eating what you want. I didn't know all that before—now that I do, I don't think I like it. If I have to stay human, I'll never get to sniff around a fire hydrant to get all the canine news, or take long naps in the sun, or shake water all over people when I'm wet. I love doing that.

I want to be a dog again.

And I want to go home.

Sigh. I look around the party at the dogs that are there, but none of them gives me a clue about how to change back into one of them. They're all happy, busily doing their own thing, and they don't even notice me. Probably every person here wishes they could be a dog. Dogs are the luckiest ones alive. I just never knew.

I see a flash of white and look up. There's Jessica with Dr. Max! I'm so glad to see them my face bends into a smile and my heart lightens instantly.

Only they aren't seeing me, they just move through the crowd. All the women in short skirts and high heels stop dancing to smile and say, "Hi, Max!" He says hi back, but he doesn't stop to talk to them. He sits on a narrow sofa that's too small for all of us. Jessica hops up beside him. A woman with a picture of a Newfie on her coat walks up to them and pats Jessica on the head.

"I think someone has a crush on you," the woman says, looking at Max and laughing. Jessica looks at her paws, but I know she's listening.

Max runs his hand under Jessica's ear, and she turns back to him. "Well, what's a guy to do? She's a gorgeous dog."

Jessica's mouth pops open. She looks self-conscious, and the tip of her tail flips up and down like a fish. If they weren't man and dog, I'd be sure they were going to mate, right here. But they won't. Not this time. The woman winks at Max.

"It's like she understands every word you say," she said. Which is funny in a million ways.

I wish Jessica and Max would come over here, so

we could all cuddle on the sofa like puppies. But they don't. I get up on my feet and head toward them, but as soon as Max sees me, he stands and looks around like he's about to leave. I say, "Hey," and try to wave, but he goes to the door. Jessica gives me a growly look and goes after him.

Now I'm left all alone. In the middle of dancing people and a party, I'm alone. This party is the worst— I'm ready to leave this place, now.

That's when I see the table in the corner, covered with food! Nothing there is as incredible looking as what I cooked at the restaurant today, but I have to go closer anyway, to get a better look. The cookies are round, not bone-shaped, but they look good. I see crunchy things and big things and tiny little paw-sized treats.

And *potato chips*!

☕ Jessica

I followed Max to the door. He pointedly avoided Zoë, which pained me. There had to be a way for me to explain that *I* hadn't been the one to snub him. That "Jess" wasn't herself—and I wasn't Zoë.

As Max slid one arm into his jacket, a bubble of panic rose in my chest. I had to do something. But what?

On impulse, I ran up and grabbed the loose arm of his jacket.

"Hey, Z-dog, this is no time to play." He turned and rubbed my back. "I'll see you another time."

I wasn't about to take no for an answer. Clenching my teeth on that sleeve, I dragged him toward the door.

"Oh, you have to go out? Okay, that's different." He pulled a leash out of his pocket and clipped it on my collar. *I swear, he must have had a leash for every occasion.*

I led Max outside, then yanked him around the house and down toward the beach. A plump moon dangled halfway up in the sky, throwing pale light onto the driftwood and seaweed tangles that marked the high-tide line. Below that was a long stretch of wet sand. The beach reeked with smells—salty, rotten, mysterious odors that I was dying to investigate. But I forced myself to focus. This was more important than any decaying sea creature.

The sand felt cool and gritty under my paws. I rushed down to the wet shingle and started scraping my right paw across the sand, concentrating hard.

"I thought you had to pee," Max said, busily checking his phone for messages. "C'mon, Z, I'm not here to watch you dig."

I ignored him and kept working. When I finished, I sat back, breathing hard, and surveyed my work. It looked like a huge mess.

My heart sank. This was never going to work.

"Okay, all done? Good. Let's go."

Wait. I had an idea. A foot-long stick lay on the sand just up the beach from me. Using all the length in my leash, I stretched my neck until I grabbed it. Chomping down hard with my teeth, I went to a clean stretch of sand and started to write.

I'M NOT ZOË.

I'M—

"Are you ready to go yet, Z? Because I am. It's getting late. Zoë? What are you doing?"

My heart raced, knowing he was watching. I wrote even faster, which meant that I fouled up a few letters. My "J" looked like a backward "L" and the "S"s looked like "Z"s. I ended up with this:

I'M NOT ZOË. I'M JEZZICA.

Pretty ugly. I sat back, panting. I was tired after all that writing and I longed to run into the water and sink my feet into the coolness, but I didn't. I looked up at Max, my heart full of hope.

Max was studying my writing, his face dark. Suddenly, my mind overflowed with misgivings. Maybe this was too much for a regular person to take. Surely he wouldn't understand. And even if he did, he'd just think Zoë and I were freaks. This had been a horrible mistake.

"What the hell—is this some kind of joke? A trick Jessica taught you?"

I very carefully swung my head from side to side.

Max laughed. "Oh, shit, what was in that beer? I must be drunker than I thought."

He turned to go, but I dug my heels in and barked until he looked back at my words in the sand. He frowned at them. "A trick, huh? It's pretty clever. Too bad you can't really read and write."

A challenge, eh? I picked up my stick again, breathing hard through my nose, and wrote MAX IS A VET.

Max stared, his eyes wide. Then he dropped onto the sand.

"No way. No way did I just see that." I sat in silence, waiting. "Can you do it again?"

I picked up my stick and wrote, YES. ANYTIME. The stick was starting to hurt my mouth, but I hardly cared. My eyes were on Max.

"Oh, shit." He exhaled slowly. "I, uh, don't know what to say here. This is way, way too weird. But I *saw* you *writing*—real words. I saw it. What's going on?"

I picked up my stick again and went to a patch of sand near his foot.

HELP, I wrote.

"Oh, God." Max's face looked stark, like he'd just witnessed a car accident. The moonlight made arcs and shadows under his features.

Poor Max—I knew how he felt. I found this whole thing pretty terrifying, too. Had it been wrong of me to share my secret with him? Was it too much of a burden?

He threw up his hands. "No. No. I can't. . . . You can't ask me to believe . . ." Shaking his head, he got up and walked away down the beach. I watched his silhouette grow smaller and smaller as it trudged, shoulders hunched, away from the brightly lit party house. My heart was beating quietly, but I could hear it clearly. The night was still. And I was so frightened.

About a hundred yards away, Max stopped, hands on his hips. He looked like he was having a conversation with himself—if I closed my eyes, I could hear him muttering. Then he bent down, picked up a rock, and hurtled it into the water. It skidded into the bay with a splash, then disappeared beneath the inky face of the sea.

I heard a little quiet profanity. Then Max started trudging back toward me and my heart tripped over itself with joy.

When he was four feet away, he stopped and looked at me like I'd just stepped out of a UFO. "I'm only here out of scientific curiosity, okay?" he said, one hand up, warning me not to jump him or lick him or probe his brain. "I'd hate myself forever if I didn't learn more while I had the chance." He cleared his throat, clearly nervous. "Are you Jessica?" His voice was cautious, as if he hoped to be proven wrong.

I nodded my head.

"No. Really?"

I nodded again. He swiped his hand across his face and up into his hair. "You're a person."

I sat perfectly still.

"A dog with a person's brain—is that what you're telling me?"

I nodded my head slowly up and down.

"No. No, I don't believe it. It's just not possible." He walked away again, but this time he spun around after going a few feet. "*Really?*"

Yup.

"But how? How on earth does this happen? Is it permanent, or what?"

How I wish I had the answers. I shifted from paw to paw.

"When did it happen? Wait—were you yourself when we met, at the clinic?"

That I could answer. I nodded my head up and down.

"Well, I guess that explains some things. I thought Jess had been acting pretty weird. Kind of childlike and goofy. Huh." I hoped he saw now that Zoë's interest in Guy and that tank-top man had been hers, not mine. "Has this happened before?"

No.

"First time, then. Okay. So, how do you fix it? *Can* you fix it? Don't tell me this is forever."

An icy feeling ran through me. Forever—that didn't even bear thinking about. I suddenly wished I'd never told Max. What did I expect him to do about it? Comfort me? How could he, knowing what he knew? I'd probably ruined our friendship permanently. He'd never be able to look at me the same way again.

I thought of Zoë, dancing the night away inside at the party. She was having a ball, Max was about to go home and try to forget this whole encounter, and I was left alone, the only one trying to fix things—with no idea what to do. This was far lonelier than I'd ever felt when I was a human. What had I been complaining about for such a long time, saying I felt like an outsider in Madrona? I was further outside than ever now.

Max's cell phone rang and we both jumped. "Sorry," he said, looking at the number. "It looks like a client. I'd better take it—could be an emergency."

He strode off a few paces, leaving me alone with my thoughts. I looked over the sands that would be tawny golden in the daylight—and felt a pang of memory. I'd seen the beach on glorious days when the world sparkled, when the ever-changing salt water slid back at low tide to reveal an undersea world that was rich with color. I'd seen Crayola-bright purple and orange starfish, carrot-colored sea pens, and anemones blooming like underwater roses. My canine eyes didn't catch those fiery colors anymore. The world had shrunk in beauty, and I hadn't even noticed. What other parts of human existence had I already lost? And worst of all—what else had I forgotten about so completely that I didn't even know to miss it?

A terrible thought occurred to me. Dogs didn't live very long. What had Kerrie said when Jane Eyre died, that Labs only lived ten to twelve years? If Zoë was still a young dog, what did that mean for me—that I had ten good years left, if I was lucky?

Ten years to live. I felt too dizzy to stand. Nausea rose in my chest. Ten measly years!

Max ended his call and clicked his phone shut. "I'm really sorry, Z—Jessica." He winced, clearly remembering the horror I'd placed at his feet. "I've gotta run. That was Carol Johnson—her Great Dane has bloat. If I don't get there soon, the dog could die. It's really serious."

His feet were already turned toward the road. He paused and looked at me over his shoulder. "I wish I could help," he said earnestly. "Really, I do. But I can't. I'm a vet, not a magician." My ragged heart gave a twinge of pain as I saw that he was right. I raised my paw in a wave good-bye, and gorgeous, handsome, heroic Max turned away, trudging through the sand. He waved once from the top of the beach, then was gone.

My spirits were low enough to sink into my paws. Rather than stay there in the romantic moonlight, thinking over all the things I had lost, I turned my feet to the dry sand and walked away toward home.

19

One Paw in Front of the Other

 Jessica

I don't remember a thing from the walk home. Some-how I arrived at the sliding glass door, slumped in, and heaved my body onto the couch. Zoë arrived a little later, her pockets filled with potato-chip crumbs, which she offered me. I couldn't even get excited about food.

She snuggled into the couch beside me and promptly fell asleep, snoring softly. I stared into the darkness, blinking, while images bounced off the walls of my mind. Over and over, snippets of conversations re-played themselves. When I rolled over, I saw the hurdles at the Agility Competition, felt the joy of winning the Pet-and-Person Beauty Contest. For the first time in my life, smells accompanied every memory—smells so pungent I experienced them all over again, just as vividly as when I'd first sniffed them.

Sadly, for every happy vision my mind showed me, I had to endure two scenes from my time at the beach with Max. The scent of seaweed and burrowing clams grew strong enough to make me feel ill. Max's words formed an endless loop in my head: "I wish I could help, but I can't. I'm a vet, not a magician."

The pained look on his face haunted me. It was too clear a reflection of my own thoughts and feelings— that I was a freak, a horror who was going to die far too soon. My life had ended at the moment of that lightning strike. Now I was going through the motions, playing out the tragic epilogue.

After a while, the sound of Zoë's sleeping snores annoyed me, so I pulled myself off the couch and paced around the apartment. What would life be like for me now? Could I still live here? How would Zoë pay the rent? I thought of the bills that might be piling up in the mailbox already and started to shiver. I couldn't help Zoë with any of this. I couldn't write, couldn't type, couldn't talk. In my brain, I knew how to balance my checkbook and hunt for errors on my credit card statement—but I couldn't convey any of that to her. I was like a mummy. Like a person in a coma. Forget about having ten years to live—the stress of this was probably going to kill me within one.

I stood at the sliding glass door and looked out at the moon. I wanted desperately to cry, but I seemed physically unable to. Howling was a good alternative, but I couldn't risk waking the neighbors and getting Zoë in trouble with the landlord. If he called, she might say something wackadoodle and wind up in serious trouble. Instead of howling, I slumped down on my belly and set my chin on my paws. My heart felt so heavy, I thought it would break my ribs.

Things seemed so clear to me, there in the moonlight. I'd missed my opportunity with Max. At any time while I was a human, I could have struck up a conversation with him and started a relationship— but I'd been too afraid to take the first step. And a relationship with Max wasn't the only one I'd been too afraid to pursue. With my heart beating hard, I stood up and went to the front door.

The lavender envelope still sat on the floor, looking innocent. I nosed it, taking in the smells that clung to the paper. Breath mints. Instant coffee with nondairy creamer. My breath came in short puffs as I picked the envelope up in my teeth and carried it back to my place by the glass door.

For a long time, I lay with the envelope on my paws, looking at it. I'd made so many assumptions about what might be inside—about what excuses she would make, what claims she would try to lay on my affection. But I had no idea what she'd written. I didn't have the first clue about her.

In a rush, I stood up and grabbed the envelope in my teeth, holding one corner down with my paw while I worked a tooth under the flap and gave it a tear. I tore the back off the envelope and shook the card free— lavender, to match the envelope, with a bouquet of violets on the front. My pulse boomed in my ears as I picked up the card and dropped it repeatedly until it opened. Then I carefully turned it over and consumed the words like a starving person.

Dear Jessica,
    I know I don't have a right to hope, but it's my one prayer that you might forgive me—someday.

I was never fit to be a mother, as much as I longed to be.

I want you to know how incredibly proud I am of you.

Debra

I blinked because the page was swimming. Each time my heart pounded, it replayed a piece of her message. Debra. Proud of me. Never fit. Longed to be my mother.

Could that be true?

No. No—I shook my head and pushed the card away. No, this woman abandoned me. She left me in state care when I was only two years old. She had one thing correct, though, she didn't have any right to hope for my forgiveness. I would carry the scars—physical and mental—of my childhood the rest of my life. It only seemed fair that she should, too.

I set my jaw and turned back to the moon, determined to think more angry thoughts. But that last sentence kept creeping through my mental chatter. Proud of me. She was proud of me. Was she really? How could she be?

Debra didn't know me. She hadn't been there for a single one of my successes—or my failures. She was like a fictional character in my life. I might have thought about her, and wondered what she was like, but she'd never made herself known, not even once. The fact that she suddenly wanted to get in touch didn't even come close to making up for twenty-plus years of neglect.

This kind of thinking wore me out, and I must

have fallen asleep. When the phone rang, I sprang to my feet, every hair standing on end. My thoughts flew in all directions. Had I howled accidentally? Was this Mr. Deeb calling about the noise? No—I hadn't howled. I was pretty sure, anyway. Who was calling at this time of night?

On the couch, Zoë moaned and flapped her arm, trying to push the noise away. The phone rang again. I ran over and squinted at the caller ID.

It was Max.

＼ Zoë

Jessica pulls me off the couch, tugging on my shirt with her teeth. I almost fall on top of her. Even though I know I have people feet, my sleepy body doesn't quite remember, and I stumble around before I'm steady. She clamps her teeth on my shirt again and drags me to the loud white thing on the desk.

I give it a long look. I've seen these before—my mom and dad used to spend hours talking into theirs. But suddenly I can't remember how it works. I know I'm supposed to hold part of it in my hand, but it's square and awkward, and I don't know what to do. The ringing jars my brain until I can hardly think.

Jessica gives me one of those looks she has where her ears go in different directions, like she hears a rabbit on one side and a dog barking on the other. I think she's frustrated with me. "I can't help it—I don't know what you want me to do!" I say.

The loud noise goes off again. I use both hands to

cover my ears, but Jessica pretends it doesn't bother her. She puts her front feet up on the desk, just about knocking me out of the way. She stares at the thing and raises her paw as if she's about to poke at a fish in a pond. Moving very slowly, she sets her paw on the little buttons. The noise stops. Instead the thing says, "Hello? Hello?"

Jessica is panting, looking at the machine like she wants to eat it, her ears standing straight up. I feel like my ears are perking up, too.

"Dr. Max? Is that you? What's going on?" I give Jessica a rub on the back in gratitude for making the ringing stop at last.

"Oh, good," he says. His voice sounds tired and far away. "You're there."

"I'm here," I say. "Where are you?"

"I'm at home. Is, um, is the dog with you?"

"Of course," I say, not sure why he's being funny. "*The dog* is right here."

"Listening?"

Jessica, who's been smiling at the talking machine with her mouth open, lets out a little bark.

"Right," says Dr. Max. "Okay. I, uh, I wondered if I could come over? I wanted to talk about this some more."

Jessica barks again, two times. Her paws slide on the desk and she has to scramble to balance again. Her ears are up as high as they go.

"Yes!" I say. "Come over! How will you get here?"

"I have the address from the clinic's records. Be there in a sec."

The machine makes a little click, and then it's quiet.

"Dr. Max?" I say. "Are you still there?" No one answers. Jessica gets down off the desk and goes to the
glass door. It's dark in the apartment, but I can see her
white tail wagging slowly as she looks out at the night.
She looks so hopeful it somehow almost breaks my
heart.

 Jessica

When I saw Max's shadowy figure outside the sliding
glass doors, my pulse tripled its intensity. I panted
hard as I watched him come up the walk, check the
apartment number, and knock softly on the glass. I
pawed at the door until he got the hint and let himself in.

"Dr. Max!" Zoë jumped off the couch, her hair
poufy on one side, flat on the other. Even in the dim
light, I could see the crosshatch marks on her cheek
from the sofa fabric. Fortunately, Max didn't seem to
notice. His gaze hovered on the floor, as if he were
too afraid to look at either one of us. I started to feel
sick all over again.

Max reached into his pocket and jangled his car
keys, then walked across the room and switched on
the overhead light. We all squinted, blinking through
the pain of sudden brightness. Swallowing rapidly, he
looked from one of us to the other, barely flicking his
eyes over me before settling them safely on the floor.

"I've been thinking for hours and I can't make my
brain get this."

"Get what?" Zoë perched on the arm of the couch,

enjoying the game of almost rolling off one way, then the other.

"Um." His eyes darted at me again, then away. "The switch. The whole thing. Jessica told me. I know."

Zoë gaped at him, dumbfounded enough to stop rolling for a minute. Max elaborated. "I know about what happened to you and Jessica. I know you're really Zoë."

"You do?" Her eyes grew large with amazement. She sat perfectly still. "You know that I'm—me?"

"Well, you're Zoë," he said in a strained voice. "Right?"

"Yes! You know? Oh—that's great!"

"I'm glad you think so."

Zoë looked over at me, grinning broadly, showing all her teeth. I wished I felt even half as elated. "I should have thought of this before," she was saying. "You're a vet—you fix dogs. You can put us back!"

"No. No." Max shook his head as he crossed the room, reaching her in the space of a second. "No. I'm sorry." He bent down slightly, hands on her shoulders, so she could see his face. "I don't know how to fix this. I wish I did."

Zoë practically deflated before our eyes. "Oh. I really thought—just then—"

My chest ached like I'd been hit with a cannonball. Watching Zoë go through the topsy-turvy emotions of hope and disappointment was almost worse than experiencing them myself. Max looked miserable, too. I started to wonder why he'd come. What did he hope to gain? We all knew the situation was hopeless.

Please don't let him be one of those people who likes torturing themselves.

For a long while, we all sat and stared at the floor. Even Zoë had nothing to say. My mind did turn to food a few times, but as soon as I remembered the sick feeling, I didn't want to eat. Imagine that—a dog that didn't want to eat. Zoë would call that impossible.

At last Zoë lifted her head. "Let's go for a walk," she said. "I always feel better when I'm outside."

No one could argue with that. Seconds later, the three of us were ambling down the street, Zoë and Max walking side by side. I was in third-wheel position behind them. Amazing smells drifted up from the lawns that edged the sidewalk, but I stoically ignored them—I wanted all my attention fixed on Max. He'd come for a reason, and I wanted to be paying attention when he told us what it was.

After about half a block, right near a lilac hedge that every dog in the neighborhood must have peed on, Max said, "I could barely focus on Carol Johnson's Great Dane tonight. The whole time I was working on him, I kept thinking, what if he was like you? What if he looked like a dog, but inside he had a person's brain? A person's memories? Can you imagine—a person inside a dog, there on the exam table, hearing me talk about odds and risks and treatment choices? I couldn't shake the feeling that he was lying there, listening to me talk about his condition, understanding every word. And the pain he must have been in—I wanted to stop everything and tell him that I understood, that I was going to do my best. But how could I with Carol Johnson standing right there? She would have thought I was nuts."

He fell quiet. As I walked on, I pictured him in his clinic, wrestling with this, and guilt draped over me, making my head and tail droop. I'd brought this upon him. If I hadn't insisted on showing him my words in the sand, he would never have had this crisis.

I felt awful. If there was one thing I knew about Max for absolute certain, it was that he loved animals. He had a true passion for his profession. I thought of all the people I'd known—from my foster parents on down the line—who hated their jobs. Most people slogged through their workdays with one eye on the clock, toting up vacation hours and holidays, living for Fridays and hating every Monday morning. It was rare to see someone doing work they loved— work they were meant to do. To hear Max doubting all his skill and knowledge hurt me physically. Realizing that I was the one who had made it happen made me want to vomit right on my own feet.

Thank goodness for walking, I thought. At least it gave my body something to do while my conscience gave myself a good flogging.

A few blocks away, a dog barked, and we all stopped to listen. When it quit, Max spoke again. "I mean, I know dogs understand us. I've never doubted it. But I always thought they knew what we *meant* more than what we said. Like they could sense our intentions. They're smarter than we are emotionally, that's what I think. More genuine. And consistent."

Zoë nodded vigorously. "Yep, that's all true. But most dogs don't understand words—not all the words, anyway."

"No? Are you sure?"

Zoë was quiet for a minute, watching her own shadow stretch under the streetlamp in front of her feet. "Well, I never did, that's for sure. I do *now*, which is funny. Now that I'm in this body, I know all kinds of words and what they mean. I can even read!"

Max chewed on that for a moment. I noticed that he hadn't looked at me once since we'd started walking. Was it strange that he found it easier to look at Zoë? Was it just because she looked like a human? Or because it bothered him more to think of my having both a human brain and a tail?

He took a deep breath and let it out, making a cloud of steam in the night air. "I don't know. Maybe I'll be a better vet if I think the animals can understand everything I say." He gave Zoë a quick up-and-down look. "So you're . . . Zoë. A dog."

"Mm-hmm." Zoë swung her arms as she walked.

"Um, don't take this the wrong way, but how do I know you're not really still Jessica, just . . ."

Crazy. The second he asked the question, I saw how it could look. What if I was still me, only I'd snapped and now believed I was a dog? Wouldn't that explain all of my odd behavior this weekend? A psychotic person would have no problem licking people's faces and trying to pee in Hyak Park—not if they really believed they were a dog. Of course that

was what he would think. It was what the whole
world would think. *That,* I told myself acidly, *is why
you never should have said anything.*

Zoë was laughing. "Oh, no, Dr. Max. I'm not crazy,
and I'm for sure not still Jessica. I was a dog my whole
life before the lightning thing happened. You should
have seen me trying to walk on two legs the first
time. Really. Also, I can tell you that this person nose
is terrible."

Behind her, I shook my head. None of this was real
evidence. A crazy person could have made up all that
and more.

"But can't you prove it?" Max asked.

"Of course I can't prove it. It happened! I'm not
sure it's ever happened before. Ever, ever. But can't
you tell from looking at Jessica? She knows absolutely nothing about being a dog."

I allowed myself an indignant look—not that either of them turned to see it.

We turned a corner. The wind picked up and tossed
leaves across the empty road. Zoë shivered and
wrapped her arms around herself as Max asked to
hear how it all happened in the first place. She told him
how we were walking across the square when lightning struck us both. "When I woke up, I was terribly
cold. And I couldn't smell anything. I tried to stand up,
but everything about me was wrong." She bit her lip
and sniffed. "I really miss being a dog."

"I'm sure you do," he said, though I heard a note
of skepticism, still, in his voice. "It's just such a lot—
too much—to take in."

Zoë snorted. "Sure, but you only have to think

about it. Imagine having to *do* it. That's much worse. Besides, it's Jessica we should feel bad for. It's harder for her."

"Why?"

"Well, you know. You people have so many problems. You get so tense about things. Worried about this and worried about that. People are always moping around over nothing. Imagine how it is to be faced with a bad problem that's really real!" She snorted. "People are always trying to make things better with their cheer-me-up drinks and cheer-me-up food, and all they ever do is make you smell bad and act angry. People leave home for weeks and weeks, just to come back more miserable than when they went away." She shook her head. "I tell you, it's hard being a dog, watching your people do things that only hurt them in the end. Over and over and over again. It's hard to keep forgiving them. But, I guess, that's part of the gift dogs give. We're pretty forgiving."

She shook her head and took a few more steps before speaking again. "It is tough to understand, though. People have all this elaborate stuff—machines and fancy electronic gizmos. And how much joy do they really get, locked in the house all day? I don't see what the big deal is. Happiness is easy. All you need is a ball."

Again, Zoë's observations surprised me. Did she really think people were the ones that needed pity, and that dogs had it all figured out? Well, maybe they did. After all, dogs had managed things so that they didn't have to work, or pay mortgages, or wade through health insurance options. They spent their days snoozing on the couch. Sure, maybe they had to wake up to bark at something or take a walk, but all in all, they had it pretty good. Maybe she was right, maybe dogs were smarter than people.

But if that was true, why did I miss being human?

Max was shaking his head. "Sometimes it isn't easy to be happy," he said, picking up on Zoë's comment. "Not when the, uh—" he glanced back at me, so quickly I thought I might have imagined it "—person you like isn't a human anymore. It's pretty freakin' depressing."

My breath caught in my throat. That moment felt like the end of everything. I'd never wanted to touch him this badly—to hold him and pretend everything would be all right. But I couldn't pretend, not even to myself.

We walked in silence for a long time. Eventually, Max noticed Zoë shivering and suggested we head home. No one spoke the entire way. When we reached the apartment, Zoë yawned and stretched so far she nearly hit Max in the head. "I want to go to bed," she said. "Last night I was so cold. My blanket fell off and I got shivery."

Max glanced down at me before responding. "Maybe you need some pajamas."

Zoë cocked her head. "What are pajamas?"

"Comfy clothes you wear at night, to sleep in. I'm sure Jessica has some in her, uh, bedroom."

What a considerate guy he was. I trotted into my bedroom, knowing Zoë would follow, and nosed the drawer that held all my pjs. When Zoë opened it, I hoisted myself up on two paws and pulled out my favorite, a pale yellow, summer-weight sleeveless nightgown. Zoë took one look at it and sniffed.

"Look at these!" she crowed, holding up a pair of blue flannel footie pajamas. "These have rabbits on them—I love rabbits! And what are these at the bottom? Bunny ears, down there?" She was still mulling over the mystery of rabbit faces on the feet of pajamas when Max called from the door.

"Zoë, do you want help finding something to wear for tomorrow?"

"Nope, that's okay. I have clothes for daytime already."

I let out three panicked barks in a row. She couldn't possibly wear the same clothes for a third day running. I would die of shame.

"I don't think Jessica wants you to keep wearing those," Max said from the door, barely hiding the laughter in his voice. "People don't usually think that's appropriate. You're supposed to change into new clothes every day."

Zoë scoffed. "Every day? That's ridiculous."

I barked again and rammed her knee with my head.

"Ouch, okay, okay. I'll change, but I don't see why. It isn't like *you* change," she said to me. "Ever. But all right. If it's what people do. What should I wear, Dr. Max?"

There was a long silence on the other side of the door as Max pondered this question. *I'd better move quickly,* I thought, *before he comes up with something hideous.* I ran to the half-open pajama drawer, and started beating my paw against the one above it. To begin with, she needed clean underwear.

Zoë came over to look into the drawer, as curious as a kid opening birthday presents. I nudged the plain-but-practical blue panties on the top and a nice gingham-checked bra, but Zoë grabbed for the one underneath it.

"Ooh, red! This is pretty." She held the bra upside down in front of her and nodded in approval. If I could have spoken, I'd have tried to talk her out of it (she wouldn't be able to wear a white top over it, after all), but I couldn't, so I decided to let it go. Getting her clothed was my main objective. Color choice was a subtlety that could wait.

Within seconds, Zoë had stripped naked. With her bare butt pointed at me, she bent over the drawer and dug around until she uncovered the red panties that matched the bra. She got into the panties quickly enough, but the bra caused her some trouble.

"How does it go on?" she asked me, as she tried to stick her head through one of the arm holes. She knelt on the ground so I could help her, guiding the straps over each arm until she had it on, more or less. *And let me just say that one thing that's weirder than seeing yourself naked is helping your naked self put on clothes.*

I was about to help her clasp it—or try, at least—when Zoë bolted up, ran to the door, and pushed it open. "Look, Dr. Max, look at my pretty red suit!" She danced in a joyful circle.

Max's eyes could not have been wider. He stood there, mouth hanging open, completely transfixed by the half-naked creature in red before him. "Uh," was the only sound he uttered. When he closed his mouth and swallowed hard, I felt a faint flush of pride— Max liked the way I looked! But then he saw me, and we both snapped back to reality. By his eyes, I saw that he clearly remembered Zoë was a dog, not a woman. And I remembered to be humiliated by what Zoë was doing.

Max stammered out, "Okay, Zoë, why don't you pick out the rest of your clothes? People have to wear more than just that."

She nodded, but as she turned to reenter the bedroom, she stopped. "Dr. Max, can you hook it in the back for me? I can't do it."

Max swallowed audibly again. I wanted to hide my face under my paws, but I made myself watch as Max gamely stepped forward and fastened the hook-and-eye closures. "There," he said, patting her on the shoulder. I'd never seen him look so awkward. "All done. Now what about tomorrow?"

"Oh, we don't need to hook it again tomorrow," Zoë said. "I'll sleep in it! Where are those pajamas with the bunny feet?"

Half an hour later, Max and I had Zoë tucked in on the couch, proudly twitching her bunny feet which she'd insisted we not cover up with the blanket. A twinset and skirt lay on the coffee table, ready for her to put on in the morning, along with clean panties (my addition) and sandals that Max had dug out of my closet. I was so indebted to him for going through this with me. It almost felt like we were Zoë's parents.

When Zoë was settled, Max strode over to my desk and opened my laptop. A shiver of excitement shot through me, running from my nose to my tail, which started to wag. I stole up beside him and set my chin on the edge of the desk to see the screen.

"We might as well give this a try, don't you think?" he asked me. My tail thumped the floor. "You never know what we might find."

After three hours, we hadn't found much of anything. Well, not much that sounded sane, anyway. Max had clicked on plenty of sites that listed out-of-body experiences . . . right alongside lizard people in Congress, Area 51 aliens, and Sasquatch sightings. He read through page after page, finally giving up with a soft, incredulous snort. Then, drumming his fingers, he'd type in a new search string and start again.

My eyes had a hard time staying focused on the screen, and in time I gave up and lay down on the floor. I had a strong urge to lie with my chin on Max's feet, but I resisted. This was all strange for him—I needed to be grateful that he was in the same room with me and not push for more. And I was grateful. Deeply. Sitting together like that, with just the gentle click of the mouse and occasional under-the-breath murmurs from Max, soothed me like hearing rain on the roof while I waited to drift off at night. Just knowing he was there made me feel safe. Before I knew it, I'd fallen asleep.

I woke with a start to find Max stretching kinks out of his shoulders. Those handsome, shrugging shoulders. He looked down at me, and our eyes met in the pale glow of the computer screen. I could tell from his face that he hadn't found a solution. There was no brilliant NASA scientist ready to take on our case, no examples of situations like ours being cured by deep meditation. We were still stuck.

"I found a little, not a lot," he said in a hush, taking care not to wake Zoë—who snored on the couch, her face smooshed into a throw pillow. "One thing, though—if the Internet is anything to go by, out-of-body switches happen more often than people think. There's plenty to read. Could be all garbage, of course, but at some point you have to ask yourself, why would so many people spend their time writing about something that didn't exist?" As he rubbed his hand down his face, it was clear that he'd asked himself that question.

"I tell you, a week ago I'd have laughed at most of the stuff I found. It seems just ridiculous. But now, knowing you . . . Well." He gave a little shrug as if to say that knowing me made all the wackos of the world look sane. Which, I suppose, it did. "Anyway, almost all the sites had a couple of things in common. They all agree that the switches happen spontaneously, and that communicating about it afterward is the worst part for the people who get switched."

He stared at the screen and fidgeted with the mouse. "It was really kind of agonizing to read about. A lot of people said they were depressed and wanted to kill themselves—only they couldn't because they were horses or whatever without any hands. Super sad stuff." His lashes flicked in my direction. "I hope you aren't in a dark place like that. I mean—I had a girl-friend back in high school who would get depressed. Really depressed. It's the worst thing I've ever seen."

I wanted to hear more, both about the girlfriend and what he'd learned online. I licked my lips and concentrated on giving him the most attentive face I could muster.

He bent his arms behind his neck until his elbows cradled his head. "There's nothing worse than stand-ing by and seeing someone in pain—and not being able to do anything about it. It drove me crazy." He gave a wry little laugh. "And here I am again, huh? In the same situation. I'm supposed to be a man of sci-ence, but I can't figure out a thing to help you. I mean, I always knew I couldn't cure half the things that go wrong with dogs. But I never expected to be beaten by something like this."

We were both quiet for a while as Max stared off into the corner of the room. I tried with all my might not to be depressed. I wanted to buoy Max, to be anything other than a sad weight around his neck—another broken woman that he couldn't fix. Still, the melancholy kept creeping in. Without being able to hug him, or kiss him, or even touch his hand, it would be hard for me to feel total joy. Not now that we'd been through so much together.

As I looked around my dark apartment, however, I had to pinch myself. What was I doing? Before this happened, all I could do was moan about how lone-some I felt, how isolated I was in this town of dog people. I would have given anything just to know that Max liked me, let alone get to spend a whole night with him.

I needed to whip my moping brain into shape. It was time to appreciate what I had instead of whining about what I lacked. With a contented sigh, I shuffled closer to his chair and sat with my tail almost on his feet. Ever so gently, slowly enough that he might not notice, I leaned against his legs.

He didn't say anything, but he didn't move either. And when he spoke again, I could have sworn I heard a new note of optimism.

"One of the common themes was that people think things in their past play a part in the switch. That it's something big in their personal history that keeps them from changing back when they want to. One woman—" He stopped. I couldn't see his face, but I imagined that he was shifting his jaw, debating whether to tell me. "All right, this sounds totally loony, but one woman claimed she got turned into a spider because, when she was young, she flushed every spider she found down the toilet. Getting changed into one was what she deserved—that's what she believed. She said she still has nightmares about being swirled down the toilet pipes.

"Anyway, she didn't turn back until she'd accepted how cruel it was to kill spiders that way. She made a vow to protect spiders for the rest of her life. And then she turned back. I don't really know what it means, but . . ." He trailed off.

I sighed. Weirdly, hearing about the batty spider lady made me feel a lot better. Not that I could see

what amends I could make to the canine community—
I'd never harmed a dog in my life. Still, a lead was a
lead, no matter how crazy. I'd have to sleep on that
one. Not now, though. It could wait until after Max
had gone.

20

'Til Death Do Us Part

 Jessica

I woke up on the couch, my legs wrapped up with Zoë's arms like we were a pair of puppies. I yawned and stretched, feeling content—until memories of the night before swamped my brain. What I wouldn't give to delete that whole scene on the beach from history and wipe it out of both my memory and Max's. Of course, if I had that kind of power, I probably wouldn't be in this mess at all.

My shuffling around woke Zoë, who opened one eye at a time, then rubbed her hands all over her face. She was scratching her scalp when the phone rang.

I got to the phone before she did and glanced at the caller ID. *Oh, no, not her. Anyone but her.* In a flash, Zoë was up and bounding to the phone. I tried to box her out with my butt, but she reached over me. "This time I know ho-ow," she sang, punching the speaker button with her index finger. I sat frozen, afraid to listen, but too frightened to move. "Hello?" she said eagerly, winking at me. She probably thought it would be Max again.

"Hello, Jessica?"

The voice on the other end made my lungs clench. It was half familiar, half foreign, and younger sounding than I'd expected. I could feel my pulse rising as I shifted from paw to paw. *Hang up,* I mentally screamed at Zoë, *hang up now! We can still escape if you'll just hang up now. We can keep on hiding from her, if you just—*

"Yes, this is Jessica," Zoë said, grinning like a dope. Clearly she was too clueless to hang up—I would have to do this myself. I jumped to my feet and lunged for the phone, smacking at the console with my paw, a motion that threw me off balance and made me crash into the desk.

"This is Debra," the voice said. Apparently, I had missed the phone. "Debra. Your mother."

My stomach spun and twisted. I heaved my paw at the phone again, but this time Zoë swept the whole phone box out of the way just before I struck. "My what? My mother? I have a mother?"

We both held still as I panted, waiting while the voice on the other end decided how to respond.

"Yes," Debra said. Then, "I'm so sorry for everything, Jessica. I want to tell you so. In person, if you'll let me."

Zoë frowned at the phone. I tried to sidle up close enough to hang up with my nose, but she lifted the phone out of reach. "What do you mean, in person?"

"I mean I'd like to meet you. If you're willing." Debra rushed on. "I know you might not be, and I understand—I'll understand anything you want to do. I don't want anything from you, just to talk. I know you must hate me. I just want to say I'm sorry." She paused. "And to see you."

I could barely breathe. She wanted to see me. She was proud of me. She'd ditched me when I was an apple-cheeked two-year-old, and now she wanted to see me. To apologize. What was I supposed to make of that? Could I trust her? Did I dare meet her?

"Okay," Zoë answered without hesitation. "Sure. When? Where?"

"Um, how would today be? I know you live in Madrona—I have to be in the area and I thought I could stop by."

Today? Today? No, absolutely, unequivocally, no. Today will never work, never, ever—

"Today's good," said Zoë. "At the park?"

While I sat there, numb, Zoë and Debra—my *mother*, Debra—agreed to meet in the park at two that afternoon. I glanced at the clock, stunned to see that it was already ten in the morning. That meeting would be in four short hours. I was going to be sick. No, not sick. Gone. I'd be gone, that was it. Zoë couldn't make me go, not if I flat-out refused. She could do whatever crazy-stupid thing she wanted, but I wasn't going. I just wasn't.

Zoë hung up the phone with her index finger and turned to me, her face full of light. "Your mother! Aren't you happy? Aren't you excited? You get to see your mom today!"

I looked away. She ran around to the other side of me. I found myself staring at that scar on her arm, the

one I'd always had but didn't know why. I probably
didn't want to know.

"This is so great! Maybe I'll see my mom today,
too, then it'll be the best day ever for both of us." I
looked away again, swinging my head back in the
other direction. "Why are you being like that? Aren't
you happy? Don't you want to see her?"

I kept my face averted. I just couldn't look at her.
Even though she didn't understand how or why, she'd
betrayed me—she'd undercut all the quiet and safety
I'd spent years putting in place. I wasn't ready to see
Debra. I wanted to hate her, more than any other human being alive. Zoë couldn't understand, and I
couldn't explain it to her. She'd just have to grasp the
fact that I wouldn't be going to the park at two. I
wouldn't meet Debra, not today, not ever.

I thought making that decision would give me peace,
but it didn't. I paced around the apartment, unsure
what to do with myself. I felt anxious, but when I
asked myself what I was worried about, I only came
up with one answer, that I was afraid Zoë would clip
a leash on me and force me to meet Debra. And of
course I hated the idea that, even if I boycotted the
meeting, Zoë would probably still go. She'd go and
give Debra a great big hug, welcoming her back into
my life with open arms. Well. There was only one
way to make sure that never happened. I had to get
back into my own body before two o'clock.

Which, of course, was easier said than done. I'd

been working this problem for so long I didn't think I had anything new to give it. But Zoë wanted to switch back, too—she'd said as much last night. If she were on my side, working with me, did that make a difference? Was there any last idea I hadn't tried?

Yes. Yes, there was.

I heaved myself up off the couch and went into the kitchen to check the time. It was 10:15. At 5:30 I was supposed to make a speech in the square, in front of everybody. Funny how that had become the least of my worries.

I roused Zoë with a bark and nudged the twinset, reminding her to change her clothes. That process took three times longer than it should have, but we finally made it out the sliding glass doors, clothes on and sandals buckled. We had half an hour to find something to eat and get ourselves to the Doggie Wedding Chapel on the green. It looked like a good day for a wedding— and the second biggest shock of our lives.

Doggie weddings were a long-standing Woofinstock tradition, but if you asked me, they were one of the weirder events ever created. The furry brides and grooms went through everything from the vows to the ring exchange, but they never got to enjoy the "happily ever after" part. Their owners got snapshots and memories for a lifetime. The dogs got to eat chicken-flavored cake.

Some people on the committee were gaga over this event, and they spent half the year planning the look of the wedding chapel, which was a big white tent erected in the middle of the green. This year's theme colors were sea-foam green and apricot.

"Mrs. Sweetie's been married five times," Malia Jackson had gushed every time the Canine Chapel of Love came up for discussion. "This year she's going to step away from tradition and wear a lilac gown. Aren't you, Mrs. Sweetie?" Malia always turned at this point and chucked Mrs. Sweetie under the ear. Which, I have to say, Mrs. Sweetie seemed to enjoy.

As we neared the tent, my insides started to twist with anxiety. *Zoë had better not get any crazy ideas about marrying me off*, I thought. *She's done enough to mess up my life already.* I couldn't imagine anything worse than being wedded to another dog—especially a dog of Zoë's choosing. At least, if we did manage to switch back, she'd be the one married to the incontinent pit bull, not me.

The tent was in sight, but Zoë made us veer toward the avenue of vendors, so we could snack our way through breakfast. Not that I objected. I got pretty excited about the snacks. In fact, I'm ashamed to say that dog cookies were starting to taste incredibly good to me. Especially the cheese-and-liver ones.

At last we made it inside the tent, where dozens of pet-and-owner pairs were already sitting in rented white folding chairs. Zoë's attention was captured by a woman in a lemon-yellow suit in the back row, who kept saying, "I just love weddings," in a loud voice. Lacy veils were everywhere—hung on the backs of chairs, draping off canine heads. A number of dogs had costume suits and gowns that hung from their necks, creating the illusion of tiny human bodies with doggie heads.

At the front of the tent, a raised dais held a daisy-covered bower and a wooden lectern. A red carpet ran down the center aisle, up the steps, and under the bower. I looked around, anxious to spot the things I needed, but instead my eyes landed on Max.

He was dressed in a dark suit with an apricot-colored gerbera daisy in his lapel. On anyone else, this might have looked ridiculous, but Max gave the suit distinction. He looked as comfortable in the suit as he did in his Sounders T-shirts. It fit him beautifully across the shoulders, the black wool bringing out the deep shades in his hair and eyes. A light smile played over his face, making those stellar cheekbones pop. My heart gave an odd lurch when I saw him, standing near the bower like an expectant groom. *He's not the groom, though, you dodo*, I scolded myself. *You know he's the officiant. Poor guy.*

Max spotted me. Our gazes met over the tops of heads and furry ears. His two dark eyes held everything I really wanted—but the light in them was tempered by weariness, frustration, and a shortage of decent solutions to my problem. I let my head sink to the floor as I turned around and shuffled back down the aisle. People and dogs bumped into me, but I hardly noticed.

I almost wished I'd never met him in the first place.

The weddings were about to start. From speakers in the back, a canned prelude to "Here Comes the Bride" snapped and crackled. The guests were all abuzz, turning to adjust their dogs' veils and costumes. The dogs, all of whom seemed to know about the cake, beat their tails against the floor in overlapping, jubilant rhythms. My own tail drooped until it almost trailed on the red carpet.

Malia Jackson, with Mrs. Sweetie nestled in the crook of her arm—in lilac, as promised—came to the front of the room. "Good morning, everyone," Malia said in a quavering voice, "and welcome to the Canine Chapel of Love, where we celebrate love in all its shapes and sizes, furry or otherwise." She began to explain how the order of the ceremonies would work, emphasizing that afterward we would all gather outside to shower the new couples with birdseed (rice, apparently, was bad for birds).

Suddenly, I felt a gentle hand on my neck. "Hold on there," said Max's voice. "They won't understand if they see you off leash." His eyes indicated the Woofinstock committee members, who were stationed around the edge of the tent like proud mothers of the bride. His hand moved softly around my neck to the ring on my collar. My mouth popped open in a pant.

I don't know how I dared to glance up at him, but when I did, he gave me a look of such kind understanding, my heart almost stopped. He wasn't shying away, no matter how bizarre this was. If I'd had this moment as a human, I probably would have wept. As a dog, I felt light with joy.

He walked me back to Zoë, who sat on the aisle, staring at the lemon-yellow woman. Zoë was chewing on one of her fingernails. Max carefully took her hand from her mouth, shook his head no, and curled the handle of my leash into her fingers. She smiled at him, and he patted her on the head. Then he left us and returned to the dais.

🦴 Zoë

I *see* her, right there, sitting in a chair. She doesn't see me—her eyes are on the flowers and the lacy, poufy things on the stage.

She looks happy.

That pleases me. I want her to be happy. In my perfect world, she'd be happy forever—together with me, as a dog. Maybe, if Jessica can fix us soon, I can go home today.

I want to run up to her, like I did with Dad in the park, but I don't. People have their funny rules, one of which is *don't push other people over*. It's a boring way to live if you ask me, but I've learned the hard way that you have to obey these rules. Otherwise everyone turns cold and stops treating you like a part of the group— it's worse than getting swatted with newspaper.

Instead of running, I sit behind her and look. When I lean forward, I can smell her flowery scent, and it makes my heart ache for home. I have to get her attention, to show her that I've changed. I've excelled at obedience and beauty and agility—I'm ready to be the perfect dog for her and Dad.

All I want is for us to be together forever. I'll be the cleanest, quietest dog ever. If Jessica can just fix us, everything will be perfect.

☕ Jessica

As I sat in the back, watching Max, resolution hardened in me. My plan was drastic—dangerous, even—but at this point, I had no choice. I couldn't go through life as a dog, and I knew Zoë wanted to be herself again. The longer I looked at Max, the more desperate I became.

I shifted back and forth on my front paws. Next to me, Zoë was lost in space as she watched a woman with Jackie O–type button earrings who was dabbing her nose with a tissue. I didn't try to understand what she was thinking—I had more important things to worry about.

At the back of the stage, a complex network of extension cords ran to the massive box speakers on each side of the dais. More cables, some stuck to the floor with electrical tape, snaked the length of the tent, heading back to the sound table. A black cable connected the microphone to the speakers. I didn't know much about electricity, but it seemed likely that somewhere in all those wires was enough power to jolt Zoë and me back into our rightful selves. At least, that was my hope.

Everyone's eyes were glued to the front of the room, where a Great Dane in a bow tie was exchanging "bow-wow vows" with a nervous-looking golden Pomeranian. The Pomeranian was snowed over with lace, and she kept stopping to scratch herself. The Great Dane heard a garbage truck rattle by and let out a woof that made his bride piddle on the floor.

Max smiled benevolently at them both. This was the stuff that doggie weddings were made of.

"Do you, Mitzi, promise to share all toys with Brutus, even your very favorite squeaky ball? And do you, Brutus, promise never to drool on Mitzi's head?"

Brutus and Mitzi apparently did, because, even though neither of them said a word, Max produced two shiny rings for them to wear on their collars as a symbol of their lifelong devotion. Mitzi sniffed her ring and licked it. Brutus tried to bite his and had to be distracted with a biscuit from his owner's pocket.

The second the biscuit appeared, my tail started to wag of its own accord, beating the floor along with two dozen other doggy tails. *Not now, not now!* This was a critical moment, no time to be distracted by mouth-watering, gravy-licious, chicken—no, liver—no, *bacon* flavored treats. I gave myself a shake and refocused on the lectern.

Max nodded solemnly at each of the dogs. "I now pronounce you dog and dog," he told them. The audience burst into applause, the Great Dane and Pomeranian were led away, and I stood up to make my move.

I gave the leash a tug, bringing Zoë to attention, and started for the center aisle. She reined in close so she could keep up—I felt her footfalls on the red carpet behind me. My heart thudded against my rib cage. I hauled us to the front of the room, avoiding eye contact with Max. The last thing I needed was a questioning look from him, putting me off my game. If this went well, we'd have plenty of time to talk it over later.

Blocking out all the sounds of the crowd, I slipped

up onto the dais, pulling Zoë, and ran behind the speaker on the right side of the stage. Clamping my teeth down on the extension cord, I tugged with all my might. Miraculously, it sprang loose. Just like that, I had a live wire sprouting from my teeth.

My next step was to get to water. I'd seen a pitcher on the side of the room next to the chicken-flavored cake, and I headed there. I charged toward the table, taking the fastest route—straight past Max and his lectern. But when I neared the microphone, a horrific squeal stopped me cold.

Sound—more painful than I'd ever experienced— shrieked from the mic. Every hair on my body bristled. I couldn't see, couldn't think. It felt as if the world were ending.

My jaw popped open and I dropped the cord. Running like the demons of hell were after me, I leaped off the stage and dove under the cake table. Hiding behind the table skirting, I quivered. And peed on the floor.

Mercifully, the squealing stopped. As I panted, my head close to the ground, thoughts finally started to flow through my brain. *Feedback,* I thought, *that's what that was. The cord must have caused the mic to give off feedback. It's okay—I'm okay. I'm not going to die.*

Still, I felt shaken and half drunk. Slowly, as my vision cleared, I gathered the courage to poke my head out through a break in the skirts.

The tent had erupted into utter madness. Every dog in the place had gone haywire. Dogs had knocked over chairs, knocked over people, knocked over the daisy-covered bower. Half the dogs were barking, half yipped in shrill small-dog voices. Some had tried to dig their way out of the tent, pushing on the fabric until the tent poles started to lean.

In the back, a bulldog and a border collie were in a fight. Owners ran everywhere, their leashes turning into hazards as the people fell and were pulled into piles of chairs.

The dogs moved in mobs, racing from one end of the tent to the other—just like me, they were all trying to run away. Within seconds, five dogs joined me under the table. One of them, the Great Dane groom, got tangled in the skirting and started pawing with his giant feet, taking swipes at loose skirting, women's dresses, and his poor, unfortunate Pomeranian bride, who was hiding under my legs.

The Pomeranian started yipping. The Great Dane pawed at everything that moved. Three more dogs shoved their way under the table. Someone growled. I showed my teeth.

Before I knew it, fur was moving fast, and I couldn't tell one dog from another. The Great Dane jumped, hitting the underside of the table with his massive head. I heard a yelp, a snap, a snarl. Two dogs, each trying to get their head above the other's, jumped at the same time. The table lifted, rocked, and dropped back to the floor. Then someone bit the Great Dane's tail.

Just as he hit the roof, a corner of the skirting flipped up and a human hand reached in. It caught my collar, hooked around my rib cage, and dragged me out like a fireman pulling a child from a burning building. I came out gasping for air, my ears ringing with pain.

Behind me, the table went over and landed with a bone-chilling thud. Everyone, human and canine alike, fell silent, waiting to see what would happen. Then a woman's wail broke the silence.

"Nooooo! You idiot, idiot dogs! You've ruined it—*ruined it!*"

Not waiting to find out what they'd ruined, dogs scattered from behind the table. All except the Great Dane, who was still caught underneath the skirting. I trembled next to Zoë, trying to catch my breath. When I opened my eyes, I noticed things—Max, catching up leashes and wrangling dogs at the door of the tent; the lady with the button earrings, lying like a bug on the floor with the entire chicken cake on top of her—but I preferred to keep my eyes closed. I leaned against Zoë, and she held me with arms as solid as steel.

I had failed. I hadn't managed to change us back, or even shock us. All I'd done was ruin a great Woofin-stock tradition.

And yet, sitting there, wrapped in Zoë's arms, I felt a sense of gratitude that was almost like peace. Zoë had saved me. In spite of her own wants and needs, she'd thrown herself into the chaos and dragged me free. I would never forget this gift she'd given me.

I turned to her and licked her face.

 Zoë

Jessica is licking me, and her tongue feels wet on my bald skin. That makes me laugh, and when I do she licks some more.

I'm also worried about what to do. My mom from my old life is lying on the ground with chicken cake on her stomach, looking like a big dog dish. I really want to go eat some cake, but I don't. A crowd of other dogs is already doing that.

The dogs are licking my mom all over, but she isn't laughing. She's yelling and her face is red—an angry, out-of-control sort of red. I want to talk to her, but I also want to say the right thing, people-style. I don't know if I can.

I see her bare her teeth at a dog with pointy ears, and then I know what to do. I go to her and push the dogs away. She looks up at me like she's a puppy, like she wants me to pick her up. So I do. I stand her up on her feet and only eat a little bit of chicken cake off her dress. When she's not looking.

My mom looks all jumbled, like a long-haired dog that's been rolling in a pile of leaves. She keeps brushing things off herself, even after all the chicken cake has fallen on the floor. I resist the urge to eat cake off the floor. I'd like to, but a terrier eats it all first. Two slurps and it's gone—terriers are quick like that.

My mom turns to me. "Thank you," she says. "That was such a nightmare. I knew I shouldn't have come to this, not with this many uncontrolled dogs. But I just love weddings and my friend said it would be fun."

"You didn't have fun?" I say. I had a great time.

She shakes her head in an *absolutely not* kind of way. I'm sad to hear this—it worries me that she didn't enjoy something I thought was such fun. We both put on a sad face.

Then a woman with an angry look comes up to us. She's holding a poodle in a purple dress that's growling at me. When no one is looking, I show it my teeth and it stops.

The angry woman talks right in my face. "Jessica Sheldon, I expected you to be a more responsible dog parent than that!"

What—why is she yelling at me? Didn't she see me pull Jessica out from under the table?

"Letting your dog run up on the stage like that—she could have been injured! Or killed! Electricity is nothing to play around with."

I start to say that I don't know a dog named Electricity, but my mom speaks first. "I must have been dizzy—I didn't recognize you. This was all your fault! You should be arrested," she said. "Fined by the city. Your dog is a public nuisance." She backs away from Jessica and me like we stink of poop. My face feels hot and uncomfortable. This isn't what I wanted at all. I wanted Mom to hear about our awards and our talents, not to remember how she was covered with chicken cake because Jessica was a nuisance.

But here comes Dr. Max! I'm overcome with relief. Dr. Max always knows what to say—I think he really is an alpha. He turns to my mom and the angry woman and says, "Jessica's taking on a big burden, taking care of a stray like Zoë. I'm sure she did her best to keep the dog under control. And no one was actually hurt, were they?"

"No," says the angry woman, "but the Chapel of Love is ruined!"

Max gives her a sympathetic look, and she likes that. I think she likes Dr. Max.

"Well," he says, "let's look on the bright side. That cake was a huge hit."

Behind me, Jessica makes a funny snorting sound. Everyone turns to look at her. Even my mom stops wiping invisible cake specks off her dress and looks. Her eyes grow wide.

"Did you know she won the Pet-and-Person Beauty Contest?" I blurt out, pointing to Jessica. "She was crowned as the most beautiful dog in town. And she won the silver medal in Agility—that's how good she is."

My mom makes a little disbelieving noise.

"It's true," I say, "we have the medals. She's a wonderful dog. Anyone who took her home would never regret it. Never."

She makes a crowded noise in her throat and turns around. I start to say, "You can take her," but it's too late. Mom is gone.

21

A Doggone Shame

 Jessica

After the cake disaster, people cleared out of the Canine Chapel of Love pretty quickly. Max got all the dogs and owners reunited, and he even stepped in to defend Zoë to Malia Jackson. Poor Malia. I wished I could tell her that it hadn't been Zoë's fault that the doggie weddings were ruined—it was mine. Frankly, I wished I could say a lot of things to a lot of people.

The volunteer crew swept in to clean up the decorations and prepare everything for the rental company that had provided the tent and chairs. The sound crew packed up their speakers and sound table and extension cords. Malia took apart the daisy-covered bower, and Max collapsed the lectern. And just like that, the Canine Chapel of Love closed down, shutting its doors on doggie love for another year.

Zoë moped around, trying to nudge bits of cake out of the grass with her shoe. She'd had a strange interaction with the woman in yellow that I didn't fully understand. I was having a hard time concen-

trating on human talk and conversation—strange
smells kept distracting me. For example, I knew Zoë
would never find any cake in the grass because I'd
already spent ten minutes methodically sniffing the
area. Now I was tracing the edges of the tent, stopping wherever dogs had peed.

The wonders of my canine nose were startling. I
could pull in a scent, say the urine of a geriatric shel-
tie, and hold it in my nose for several minutes. As a
person, I would have had to exhale and take a second
sniff to learn more. As a dog, I pulled the scent in,
kept it, and when I sniffed again I brought in fresh
lowlights and highlights filled with information. Every sniff was like reading a new chapter in the world's
most fascinating book.

When Max came up to me, he had to tap my shoulder to get my attention. I turned reluctantly—not
only because I'd caught an amazing smell, but because the sight of Max made me feel more woeful
than ever. If I couldn't change back into a human, the
two of us had no future. We'd be over before we'd
even begun. A part of me wished he would just go
away and leave me alone.

"Hey there," he said softly, crouching down to my
level.

My ears and tail sagged. Remembering last night's
resolution to be more upbeat, I tried to wag my tail,
but the rest of me still played Droopy Dog.

"Don't worry. We'll get this thing figured out." He
reached out to pet me, then hesitated. My humanity
put an awkward wall between us. That made my
spirits sink even lower.

I did manage one thing. I kept just far enough away from Zoë that she couldn't put me on a leash. Sure, I was willing to hang around with her for the rest of the morning—what other choice did I have? But I planned to make myself scarce in the afternoon. Zoë could meet Debra without me.

I had to hand it to Max. He was sure good with dogs, even the kind that looked like humans. Now that he knew the person in my body was really Zoë, he seemed to know just how to treat her. He patted her playfully on the head, got into shoulder-shoving matches with her, and—when in doubt—offered her things to put in her mouth.

I was amazed and grateful to see that the Glimmer-glass staff had set up wrought-iron tables and chairs outside the restaurant in the square, where people clustered with their dogs. It was a brilliant idea. I wondered who had come up with it. Max and Zoë sat down at a table on the edge and placed their lunch orders. I, a second-class citizen, lay down under the table on the opposite side from Zoë. *Just as long as no one spills coffee on me, I'll be fine right here.*

I was relieved to see that the café was doing just fine. Every outside table was filled, and a healthy line ran out the door from the espresso counter. When we arrived, I had to fight the urge to sneak inside and see if Kerrie was still cooking, but I was glad I'd re-sisted when I saw the first entrée that came out. No one made calzones quite like Kerrie. And no one gar-nished plates as artfully as Theodore. The kitchen was better staffed than it had been in months—the best thing I could do was to leave it alone.

In spite of the heavenly smells of chicken salad and fruit sorbet and *hamburger,* I dragged my mind away from these things of the dog world and back to my human worries. As the minutes clicked by, I felt more and more restless. I hadn't managed to switch us back, and now I was out of ideas. What else could I try?

Kerrie came out of the café, her apron messy with chocolate smears and pumpkin smudges. I hopped up and came out from under the table, happy to see her. She rested a hand on my head and laughed.

"Here's the dog that forced a spoon in my hand," she said, grinning at Zoë through amber-framed glasses. "I suppose you had something to do with that?"

Zoë gave a look that was so blank, it was worthy of an Oscar.

"Of course you did," Kerrie went on. "Well, it doesn't matter. I'm not upset. It feels great to be back in the kitchen." She looked down at me and gave me a wink. "Though how you possibly could have known that, I haven't a clue. I guess Ariel was right about you."

After a minute Kerrie left me and went to stand by Zoë. "Jess, my friend, I have to hand it to you. This Woofinstock has been an absolute hit. I had no idea you knew how to be a one-woman public relations machine. It's going better than I'd ever dared to hope." She reached out and squeezed Zoë's arm. Zoë beamed.

"Not that it started out so well," she added. "For a

while there, I was ready to strangle you. Luckily, though, I couldn't find you!" Sunlight glinted off her dangly yellow earrings. "But it's all worked out beautifully. Even the waitstaff has been working together without too many squabbles. And boy, are you ever famous! I swear, every other customer who comes in says they saw you somewhere around town and thought they'd give the Glimmerglass a try because of it. Everybody's heard of you and the white dynamo dog." Kerrie winked at me again. "You and that T-shirt of yours have sent a ton of business our way."

That was my turn to beam.

"Yeah, we did win a lot of contests," Zoë agreed. "Zoë is the best dog ever. You should tell that to anyone who asks. Hey!" Suddenly, she was up, out of her seat. "That dog's pooping over there!"

Off she went. As Kerrie gaped, Max tried to cover. "Oh, good, I'm glad she's stepping in," he said. "People really need to learn to clean up after their dogs."

Twenty feet away, Zoë stood near the dog, the picture of indecision. She clearly wanted to crouch down and get a good sniff, but not with so many people watching. With an internal sigh, I realized that in just two days as a human, Zoë had learned to be self-conscious. I thought wistfully back to her uninhibited dancing to "Louie Louie" and wondered if that freedom was a thing of the past. If so, that was a tragedy.

Kerrie slipped into the seat my body had vacated. She glanced in Zoë's direction and leaned in toward Max. "It's nice to see you two getting to know each other. I know Jess has had a hard time meeting people."

Oh, great. Here comes the part where Kerrie reveals all my flaws.

"Is she shy?" Max asked.

Kerrie shrugged. "Not really. I think her family situation growing up really set her back. Keeps her from feeling . . . I don't know. Deserving, I guess. You know what I mean?"

I gulped and looked away. A painful feeling, like a clenching fist, groped around in my chest.

"I don't, actually," Max said. "What do you mean?"

"Oh, she didn't tell you about it?" Kerrie bit her lip and looked down at the table. "Well, I don't want to tell tales out of school." I held my breath and waited. Kerrie was like a big sister to me, and I knew that one of her protective devices was to tell people things that she thought I would never share. She liked to get all the dirty laundry out there at once. Sometimes this has been a help, but sometimes it hurt. "Well, Jess had it pretty rough. She was a foster-care kid. Got passed around quite a lot. Her real mom dumped her into the system when she was just a baby—can you believe it? I don't know how any mother could do that. When I think about how it would be to feel unwanted . . ."

Kerrie let out a ragged breath. I knew she was thinking of her own son, imagining how a childhood like mine would have twisted his spirit. Hearing her, I saw myself as a warped pretzel person, covered in a thick layer of scar tissue. Bent like I was, how could I ever stand up next to someone else . . . someone like Max?

"It would be awful," Max said. He looked down at

me, but I couldn't hold up under his gaze—I moved under the table and looked off across the square. A family strolled across the cobblestones, each parent holding the toddler's hand. One, two, three, jump! One, two, three . . . "But a lot of people have rough childhoods," he continued. "It doesn't have to be a life sentence."

No?

"In Jess's case, I have to wonder." I heard Kerrie's earrings jangle. She must have shaken her head. "Everything in her life goes back to that—her work ethic, the hard time she has relaxing and being herself. Even this weird thing she has about dogs is tied to it somehow. I don't know what to make of this white dog she's palling around with. I'm afraid she's trying to force herself to get over her fear through sheer will. It worries me."

Suddenly, I couldn't stand their conversation for another second. I hated being pitied, and listening to them bemoan my rotten childhood was somehow worse than living with it. It killed me to have my past unveiled before Max like that. It would only push him away.

Far behind me, Zoë yelled, "Hey! Someone left gum over here!" That was my moment. Moving as lightly as I could, I slipped out from under the far side of the table and trotted across the square. I ducked into the narrow alley that ran next to Eggs About Madrona. In the shadows, I paused and cocked an ear back at the square, then stood still, waiting for my heart to quiet. I heard nothing.

They hadn't noticed me leave.

🦴 Zoë

Dr. Max hears me say "Hey! Someone left gum over here!" and he comes over. I point out the bit of gum to him. I would pick it up and give it a chew, but that kind of thing makes people give you funny looks. I'm tired of getting funny looks. So instead I show him the Frisbee I found.

"Throw it!" I say. He does and I run after. Only when I get it and bring it back, I feel flat, like a ball with no air in it. Frisbees make me think of home. One time at home, a boy came to visit and he threw a Frisbee for me in the front yard. It was one of my favorite days ever.

Dr. Max says, "What's wrong?"

I say, "There are some people I really need to visit, but I don't have a way to get there. Can you take me to their house? No one else can find it. Can you?"

Dr. Max looks thoughtful and then he asks me a million questions about my family. He wants to know what their house looks like ("Really big, with grass in front") and how long I lived there ("Forever!"). He asks about Mom and Dad, and I tell him about how Mom got cake on her dress at the Doggie Wedding Chapel.

"She was wearing yellow. And she smelled like flowers. She always smells like flowers."

Dr. Max goes inside the café for a long time, and when he comes out he has a paper in his hand. "I'm sure Jessica will wait for us if we just pop out for a minute," he says as he leads me to his car. Dr. Max rolls down the window so I can put my face out, if I want. He plays music and it makes my feet twitch. Finally, I might be on my way home. Every time we pass a corner I recognize, I say, "Hey, I know that place!" and point with my pointing finger. Max gets a kick out of this.

"I have a hunch about something," he says. "I think we aren't just going to see your friends. We're going to your home, aren't we?"

I knew Dr. Max was a genius.

"Yes! Yes, we are!" I feel such gratitude toward him. If I were a dog, I'd lick his cheek, but as a person I have to put together the right string of words to show my emotions. It's all so removed—if I feel love, why don't I just show it? Why do I have to talk about it? But, I've learned, that's the way people are. They'd rather discuss something than demonstrate it.

"Thank you, Dr. Max," I say, and I mean it with my whole being. "Thank you for bringing me. I asked a lot of people, and none of them would help. No one else would take me home."

He smiles, and I'm relieved that I said the right thing. I put my face out the window, but only for a minute because the wind makes my hair go in my nose. When I come back inside, Dr. Max says, "Can I ask you some more questions? About what it's like to be a dog?"

" 'Course," I say. "I know all about it."

He asks me how it feels to go to the vet, how much it hurts to get a shot, if I'm ever scared and when. I tell him about how big noises and bad smells make me nervous. And I tell him why I don't like having my nails clipped. Really, I don't like it when anyone touches my feet at all. He asks a lot about pain and seems glad when I tell him that things hurt more in my human body than they did in my dog body. Then he asks what I used to spend my time thinking about (hot dogs) and what I dreamed about when I slept (running). They're all easy questions.

"I liked the way you smelled when I first met you," I say. He seems surprised. "You smelled like the real you, not all perfumed with soap. That always calms me down. And I never minded going to the vet. It's exciting there because it smells like cat."

We spend some time talking about cats. Dr. Max knows a lot about them.

"Can I tell you something funny?" He looks at me out of the corner of his eye, and he looks so much like a rolly-eyed dog, I laugh. "It's not a joke," he says. But then he laughs, too. "When I was a kid, I really, really wanted to be a dog. Seriously. When grown-ups asked me what I wanted to be when I grew up, I said a German shepherd. Isn't that crazy? And I had this idea that little dogs were all young, and that when they grew up, they turned into bigger dogs. You know, like toy poodles were babies that got older and became standard poodles."

He shakes his head. I shake my head, too. And because I'm being nice, I don't tell him how *crazy* his idea is. Dr. Max is the furthest thing from a German shepherd. "Um," he says, glancing sideways at me, "I hate to ask this, but can you tell me one more time how the switch happened?" I roll my eyes, and he says, "I know you told me already. But I can't help thinking that if I can hear all the details, maybe I can find a way to help. You never know."

I tell him absolutely everything I remember, but he just frowns more. He mumbles things about "electrical impulses" and "transfer of energy," but I can tell he's just barking at nothing. I've done that plenty of times. It's fun while it lasts, but it doesn't get you anywhere.

Finally, he gives up on that. But he's still full of questions.

"How did you get separated from your people in the first place? Do you remember?"

My heart shrinks a little when I hear his question. I don't really want to think about that. I can remember being home, in my crate, and I remember later when I was walking around in Madrona by myself, smelling the ocean. But I felt terribly alone then—even thinking back on it makes me uneasy. I was scared of everything, and nervous, and my heart ached constantly. That only started to change when I met Jessica.

"I don't want to talk about it, Dr. Max." And even though he nods and doesn't pursue it, my eyes fill up with water.

 Jessica

I shuffled down the dark alley, drawn forward by the smell of hot dogs cooking and a need to be as far away from my friends as possible. I felt like I'd swallowed rocks, my chest ached that much. As far as I was concerned, things with Max were ruined. I was a dog, he was a human. And if that weren't enough, Kerrie was currently telling him every detail of how I'd been ditched by my mother. And how I never knew my father. The closest things I had to parents were people who were paid to look after me. It wasn't the sort of family anyone would look forward to marrying into.

The hot dog smells grew stronger—beefier, richer, fattier—the closer I got to the back of Eggs About Madrona. In my scent-induced delirium, all I could think was that they were called hot dogs because dogs should eat them *all the time*. I heard voices as I neared the corner. I slowed down, salivating, and took a look.

A small, cluttered backyard, devoid of grass and scattered with old kids' toys, sat behind Leisl's restaurant. I'd forgotten that she lived above her business. I looked around for the other dogs that she bred, but only saw Foxy, playing in the dirt with a ten-year-old girl in braids. Right, Leisl had a daughter. Pulling her name out of my memory was like yanking an anchor through fifty feet of mud. *Anya*.

They must keep the breeding kennels somewhere else. Or maybe Leisl had gotten out of that business?

An older woman with steel-gray hair sat at a patio table, smoking. For a second, I wondered if Leisl had ever considered clearing all the junk out of this area and making an outdoor seating space, like we had at the Glimmerglass. An instant later, the idea was gone, replaced by an overpowering urge to eat hot dogs. Then I saw why. Leisl had come out the back door, carrying a platter of hot dogs and scrambled eggs.

Anya moaned. "Moooom, not eggs agaaain."

The older woman tapped her cigarette against a flimsy silver ashtray. "You'll be grateful for what you get, young lady." To Leisl, she snapped, "It's about time."

"The kitchen got a little behind with the lunch service. I had to pitch in for a bit," Leisl said, setting the platter down on the table. She turned and put her hands on her hips, her voice bristling with irritation. Inside, I cringed on Anya's behalf. *Be perfect,* I wanted to whisper to her, *just be good, clean, and perfect, and she'll always love you.*

"Anya, you have mud all over your pants. And look at Foxy! I just had him all clean—he has burrs all over!" Leisl stomped over and caught Foxy by the leash, even though he was perfectly capable of coming when called. His ears hung down tragically as she dragged him toward the door. "You stay right there," she bellowed. Foxy stared at the ground.

"Maybe if you'd kept him cleaner, you coulda won that Pet Beauty Contest you were in," said Leisl's mother.

Leisl gave her a glare. Then she turned to her daughter. "And you, young lady, get over here and eat. I don't want to hear a single whine, you got it?"

The family sat down at the table and began to eat. Hostility breezed off them in clouds. A pang shot through me, and not just because they clearly weren't intending to give away any hot dogs. I should have been disgusted with them—they had the family I'd always dreamed of. But instead I felt sorry for them. They were here, inches away from one another, yet they weren't making the least effort to be kind, to be gentle with their relationships. Leisl's mother bruised her, and she bruised Anya. So Anya whined, which grated on Leisl's nerves and made her snap at her mother. None of them could change what they were doing because their thoughts were caught in a groove.

I'm glad I don't have a relationship with Debra, I thought, *if this is how it would be. Snipping at each other all the time. I don't need that.* Better to stay as I was, hidden here in Madrona. Sure, I had questions, things I wanted to know. And yeah, I was curious to see the woman who gave birth to me. I wondered what she would say, how she would act. Whether we'd have mannerisms in common. But no answers were worth trading my privacy for the venom I felt coming off Leisl's family.

Just then, the wind picked up, building gusts out of nothing. The sky was perfectly clear, but a taut breeze poured down the alley where I stood, billowing the T-shirt around my body. In Leisl's yard, it wrapped into a funnel, picking up dust and bits of paper from the ground. Anya, her blond hair flying, started to sway as the wind rocked her chair from side to side. The feet lifted from the ground—it seemed like the whole chair was about to fly off into space. In a flash, both women were up, planting their arms on either side of her chair. And just as quickly, the wind stopped.

"Whoo, we almost lost you there." Leisl laughed, touching the top of her daughter's head. Anya looked up at both of them, her eyes full of fright and relief. She looked nervous enough to cry, but instead she took a cue from her mother and started to laugh. Pretty soon all three of them were chuckling, their shoulders lifted up toward their ears in the exact same way.

Mothers and daughters. Kerrie called the mother-daughter relationship "the ultimate mystery." I'd always felt envious when she said that, like I was standing in the dark, just outside a glow of lamplight that shone on everyone else.

Another breeze zipped past, teasing my ear. I wanted to be in on that mystery, even if it caused me some pain. Maybe my thinking was caught in a rut, too. I turned around quickly, before I could change my mind, and started running back to the Glimmerglass.

22

Homeward Dog

 Zoë

At last, my very own house! I'm almost shaking with
excitement. Dr. Max stops the car and gets out, but I
stay where I am. When he opens my door, he says, "Is
something the matter?"

I don't know how to tell him that I'm nervous
about what will happen. Before we got here, it was
easy to pretend that Mom and Dad would be thrilled
to see me. After all, I'm dying to see them. But I can't
forget the way Mom looked right at Jessica and didn't
say a thing about taking her home. Why would she
do that?

Dr. Max reaches out a hand. I put mine in his, and
I can feel his strength running through our palms, up
my arm. He helps me out of the car, and I think that
if he weren't here, I would never be brave enough to
walk up to the door. It was one thing to think ahead
to this moment, but now that I'm here, I feel pretty
queasy.

I stand on the front path and look around at the

yard. Things have changed. There's less grass than there used to be, and someone built a new flower bed in the front, near the street. We never had one there before, just the one in the back where I used to dig holes. I wonder if they put the new bed in because I'm not here anymore?

Dr. Max leads us up the front walk and stops right before the porch.

"Okay, let's get our game plan ready. We're going to go up to the door and knock on it. Someone will probably come. Do you want me to do the talking? I think it might be best."

I nod my head.

"Just remember," he says, "to them, you're not a dog. You're not Zoë. You're Jessica. We're here to ask if they'll take a *dog* back, not *you*. Even if they say yes, you can't run right in."

As he talks, my throat feels pinched all over. "Dr. Max," I say in a quiet voice. "What if they don't say yes?"

He presses his mouth into a thin line. "We'll deal with that when it happens. If it happens. And if they say yes, then you and Jessica have to switch back first. Your people don't want to have a human come live with them."

"But I don't know how to switch back into a dog," I whisper.

"I know. Neither do I," Dr. Max says. "I'm just hoping that coming here—and doing something—will help. You never know, right? It might . . . shake something loose. Cosmically. I don't know, but it might. So let's go talk to your people and see what happens. Just remember that, to them, you don't look like the Zoë they know. You look like Jessica. A person."

"Right," I say. Dr. Max smiles and squeezes my hand, and for a second I feel excited again. After all, my people can fix anything. They can make beef-and-liver dog food come out of *nowhere*. Maybe they can make everything all right.

We go up the steps to the door and Max thumps on it. Then we wait. And wait. I chew my lip and try not to worry.

The door opens and it's my mom. She's wearing a pink dress, which makes me hopeful because pink is a lot like red. And *Mom's* wearing it. She has her button earrings on, too, and smells flowery, just like she's supposed to. She looks at me and looks at Max. Then she looks at me again.

"You—you're the one from this morning? With that awful dog?"

I'm scared of saying the wrong thing. Instead of answering, I look at my foot.

Max says, "Hi there, I'm Dr. Nakamura. I'm a vet in town. It was actually a dog we came to see you about. Your dog, Zoë."

I flick my eyes up at Mom. She looks funny, like she just got caught eating garbage.

"We don't have a dog."

Dr. Max's voice gets gentle. "Your dog, Zoë. She showed up at the clinic. I thought you'd be relieved to hear that she's okay."

Now Mom looks funny and sounds funny. She says, "Are you with the police?"

Dr. Max says, "No, ma'am. We just want to hear what happened. And to reunite a lost dog with her family. No one's in any trouble here."

Mom's eyes shift back and forth. Then they settle on the porch under our feet. When she speaks again, her voice is thready and distant. "She just—she was never the right dog for us. Too rambunctious, too rowdy. Too big. We only got her because we wanted to fit in here and this town is head over heels for dogs. We picked her up at Woofinstock two years ago—they had a bunch of little puppies for sale. But she got so big, and she was just a disaster. Always breaking things and digging holes and tearing things up. Charging through doors. Howling in her crate. Chasing the cat."

My heart sinks as she lists my faults.

"She's still a young dog," Dr. Max says. "With training, she could grow out of all those bad habits."

Mom looks Dr. Max right in the face. She looks scared, like a nasty, growling dog is chasing her.

"That dog is not coming back in this house. The mess, the dirt—I won't stand for it. Not again."

Dr. Max looks like he has a thousand thoughts running through his head. His mouth opens, but no words come out. I think he might be angry. I'm having trouble breathing.

"So you abandoned her?"

Mom starts closing the door.

"My husband did it. She should live somewhere else, somewhere with more room. With a different family. Not us."

"But you're my family!" I yell. I step toward her

and she ducks behind the door. It clicks shut in my face. I put my mouth up to the crack and yell as loud as I can.

"*You're* my family!"

 Jessica

I hurried down the alley, trying to distract my mind so I wouldn't talk myself out of my plan. As I rounded the corner into the square, I almost collided with Carmelita Sanchez, who ran the Crazy Diamond Music Store directly across from the Glimmerglass. She shied away from me to avoid the collision—or so I thought until I looked at her face. Every feature wrinkled with disgust, as if she couldn't stand to be close to me. She pulled her hands to her chest to prevent me from touching them even on accident.

Her dislike of dogs couldn't have been plainer if she'd had a neon sign over her head.

The bizarre thing was that—until now—I'd thought she was one of the dog people. I'd known Carm for years. She'd always held a committee post for Woofinstock, and everyone considered her a stellar Madrona citizen, right down to her love of wagging tails. She didn't have a dog of her own, but no one questioned that.

Now I saw her for what she was—exactly what I'd always been. A person who faked it.

I turned away from Carm, happy to relieve her of my presence. Now that I knew how she felt, I couldn't help feeling the same about her. If she didn't like me, then I didn't like her.

As I walked away, what startled me more than her antidog attitude was the speed with which I'd spotted it. When I was in my human body, Carm could have fooled me any day of the week. But as a dog, I'd recognized her immediately as the only dog hater in the square. I thought of all the years I'd spent fake-smiling at dogs when I really wanted to run away, and felt my stomach curl with embarrassment. Had they all been able to read me as clearly as I'd read Carm?

I was certainly guilty of acting like a ninny. I'd committed all the classic dog-fearing mistakes—running away, shrieking in terror, yanking my hand away from a sniffing nose. I was always tense around dogs, and that would have made them tense, too, of course.

I felt like an idiot.

When I reached the Glimmerglass, I was happy to see that the crowd out front was still sizeable. Nearly everyone had a cellophane bag of Glimmerglass cookies. I wandered through the mix of Nikes, Rockports, and Crocs, looking for anything that reminded me of Zoë. Or Max. The more shoes I examined, the more overwhelmed I became. Shoes were everywhere, and people were everywhere talking, filling up the air with chatter. My ears twitched back and forth.

"Have you tried the Four Paw Scramble? It really rocks."

"Joey, don't wander off!"

"Oh, man, I have to pee."

"Are you going to the big closing ceremonies, over on the green? What happens there anyway?"

My eyes popped open wide. The closing ceremonies— where I was supposed to make a speech! Oh, crap. I padded around in an anxious circle, whining under my breath. What could I do? Nothing. Nothing at all. That made me whine all the more.

I strained my ears listening for Max's voice, but that just made my head hurt. The human world was like a foggy cloud land that existed high above my head. I could tune in if I tried, but all in all it felt pretty unimportant. And confusing. The longer I listened, the more boggled my head became. All I could think of was finding Zoë or Max.

In a haze, I wandered over to the doggie water bowl and took a long lap. A white, skuzzy film floated on top of the water, but I didn't care. I just needed to drink, to cool down my overheated brain. After five deep swallows, I remembered.

Time. I needed to know what time it was.

I scanned the square until I spotted the big clock above the jewelry store. It was hard to read, but I squinted and strained until I made out the big hand and the little hand. Seventeen minutes to two. Time to go.

 Zoë

I'm soaked with brokenhearted feelings. We're in the car, and Dr. Max is driving. My heart is too sad to let me think of anything. All I can do is make gaspy, shuddery noises and let the tears pour out of my eyes.

Dr. Max hands me a white square of paper. I take a bite of it.

"No, no," he says, pulling it out of my mouth. "It's not for eating. It's a tissue. You wipe your nose with it."

I do that and then I'm less drippy. But only for a second—only until I remember what Mom said to us. About me. She'd said I should live with a different family. "Not us," she had said.

Not them!

I wail out loud. Dr. Max has to jerk the wheel back and forth.

"But I want to live with them! I want to go home!"

"I know you do," Dr. Max says. His face looks growly. And blurry, because I'm all wet. "I know you do."

He rolls down the window, and I put my head out and make the saddest, most cracked, deep-belly howl I can. Then I do it again. I would do it again and again and again, except Dr. Max pulls me back inside.

"I know you're upset," he says. He still has that growly look. I don't see how anyone can be growly when this is so intensely sad. "I was really hoping that would go better." He sighs. "Do you remember what happened? When they left you in town?"

I sit in my seat, trembling. When I blink my eyes, I can see parts of my memories—Dad driving me in the car, me putting my nose on the window. Me getting told not to put my nose on the window. Me barking at a sheepdog. Getting told not to bark.

Then we got out, and that was exciting. I sniffed all around like I always do. Dad seemed funny—there was a nervous smell that I didn't notice at the time. But now, thinking hard about it, I remember the smell. It makes me feel sick.

"I'm sick," I say.

Dr. Max pulls the car over right away. He comes around and opens my door.

I lean out and throw up in the street.

Dr. Max hands me another white square, and this time I know not to eat it. I wipe my nose with it. But then he shakes his head and says, "Nope, your mouth this time. It's for wiping anything."

I do that and it works, but dealing with all these people things makes me tired. Being a person is too much work. Not as much work as remembering, though. I don't want to keep thinking about that sad day, but Dr. Max is coaxing me with his eyes. I give a big, shuddery sigh and ask my memory to carry on.

I remember Dad's nervous smell, and I feel bad again, but this time I keep on remembering without throwing up. I had my leash on. Dad took my leash and tied the other end to a big metal railing. He patted me on the head. He didn't look at me, which I thought meant he would be right back. I sat down to wait.

He got in the car, which worried me. But I thought he would come right back. He always had before. Why would that day be different?

I waited. I yawned and waited some more. I lay down and put my head on my paws. I fell asleep. I woke up and waited some more.

After a long time, it got dark, and I was hungry. But I still waited.

A yellow Lab came by, and I growled at it. I was nervous from all the waiting. And hungry. And scared. Dad had never taken this long before.

I fell asleep again and when I woke up, I was cold and felt sick to my stomach—maybe sick with hunger, I don't know. The air was full of strange noises, but no matter how hard I tugged on my leash, I couldn't get away. I tried barking and that helped. I barked until someone yelled at me to shut up.

Later, I got tired, but I couldn't sleep. I tried pacing around, but my leash was too short. After I'd waited a long, long time in the dark, something big and flappy swooped down over my head. I barked at it and strained hard on my leash. This time my collar broke away from the leash and I ran away, then hid behind a Dumpster until it got light. I ate two of the wrappers that were by the Dumpster and later I threw them up.

"Dad left me there and he didn't come back," I say.

Dr. Max looks at the ground. "I'm sorry, Zoë. I'm so sorry that happened to you." He looks into the empty space over my shoulder. "This was stupid of me. I shouldn't have brought you here with me. It was a mistake, and I should have known better."

"How could you know they wouldn't want me back? I wasn't such a bad dog, I swear."

"Of course you weren't," he says. "But I should have suspected. They hadn't put up signs around town or anything. I should have guessed. It's the worst part of my job that sometimes I have to see things like this happen."

"Well, it's nowhere near as bad as having it happen *to* you," I say in a sharp voice. I look at Dr. Max, and in a flash I see that he's a person, just like all the other people. He could love me one minute and then throw me to the wind the next. How can I feel safe with him? With any of them? A part of me wants to turn around and walk away—from him, from my house, from all the people in the world. If I'm on my own, no one will ever let me down again.

I'm seriously considering leaving Dr. Max right here on the street, when I remember a horrible thing. I'm a person now, too. And even if I become a dog again, I don't know how to live on my own. I think back to how scared and vulnerable I felt when I was alone in Madrona, and I know I can't go back to that. I have to live with people in order to eat. Still, I don't think I can ever trust them in the same way again.

"What if Jessica is like them?" I ask. "What if she takes me home now, but then one day she hauls me into town and drives away? How do I know that won't happen?"

Dr. Max's eyes look bleak, like he isn't sure how to answer me. "I know this is a difficult thing to ask of you," he says, "but you have to trust her."

Every piece of me resists the idea. But what choice do I have? Besides, when I think about Jessica, I feel my heart crack open the tiniest bit, as if it wants to rely on her. Dr. Max clears his throat.

"You know, Jessica wasn't even looking for a dog

when you first met, but she agreed to take you home. That was a big risk for her. She had to trust you in the same way you'll need to trust her now. You both have to be good to each other—that's the only way this can work."

I make a snorty, sniffing sound. "I want to help her be happy," I say. I'm all wet again, but I'm not as sad, thinking about Jessica. The idea of her brightens me. "Do you think she wants that for me, too?"

"Yes. Yes I do."

I think about that for a long while. I don't like shifting my thoughts away from my family, because it feels like giving up and letting go. But I do that—and I dwell on Jessica instead. Then I say, "Dr. Max, do you think I'll get to be a dog again?"

Dr. Max makes a sighing noise. "I don't know, Zoë. I really don't. But I hope you will. Don't you?"

"Yes," I say. "I do. So very much."

☕ Jessica

The second I reached the park, I realized how stupid this plan was. Dozens of couples and families were there, sprawling on the grass and walking their dogs. *How would I ever recognize her? How would she recognize Zoë?* I considered bagging the whole plan and going back to the Glimmerglass, but I decided that wouldn't help—I couldn't find the people I was looking for there either. Instead, I climbed on top of a picnic table and surveyed the scene.

The families could be ignored. Debra would be

alone, I felt sure of that. And I doubted she would
have a dog. Something niggled at my memory while I
held that thought, something dog related, but then it
squirmed away and vanished. My eyes ran over the
crowd again and again and again.

It was a repeated motion that finally caught my eye.
A small woman in jeans was looking at her watch for
the third time in as many minutes. I jumped off the
table and trotted closer.

Her hair was lighter than mine and graying, cut
into a short bob, the kind that ended right below her
ears. I sat down about ten feet away and tried to observe her without staring, taking in her charcoal-gray
fleece jacket, her nervous eyes, battered brown purse.
It looked like we were about the same height, and her
face was oval-shaped like mine, but longer, with a
more pronounced chin. Her mouth looked different—
wider and colored with lipstick where I always wore
gloss—but then she frowned, looking at her shoes,
and I did a double take. I'd caught that exact expression on my own face a thousand times.

It was true then. She really was my mother. Her
hands looked like mine, and she was wearing turquoise
earrings that were exactly like my favorite pair. How
bizarre. Seeing her was like looking in a fun-house mirror that made my face age by twenty years. And yet she
was clearly her own person, with the pinched mouth of
a longtime smoker and an Irish promise ring on her
third finger. A string of questions bubbled up, scaring
me with their hopefulness. Did that ring mean we were
Irish? Was I Irish? Was there family in Europe? And
what about my grandparents—were they still living?

Had Debra gone on to have any other children, children she'd kept and raised? Could I have a brother? A sister?

My head was starting to throb. I turned away from Debra and closed my eyes, wishing I could shut all the sunlight out.

23

Mothers and Daughters

Zoë

"What time is it? Where's Zoë, the dog?" My voice sounds squeaky. "Why isn't she here?"

The lady with the jangly earrings bites her lip. "Oh, shoot. Oh, no—she must have wandered off. It's my fault. I got called into the kitchen and then it's just been one thing after another."

"But what time is it?"

Kerrie frowns at me, but she looks at her watch. "A little after two. Do you want us to call the Lost Dog Committee? Or start looking?"

"No." I shake my head and take off at a jog. "I'll get her. I know where to go!"

A worried feeling flutters up and down inside me as I run. It had seemed like a great plan this morning to meet Jessica's mom. But now that I've seen my own—now that I know how she really feels—I wonder if there was a reason Jessica didn't want me to make this date.

☕ Jessica

When I spotted Zoë jogging up the path from Midshipman's Square, my heart swelled. I was glad to see her, relieved that our crazy duo would be back together again. And even though I doubted she could fix this situation with Debra or even make it easier (really, she was likely to make it more excruciating), at least we'd be facing it together.

I darted a look at Debra. When she saw Zoë, her whole face brightened—then she instantly tamped down her expression, probably afraid to look too hopeful. Her hand lifted in a wave, but she paused, thought the better of it, and put it back down at her side. *Poor woman,* I couldn't help thinking. She was just as stiff and self-conscious as I'd been before I met Zoë. I guess I came by it honestly.

Zoë spotted me and came at a run. I broke away from my seat and ran to greet her, overjoyed to smell her warm, cozy scent as she wrapped her arms around me.

"Oh, Jessica," she said, her face buried in the fur at my neck, "the worst thing happened. The worst thing ever." Her voice turned thick. "Dr. Max and I went to my house and talked to my mom—my owner from before I met you. She said she doesn't want me back."

I gasped. Zoë had a family? And she and Max had just gone to visit them? Oh, poor Zoë. This must have been what she'd been after all along, to go back to the people she loved. And now they'd turned her down. My eyes glistened with sympathy.

Zoë looked down at my paws. "I thought my people wanted to live with me forever, but they don't. They don't ever. I thought they loved me. But if they loved me, they would have kept me."

Sweet Zoë. I nuzzled under her hand, and she reached around me again, dropping her face onto my neck. Together we took several deep breaths. Then Zoë made a monstrous snuffling sound, sat up, and wiped her face with the back of her hand.

"I wanted to say I'm sorry," she told me, looking me right in the eye. "I made this plan with your mom today, but that was before I knew a mom could say no and not take you back. I've been thinking about it, and I think that if your mom had been good to you, you'd have been happy to see her today. And you weren't—you were angry with me when I made this plan. So if you don't want to meet her, it's okay. I understand. We don't have to."

I shifted from paw to paw. A part of me certainly wanted to turn tail and run off with Zoë, and never look back. As small and unintimidating as Debra seemed, she terrified me. I was afraid of what I might learn, of what kind of person she might turn out to be. It would be so easy to run away. So simple.

Another part of me, though, was tired of doing what was easy, of hiding out in a safe little world where I never entered any competitions, never said anything to Hot Max, never spoke to my birth mother. That was no way to live—Zoë had taught me that. Plus, I'd seen that hopeful look on Debra's face when Zoë came into sight. She wanted this so badly. Wanted *me* so badly. She might not have wanted me when I was a toddler, but she clearly did now.

I stood up, turned, and walked over to Debra. Zoë followed me, and when I saw the smile that lit Debra's face, I was glad I'd decided to go through with it.

"Hello, Jessica. Thank you for meeting me." Debra made a timid move as if to hug Zoë, then changed her mind and extended a hand to shake just as Zoë went to return the hug. It resolved in an awkward greeting that was neither hug nor shake. They sat on a bench, and Debra picked up her purse, put it in her lap, then moved it back to its spot beside her. I sat on the grass in front of them.

"Wow," Zoë said, looking at her, "you look so much like me!"

Debra gave a nervous smile. "You're very beautiful. Prettier than I ever was. That dark hair—you got that from your dad, not me."

My dad? My mouth popped open. *Who was my dad?*

But Debra changed the subject. "I'm surprised you have a dog. Surprised to see you with one after what happened."

Zoë crooked an eyebrow. "Why? What happened?"

Debra's mouth opened and closed as if she wasn't sure what to say—and maybe regretted what she'd said already. "You don't remember?" A guilty shadow passed over her face. Zoë, quick as a fox, leaned in.

"No. What happened? What did you do?"

I scooted closer, not wanting to miss a word. My heart was thumping, making it hard to hear.

Turning her face away from Zoë and toward the ground, Debra fiddled with the zipper on her jacket. "I've been so sorry for what I did when you were a baby," she said. "There isn't a day that I don't wake up regretting what I did—how stupid I was. And there's no excuse. I don't see why you should ever forgive me. You might not, I know that. I was so scared to come here and tell you all of this. But I figured you couldn't think any worse of me than you do now. Right?" She flicked a look at Zoë, then went back to staring at the ground as if it held all the answers.

"I've had a lot of problems," she said in a low voice. "With addictions. There are no excuses—I was the one to smoke every pipe and fill every needle. But my family life was bad when I was young and I just wanted to escape any way I could. I was sneaking drinks when I was thirteen. I was still just a kid, just seventeen, when I found out I was pregnant with you. After you were born—after your dad left—I got wrapped up with a really mean guy, a crack dealer. It got pretty bad." Her eyes flicked upward at Zoë. "I never did anything while I was pregnant with you, I can swear to that. After your dad left, I got totally clean and had a job with a nice family, working as a nanny. It was one of the best times in my life, while I was pregnant with you. When I got so far along I couldn't work anymore, I stayed in a shelter. It wasn't a great life, but I was clean. Clean and sober."

Debra inhaled shakily. "It was after you were born that the trouble started. After I met him. He got me hooked and that was it—from that day, I didn't care about anything—*anything*—but the next pipe. You were just a baby, a tiny little baby, and your mom . . ." She shook her head as if there weren't words to describe what she thought of herself then. "There were times when you didn't get changed for days. When the neighbors said you cried for hours, but I was too passed out stoned to notice. I did terrible things—and that's just what I remember. I would lock you in the closet sometimes when people came over to smoke or deal. I remember—you must have been almost two— seeing your little hand reaching out from under the closet door. Reaching for me, for anybody. And I just pretended you weren't there." Her shoulders shivered softly. "I'll never forget that as long as I live. I should never have been allowed to have a little baby."

Wow. This was worse than I'd feared—and yet better, too, somehow. I'd always thought she gave me up because she just didn't want me. It had never occurred to me that she'd had dark and overwhelming problems of her own. Or that it might have been better for me to be in foster care than with her. I thought of my poor, little two-year-old self, struggling to get out of that closet, and shuddered. Suddenly, I felt sick.

Debra pulled her purse into her lap again and held it close. "That boyfriend, the dealer, he had a dog. I tried being nice to it—I've always loved dogs—but he worked so hard to keep it mean that anything I did was pointless. He liked to have it for show, to scare off people who might try to cheat him. And to be a guard dog, too. He never fed it regular meals, just gave it snacks from his hand so it would be completely grateful, completely dependent on him. I guess he kept me the same way. And it worked. That dog and I would both do anything for him."

A look passed over her face that I couldn't interpret. "More than once, I left you alone with the dog. I have no idea what happened while we were gone, but it always seemed okay until one time when you were about two. I came home—sober for once, because I didn't have enough money to score—and found you screaming with blood in your hair, streaming down one side of your face." Debra paused, breathing fast. "I think you'd pulled the cabinets open in the kitchen and had found some crackers. And that dog fought you for them. It mauled the side of your head and tore open your little arm! I was so scared I carried you all the way to the hospital. And when social services arrived, I just left. I left you there. I couldn't take you back home again, not into that. Anything would be better for you than life with me. Anything."

Debra was sobbing by this point. She dove into her purse, probably searching for tissue. I jumped up and turned away, pacing briskly. My scar—that was where my mystery scar came from! No wonder I'd been scared of dogs my whole life. Anger made my fur stand out in points. How could she have left me there? And that dog—I felt sick just wondering what had happened to the dog after that. Had her junkie-dealer boyfriend shot it? Kicked it? Because the bastard had starved it so much it fought a toddler for a cracker? Ohhh, I just wanted to hit something. Bite something. Go back in time and level that whole apartment to the ground.

When I paced back around, Zoë was looking at me. Beside her, Debra wept into her tissue. I came close to Zoë and buried my chin in her lap, letting her stroke my head, my face, my ears. I felt so disjointed, like a puzzle whose pieces had all come apart. Maybe someday I'd be glad I heard all of this, but right now I just wished I could reach into my brain and pluck the whole thing out.

Above my ears, Zoë spoke. "You were right," she said, startling both Debra and me. "You were right to give me up. I didn't think I'd say that, but you were. You weren't good to the baby or the dog." She kept stroking my head, and when I looked up, her gaze was fixed lovingly on me. Then she bent down and whispered in my ear.

"You have so much love in you," she breathed. "I think you got lucky."

Lucky, yeah, right. Lucky to have a junkie mother? Lucky to grow up in foster care?

I pictured Debra, twenty-six years younger, her face wrecked by drugs, racing me block by block to the hospital while blood ran down the side of my head and dripped from my arm. Yeah, maybe I was lucky. My foster parents hadn't given me everything I needed, but they'd always provided a safe home. I was clothed and fed. No one had ever locked me in a closet or left me to forage for crumbs on my own. Maybe I *was* lucky.

Even though it was the last thing I wanted to do, I left the security of Zoë's lap and went to Debra. She gave a little gasp of shock and sank her fingers into the fur at my neck. With gentle hands, she stroked my head. Then she glanced sideways at Zoë. "I'm so glad," she said, "that you turned out so wonderful. So very glad."

She exhaled a shuddery breath. "I've been in a program for ten years now," she said, staring down at me. "Ten years sober. It's a big milestone for me, and I wanted to mark it by seeing you. You're my only daughter—my only child. I was so young when I had you, but the years since have been hard ones. I just—I wanted to turn over a new leaf for this anniversary. I'm so grateful that you were willing to see me. You have a good heart. Thank you."

Our time with Debra was short. After the tears, we were all too tired to talk much longer. I surprised myself a little, though. When Debra asked if she could come see us again, I wagged my tail without even thinking about it. I guess I figured the next meeting could only be easier than this one, and I really did want to learn about my father and my grandparents, and what Debra's life had been like. How did she finally get clean? What did she do now? And even though she was as far from an actual mother as a person could be, a tiny piece of my heart wanted her to be proud of me. Of course, as a dog I couldn't tell her about the café or Max or my hopes and dreams. But maybe Zoë would convey enough to make Debra say those words again, that she was glad I'd turned out the way I was.

Debra said that next time she would bring her dog, a half–basset hound, half dachshund. After she was gone, Zoë couldn't stop howling over the mental picture of this dog. "It must look like a giant lizard," she said, pretending to walk like a Komodo dragon. "Long body, short legs!"

She stretched her arms over her head. "I'm so glad it's just us now. This has been such a hard day so far. My mom, your mom. . . . And people keep saying I'm supposed to make a speech or something later on." She laughed and ruffled my midsection, shaking my T-shirt around. "Why does this all have to be so hard and scary? It is *scary* to be the way we are, all mixed up in the wrong bodies."

I panted in agreement, releasing my tangled feelings into the air.

"Here you are," she said, "stuck being a dog when you want to mate with Dr. Max. And I'm stuck as a person who can't smell anything. We're going to have to be very, very brave," she said. "And good to each other. Even though it's scary, we have to keep going, no matter what bad things have happened before. At least now we have each other, and that's so much better than before. Before I found you, I was lost and scared. But now I have you for my friend. That's a pretty big improvement." Our eyes met and a bridge of understanding spread between us. "I know you really love me, just like I love you."

My heart gave a little squeeze of happiness. I did love her, crazy galoot that she was. I really did. And I felt so terrible that she'd been abandoned by her family, just like I was by Debra. Except that in her case it was even worse. Her people had probably dropped her off on the side of the road because they were tired of having a dog. At least my mother had given me up for a better life because she couldn't get her own straightened out.

I wanted to give Zoë everything she longed for—love, companionship, romps in the park. I wanted to support her as she tried to run the café. I even wanted to give her those pumpkin cookies we both loved so much.

"Jessica," she said, "I'm afraid to trust another person. If you give me up the way my people did, I think I'll just quit living. But I know you love me in a way my people never did. So even though it's scary, I want to ask you an important question." She took a deep breath. I held perfectly still, waiting. "Will you be my family now?"

She asked it in such a bare, open way that my throat choked up. Zoë—out of everyone—was saying the words I'd always wanted to hear. The aching hole that had pained my chest for all these years suddenly filled with an emotion I didn't recognize. Until I looked at Zoë and put a word to that feeling. Home.

In answer, I licked her on the face until she fell down in a heap of giggles.

Zoë

Jessica and I take a long walk in the park, then I buy us two big sandwiches with the money I have in my pocket and we eat them, sitting on the grass. She falls asleep for a long, long time, while I watch kids playing football. When she wakes up, she shakes herself and does a little dance that tells me it's time to go.

The sun it getting lower. Together we race to the restaurant, feeling light as sunshine. When I look over at
Jessica, she has a big grin on her face that's brimming
with happiness, making me smile even more.

We arrive and the woman with the growly poodle
comes, saying it's almost time for me to make the
speech. Kerrie is so glad to see us that she gives us each
a cookie. "Good luck, kiddo," she says. "I've got to
keep the dinner service going, but I'll be thinking of
you up there on stage. You're gonna be great."

Jessica and I follow the poodle woman to a big
grassy place. We have to listen to a lot of other people
talk, blah, blah, blah, while we wait. A woman from
the Lost Dog Committee says how great this year's
Woofinstock was. *It's wonderful to have so many
people in town to focus on dogs,* she says. *And don't
the dogs have fun while they're here!* The crowd really
likes that. Then, at last, she calls for me, Jessica Sheldon, co-owner of the Glimmerglass Café and head of
"Businesses for Woofinstock," and waves for me to go
up on stage.

I put my sparkly winner's hat on and make sure my
necklace looks nice. I'm really proud of how well we
did in the competitions. Even though I don't care
about impressing my mom and dad anymore, I'm
glad to wear them because of what Jessica and I ac-
complished together. As a team.

I pat Jessica on the back, and we both climb the
steps and stand behind a big wooden box with a shiny
thing on top. I think of how my hat must sparkle in
this light, and I smile. Everyone smiles back at me.

I stand quietly for a minute before I speak. So

much has happened to me—to us—during this Woofin-stock, it seems hard to put it all into words. I cough a little to clear my throat. "Thank you," I say. My voice echoes over the heads of the people listening. "I'm very happy to be here, but I have some unfortunate news." I look across the crowd to make sure every-one's paying attention. "We should be ashamed of ourselves."

The audience sucks in their breath and shifts in their seats. "That's right," I go on. "Ashamed. Because we all love dogs. But there are dogs in our very midst that are miserable. They're scared and lonely. They think the entire world is against them."

Everyone is quiet after this. I feel bad for bringing everyone down when they're here to be happy, but I can't let this go. It's too important. I see Dr. Max in the crowd and his face strengthens my conviction.

"For dogs, the bond they share with their people is the most important thing in their lives. They don't care about cars and work and making money. They don't care about looking pretty or being popular. They care about their people. Their families. And when that's taken away, when people abandon their dogs at the vet's office or along the highway, that dog's life is ruined. They're frightened and alone, left to fend for themselves in a terrifying world.

"Worst of all, how can these dogs ever trust again? They've been betrayed by the people they loved the most—how does a dog overcome that?"

I look over the crowd again as I let that sink in. Then I look down at Jess, and she blinks up at me with her tail wagging.

"Luckily for everyone, dogs have a wonderful talent. They excel at forgiveness. If a dog can find someone who loves them, someone who will never, *never* give them up, they can learn to trust again. As people who love dogs, it's our responsibility to match these abandoned dogs with the right people. With people who understand what a precious thing a dog's trust is.

"This town loves dogs," I say. "So this town needs to fix this problem. We can't sit back and pretend it doesn't exist. We have to stand up and pair these dogs with people who will take them home and be their new families. Forever."

I stop for a breath, and I'm startled because everyone starts to clap. It isn't happy clapping, it's serious clapping. And it makes me feel really good, because when people are serious, they can accomplish important things.

Out in the audience, I see Dr. Max stand up, applauding.

"Everyone has to help with this," I say over the clapping. "Everyone in this audience today has a responsibility to do whatever they can to help. We owe it to these dogs. And if we work together, we can do amazing things. I know we can. Who's willing to help?"

Two dozen hands go up, then more people stand, clapping and cheering. My throat feels tight with happiness. Beside me, Jessica is wagging so hard I think her tail might fall off. I smile at the crowd. "Thank you. On behalf of all dogs, thank you."

People clap again. I think about going off the stage, but then I feel the heat of Jessica's breathing on my leg and think of one more thing I want to say. I look around at all the dog faces in the crowd—trusting, happy faces. And I talk directly to them.

"I didn't mean to bring such a serious message to you today. But I've just had a wonderful thing happen. A few days ago, I got really, really lucky. I met her," I say, pointing at Jess, who pants some more. "This dog and I have made a pact that we're going to be together, no matter what. Forever. And that's worth more to me than anything."

I pat the wooden box, and Jessica stands up on her back legs with her front paws beside me. Then she leans her nose in toward the shiny thing, opens her mouth, and howls, louder than I've ever heard myself howl before. *A-rooooo!* It's like she's agreeing with everything I said. The people cheer and cheer, and the ones sitting next to dogs bend down and hug them until their tails wag like crazy. I reach over and hug Jessica. And she wags like crazy, too.

24

Dogs Adrift

 Jessica

When Zoë made her speech, the planet stopped spinning. From the second she started speaking, no one shifted in their chairs or coughed—she had us all transfixed with the throaty earnestness of her voice. Empathy throbbed in my chest when she talked about abandoned dogs. We'd been through so much together and we had so much to learn from each other. I felt lucky to know her.

Malia came onstage to announce the dates of next year's Woofinstock—*always the first weekend in September!*—and encouraged everyone to come again. And just like that, Woofinstock was over. Malia gave Zoë a broad wink and said the town would be glad to have her chair the Woofinstock committee next year, if she wanted. People shook Zoë's hand and told her with shining eyes how much they appreciated her stance on homeless dogs. At least a dozen people volunteered then and there for the fledgling organization, which Malia suggested we call "Forever Families." It seemed like an excellent beginning.

At some point, Max took my leash out of Zoë's hand and led me away from the crowd. We sat on the grass together, not saying anything, just being, side by side. Clearly, neither of us knew what to do. We had no solution to our problem, and yet I sensed that we weren't ready to give up, either. It was as if we sat on opposite sides of an invisible divide—hearts together, bodies apart. I shifted over until my hip brushed against his. He reached out hesitantly and stroked my head, just once. Then he leaned forward and kissed my temple. I think we both felt awkward about it, but it was awfully sweet for a first kiss. After that he sat back, blushing slightly, his hands chastely planted on the grass. I sat still and tried not to pant.

A few minutes later, Zoë ran over, clutching a silver Woofinstock collar. I recognized it as the second-place Best Dog Award.

"Look," she said, "it says *best dog*. Malia gave it to me." She showed it to me, her face beaming. "It's for us, to share, because we're the best dog."

Max smiled at her. "You did pretty well as a person today, too," he said.

She stopped smiling, suddenly serious. "It was worth being a person, just so I could make that speech. I'm so glad they listened."

"And," he added, "they're acting on what they heard, and that's even more important."

On the far side of the green, Leisl paraded Foxy through the crowd. Around his neck, Foxy wore a

"Woofie," the first-place Best Dog Award, a two-pound gold medallion inscribed with the date and an etched profile of Spitz. Foxy must have won some of the other events—Best Trick, most likely—to earn the Woofie. Zoë's was plastic and light as air, but Foxy's medal looked awfully heavy slung around his neck. I didn't envy him one bit.

"Foxy has a necklace, too," Zoë said, following my eyes, "but it's not as pretty as ours." She moved her plastic collar back and forth, watching the glitter wink in the light. "His person thinks they have the best necklace, but she's completely wrong."

She might have been wrong, but Leisl was working her win for all it was worth. In her haste to pose for every possible photo, she'd dropped Foxy's leash. With a furtive, sidelong look at her, he slipped away into the crowd, probably on the hunt for hot dogs.

Zoë, Max, and I sat together in silence, watching the people, until Max received another emergency call on his cell phone. Someone had fed their puppy too many sausages at Madrona Mesquite, and Max thought the dog might have acute pancreatitis. Before he left, his finger brushed my ear, barely enough for me to feel, like the kiss of butterflies' wings. It was just a breath, but it was a promise. Messed up though we were, he would see us both again soon.

Zoë and I stayed where we were, not moving, until a sudden shift in the air made me lift my nose and sniff the wind. Something had changed. Even though it was still early evening, the sky had darkened to a thick plum color. There was no breeze. The silent air had a heavy quality that hinted at something to come.

Something big. Like a storm.

"Your ears are up." Zoë's eyes were on me. "I see your nose twitching. What is it? Do you smell hot dogs?" She sniffed the wind. "I don't smell anything. Wait! A raindrop!"

I stood up and made a soft ruffing sound to get her attention. She popped onto her feet. If a storm were on its way, we needed to get to the heart of it. Maybe if we could get to the beach, where we could see more of the sky, we'd know which way to head.

I set off at a trot, pleased to hear Zoë's footfalls behind me. We made quick time, jogging downhill toward the ice-cream shop and then on to Waterfront Park. I ran us downhill all the way to the rocky waterfront where the old fishing pier stood. Long before I spotted the beach, I heard gulls screaming at each other as they looped through the sky. Thunder rumbled softly somewhere to the west. Out of nowhere, a chilly breeze dashed past us, rustling my fur and making Zoë's skin break out in goose bumps.

"Hey, what's that?"

She stopped suddenly, peering over the salal and wild rosebushes at something I couldn't see. I could hear it, though—a desperate splashing sound, punctuated by frantic gurgles. The sound literally made my hair stand up on end. Even without seeing the source, I knew panic when I heard it. Fear wrapped around my heart and squeezed.

Thunder crashed overhead, making the whole sky shiver. Above the trail, hemlocks and pines swayed, bending their heads together like conspirators, their branches black in the storm's half light. The waves, which usually nudged the beach so gently, nearly drowned everything out with the *whoosh* of their surge onto the shore. I'd seen storms before, plenty of times, but the shoreline had never felt this menacing.

Zoë and I plunged through the bushes, racing down a dusty path that spilled onto the beach. The water was iron-gray under the evening light, cupped with ferocious little waves. In deeper areas, the wind skittered across the top, pulling up cat's paws. Amid this chaos, the fishing pier looked like the fragile skeleton of a long-extinct sea creature.

Zoë raised her arm to point at something splashing about twenty feet from the pier, but I had already seen it. A dog's wet head bobbed up and down in a patch of flurried water. *A dog.* It took my mind a full second to internalize the horrible truth—a dog was drowning. An icy chill ran across my entire body.

I'd never felt anything as deeply as the urge I felt right then—the urge to be as far away from this place as I could. The sight and sound of that dog filled me with such terror, I tasted metal in my mouth. My stomach heaved. I could barely breathe. I wanted to hide my head under my paws and make it all go away.

I was as scared as if I were the one drowning, as if I were the one feeling the burn of saltwater in my throat as I desperately fought to stay afloat. Without even glancing in the dog's direction, I knew what he was thinking and feeling. His nose was full of murky beach scents and the cold, hard smell of the ocean. His ears heard everything that happened on the beach, but most of all they heard his own splashes, his labored breathing, and the gruesome sound of his

terrified heart. I knew what he felt. And it made me
want to turn and run.

Behind us, thunder rolled, sounding warm and in-
viting. I pictured the square, dry and pleasantly filled
with people, far away from dangers and drowning.

I turned to look at Zoë and met her eyes in the
twilight. Magic shivered through the air. Without
speaking, we both knew that this—that rumbling
thunder—was our chance. This night, this moment,
was our lone chance to run into the kind of fraught,
silver lightning that had made us switch bodies in the
first place. Lightning would strike once, maybe twice
more, and then our chance would be lost. We didn't get
many thunderstorms in Madrona. And I'd only been in
one that felt like this before—two days ago, when this
nightmare began.

With all my heart and soul, I wanted to be there. I
wanted to stand with Zoë at Spitz's doghouse and
wait for lightning to put us right. I pictured Max's
face, and Kerrie's, and thought of how wonderful it
would be to hold a fork in my hand, to stand on two
legs, to talk!

We should have turned around and run for the
square or the green or any place likely to be struck.
That was our chance. We should have been selfish,
looking out for our own interests.

Still, the sound of those terrified splashes made me
sick to my stomach. Every time the dog gasped, my
belly contracted. I couldn't leave that dog to suffer. I
just couldn't. It would be like leaving myself to die, or
like leaving Zoë. If I turned away now, the rest of my
life would be a sham. Zoë's speech still rang in my

ears—just like everyone else in Madrona, I felt
charged with a responsibility to help dogs whenever I
could. Even if it cost me my future.

In an instant, looking at Zoë, I saw that she'd
reached the same conclusion. We turned together to
the fishing pier. Side by side, we raced down the
length of the pier, the wooden slats shuddering under
our feet. Lightning flashed, turning the sky into a
sheet of white. *That was it,* I thought ruefully. *That
was our strike.*

When we reached the pier's end, we launched
through the air and shot into the water. The cold
knocked the air out of my lungs. I came up, gasping,
working all four paws to keep my head above water.
Beside me, Zoë recovered more quickly. She was
already moving toward the dog in distress. As I pad-
dled after her, I saw that the dog was Foxy. Something heavy, slung around his neck, pulled his head
under. He was fighting hard, his eyes rolling wildly
toward us as wave after wave sloshed over his ears. I
let out a bark to urge Zoë on and worked my paws
with all my strength.

When she reached him, I shuddered with relief. She
curled one arm around his chest and pulled him up-
right, lifting his head fully out of the water for the first
time. Foxy snorted and sputtered in a sick-sounding
way. When I reached them, I swam around to the
front, so we could head to the shore with Foxy's weight
supported half by my back, half by Zoë's arm. The
swim was scary—my head went under more waves
than I could count—but the sight of the gray beach
kept me going.

We stumbled out of the water and collapsed on the wet sand.

Zoë

We lie on the beach, and it's so cold I can't stop shivering. After a while, Foxy stands up, only he's woozy and he can't walk straight. He wanders a few steps and throws up. It's a pool of salty water, and I don't even think about smelling it. I've been a person for too long now, I guess. That thought makes me exhausted, but when I look at Foxy, my heart lifts again.

Jessica and I get to our feet, panting hard. Foxy is still walking in circles, slumping his head toward the sand. I can't figure out what he's up to until I realize that he's trying to shake off the thing that's around his neck. I go to him and pull it off, proud to be the one with hands at this moment. It's a thick red ribbon with a big medal hanging off it—his Woofie medal. I think of how he was pawing the water, his head slipping under and under, and I get so angry I throw the medal down the beach—even though the ribbon was red. And very pretty.

In the sky, the clouds are moving away fast. The air is quiet—the thunder is gone. Jessica moves over to me and leans against my leg. I reach down and stroke her wet head softly. We stand together, watching Foxy snort the water out of his nose.

"He's okay," I say. "Foxy's okay." Jessica breathes in and out. "Even if we can't switch back," I say, "we did a good thing. It's sad for us, but it was the right thing to do." Jessica leans in closer, and I feel like she's proud of me—proud of us. And that makes me glow underneath my downcast feelings. My happiness is like the meat inside a corn dog—you can't see it from the outside, but it tastes best of all.

When Foxy can breathe again, he looks around like he's seeing the beach for the first time. He wipes his face with his paw a few times. Then he turns around and looks at us. In a few quick steps, he pushes up against us so he's in my arms, his chest on Jessica's side, his head on both our shoulders. We cuddle against him and we all sigh. Foxy pulls away and licks us both about fifty times. He's glad and grateful, and that's yummy like the inside of a corn dog, too.

25

Blinded by the Light

 Zoë

Jessica and I walk Foxy to the big gate at the town square. We're both too tired to run. When we arrive, Foxy looks hard at both of us, and I can guess what he's thinking. His home life is complicated—his person isn't very understanding. She acts like she knows all about dogs, but she doesn't really. Not like I do. Not like Jessica does.

The sky is empty and clear. After Foxy heads home, Jessica and I both tip our heads up, but there aren't any clouds or planes or lightning streaks or anything. Just a big sheet of twilight blue. I guess, if I have to be a person forever, at least I'll get to see all these pretty colors every day. I never knew the world had this many.

We start walking home, thinking our own quiet thoughts. I'm thinking about dinner. I'm thinking that hot dogs are good enough that I could eat them all the time. Or I could go for a big, juicy steak like what they had in the café kitchen.

I'm so busy thinking about steak I don't notice that Jessica isn't next to me anymore. I guess she stopped to smell something or to leave a pee marker or to nose around for tasty garbage. One of those fun things that I don't get to do anymore. I try not to think about that and go back to thoughts of steak instead.

Then I hear a noise behind me, like a man yelling, and for a minute I think he's saying something about "hot dogs," but I'm wrong. He's saying, "Hey, you dog!" in an angry voice. My first idea is that he means me. But then I remember. *Jessica!* I spin around too fast and almost trip over my feet.

In the middle of the square, Jessica is standing across from a big man—the same man who tried to play with me in the street the day that Jessica and I first met. The words KITTIAS COUNTY are on the back of his jumpsuit. Last time, I tried to play with this man, but this time my skin prickles. Through the entrance to the square, I can see his white truck and it makes me feel cold all over. I start to run.

The man has two black things in his hands. He's pointing them at Jessica. She's backing away, but he's big and frightening and can move fast if he decides to. I run so hard my feet fly on the cobblestones. I'm frightened for Jessica and I can hardly breathe. I have to go faster, faster, *faster*.

The man hears my footsteps and turns my way, but he keeps his guns pointed at Jessica.

"Keep away, lady," he says in a you'd-better-do-it voice. "I've dealt with this dog before. It's vicious. Uncontrollable. Can't have a beast like this roaming loose. Just stand back, and I'll take care of it."

Jessica is still as a statue in front of the man. Maybe she doesn't know how threatening he is, the same way I didn't know when I was a dog. Or maybe she doesn't think she can get away in time if she runs. Either way, I have to save her.

"No!" I yell. "Don't!" He sees how quickly I'm coming and jerks his hands up, like he wants to shoot before I get there. He's going to shoot something at Jessica—I just know it.

I dive in front of her just as he shoots. Two metal pins fly out of each gun, launching right for us. Behind me, I see a flash of light—then two hot spots erupt on me, one on my belly and one on my shoulder. It burns hotter than lightning and I smell something smoking. A stream of blue light jumps from the man to us, like a long, magical tail. The light fills my eyes until all I see are ropes and swirls of brightness. Then the brightness vanishes and everything is black.

Jessica

My first thought was that my body had broken in half and caught on fire. Even with my eyes closed, the world was bright enough to make me wince. I stretched my paws out in front of me, glad to feel the cool cobblestones. At least something in the world wasn't searing hot.

I would have stayed where I was forever, eyes clamped shut—the idea of moving was too painful— but I heard Zoë groan beside me. I remembered the way she'd hurled herself in front of me when I was too paralyzed to move. She must have been Tasered. I flicked my eyes open, knowing that no matter what pain I was in, hers must be a thousand times worse.

The vague light of evening was gone, and darkness clouded the entire square. I caught a glimmer of white—the county animal control officer had opened the door to his boxy van. I heard him gasp into a cell phone.

"I was in the process of apprehending a vagrant dog," he said, his voice raspy. "Yeah, in Madrona. Yeah, I *know* I have to do things by the book here. I know, okay? Yeah. Well, uh, I was apprehending the dog when a woman jumped in the way." He paused. "Um. I think I Tasered them both."

I moved my attention away from him and squinted into the dark, looking for Zoë. My eyes swirled and spotted with dots of light, but I was pretty sure I didn't see her twinset or that black-and-white patterned skirt. Just a whitish blur that I discounted as a trick of my eyes.

Panting through my mouth, I tried to stand up, but my front feet slipped on the cobbles and I landed hard on my chest. Gasping, I blinked, trying to shake the weird streams of blue light that kept cutting across my vision. My sight was so poor I almost thought I saw . . . No.

No way. It couldn't be.

Could it?

YES—I had *hands*!

Zoë

When I wake up, the first thing I do is take a deep, full-lung smell. Then I sniff again and again. That's how I know for sure, even without opening my eyes. All the smells are back again. I can smell the eggs and steaks from the restaurants, smell the cut grass, smell the dirt at the base of the trees in the square. I can even smell the pee of the two dogs who marked the tree we're near—a tiny Chihuahua and a giant Berner. I breathe the air into my doggy nose and let it fill me with total joy.

Then I'm up on *dog* feet! I spin around and around until I actually catch my tail in my teeth, I'm that happy.

I stop, panting, and see Jessica looking at me with a big smile. I race over to her, and lick her face all over. I can feel the happiness beaming off her skin in waves.

She laughs and hugs me, and I laugh, too. Then she bends down and kisses me on the head. I feel so special it's like the light of all the stars in the sky are inside me.

We both dance and hop around, jumping through the square like puppies. But when the nasty man yells to us ("Hey, lady—are you okay?"), we both race away. We run past Spitz's house and our café, past the edge of the square, and down the alley. We run all the way home, as fast as we can, because running feels wonderful.

We get to Jessica's house and stop in front of the glass door. She puts her shoulder to it and pushes it open, then waves me in with a big grin and a sweep of her arm.

A door! I'm so excited. I wriggle, ready to bound inside. Jessica laughs at me, and I'm glad she's here. My heart feels full of happiness, like a soccer ball that's full of air. I just love her.

And I love doors! Especially this one, because this one means home.

26

Paws, Feet, and Hands

Twelve hours later . . .

 Jessica

Zoë led the way through the door, of course.

We walked into the Glimmerglass and turned down the hall together, our footsteps soft on the carpet as we headed for the kitchen.

"I'm sorry, my friend," I said as we reached the swinging doors, "but you're going to have to wait out here this time. Why don't you visit the back office and see if the garbage can has anything tasty in it?"

Zoë's mouth popped open in a grin as she turned and padded away. I slipped into the kitchen. Kerrie was at the stove, and when she turned around, I gave her the best hug I knew how to give.

"Thank you," I said. "Thank you for being the best friend on the planet. I don't know what I would do without you."

When Kerrie stepped back, her eyes looked misty.
"What was that all about?"

I smiled. "I just want you to know how much your
friendship means to me. I'm sorry I haven't always
been as forthcoming as I could have. I should have
told you everything about my past. And about those
purple envelopes from my birth mother. It wasn't that
I didn't trust you—I trust you completely. I just didn't
know how I felt about it in my own heart, so I didn't
know what to say."

"You didn't have to share it," she said. "You don't
have to tell me things."

"But I want to. And I can see now how stupid I
was, because you probably could have helped me re-
solve my feelings about Debra, which would have
been a huge help. I bottled it up, and that made me
act like a dork. I'm really sorry."

"Well," Kerrie looked down at the spoon in her
hand, "I wanted to apologize, too. I was a fool for
keeping myself out of the kitchen. I knew we needed
a chef—when I think of all the money and heartache
we could have saved if we hadn't had to hire Guy . . ."
She shook her head and her dangly amber earrings
jingled.

Dear Kerrie. I caught her hand, the one that held
the spoon, and gave it a tug, laughing. "Look," I said,
"it's been a year of growing for both of us. What's
amazing is that we had a wonderful Woofinstock, the
café is still here, and we're still friends."

"We'll always be friends," she said, swinging her
spoon through the air, pretending she was about to

swat me. "Always. Now get out of the kitchen and let
me cook!"

*E*verywhere I went, people started smiling the instant they saw Zoë—and their smiles included me.
With Zoë at my side, I was what I'd always wanted
to be, cool by association. The warmth people showed
us tickled me almost as much as the way they suddenly wanted to strike up conversations. They wanted
to talk to me and pet Zoë, and for the first time in my
life, I understood the impulse.

In the reception area of Max's clinic, Zoë saw another dog—a French bulldog—and dragged me to it.
It looked like a friendly dog and its owner gave us a
nod, so I crouched down and offered my hand, smiling with welcome. When it let me rub its chin with my
fingertips, a sense of honor and gratitude ran through
me. For once, I felt sure no random calamity would
strike as a result of being near this dog. I'd had that
all wrong. I'd been the one causing all the problems
with my standoffishness and negative attitude. It
turned out that I had to like dogs before dogs could
like me.

We didn't stay with the bulldog long, because a familiar voice rang out in the back. I saw Zoë's ears
prick up and felt my own do the same, then laughed
when I remembered that I didn't have dog ears anymore.

I don't know who moved more quickly, Zoë or me.
Even though we probably weren't supposed to barge

into the back of the clinic, we did it anyway, strolling past the front desk like we belonged there. Max was talking with a vet tech when we arrived.

"We're going to need a full blood workup on Roscoe," he was saying, handing over a chart. "Be sure you get his—"

He stopped when he saw us, his mouth still forming the next words. I don't know what told him we were back, but he clearly knew. His eyes glowed with it. Maybe it was the fact that I was wearing clean clothes, all right-side out? Whatever it was, it made Max look at me in a way that tripped my heartbeat into a double-fast pace. I swallowed and smiled nervously. Even with his assistant there, he was looking at me in a way that made me feel naked. And warm from head to toe.

"Uh, Marcie," he said, not taking his eyes off me, "give me a minute, okay?" He stepped past her and opened the door to his left, leading us into one of the little exam rooms. Except instead of standing behind the metal table, he crossed the room and sank into one of the padded chairs.

I shut the door and stood in front of it, smiling. Zoë bounded to Max and got so excited she practically climbed in his lap. He rubbed her ears, massaged her face, and let her lick his cheek—but all the time, he was watching me as if he thought I might shatter.

"Is it really true?" he said at last. "Really?"

I shrugged happily. "Seems to be. I feel pretty solidly me."

His smile deepened. "Well, come over here, then." He extended a hand to me, and I took it, allowing myself to be led to the chair next to him. Zoë leaned over and licked my cheek, and Max and I both scratched her neck, letting our hands touch as often as they happened to. After a while, he stopped petting her, and ran his hand over the top of mine instead.

"I'm so glad," he said. His eyes met mine, and I saw a world of thoughts and feelings there—things that would take a lifetime to truly understand. My pulse quickened at the very thought. I had that lifetime now. I really did.

"Me, too," I said in response, my voice thick with emotion. I stroked Zoë's forehead, knowing I spoke for both of us. "Me, too."

He leaned forward and I leaned forward. When our lips met, my heart hammered in my throat. His were so soft, so perfect. As the kiss deepened, I couldn't help reaching up to run my fingers through his thick black hair.

His hands splayed against my spine, pulling me close. I wanted to be closer still, to be part of him, one with him. We'd been waiting so long. When we pulled apart, just for a second, we both gasped from the intensity. Then Max cupped my cheek and drew me back to him, and my mind went blank as I lost myself in kissing him.

It was Zoë who broke us out of it, barking impatiently. Max laughed at her and kissed me again. And when he pulled away, I lifted my face and kissed him on one famous cheekbone, then the other. *This is just the beginning,* I told myself. *Only the beginning.*

Zoë

Dr. Max has a talent for petting dogs. When he pets me, I can't stop wagging, that's how skilled he is. When he looks at Jessica, his eyes have that wanting look, like a border collie looking at a tennis ball. Her face keeps turning colors that I know are red, even though it doesn't look that way anymore. Probably her face is hot, I think. I know people well enough now that I should have a collar that says "Genius Dog" on it.

Jessica and Dr. Max are deep in conversation. She tells him about the great news at the Glimmerglass. They made all the money they needed from Woofinstock—even enough to buy a generator. And *Woof! Magazine* is coming to do a story about Jessica and me. They're going to take our picture, Jessica says, and we'll wear our sparkly winner's hats.

When they laugh, I laugh, too. And when Dr. Max leans close, and Jessica leans close, they kiss, and I laugh even more. They're incredibly lucky to know me. If I hadn't brought Jessica here, Dr. Max would never have known that he wants her to be his family. And she wouldn't have known what an alpha he is. Honestly, I don't know how people get by without dogs around to show them the way. My old people never appreciated what I had to share, but Jessica does—she understands better than anyone in the world.

I get tired of their kissing and wander around the room. It smells like dog biscuits, and I waste some time looking for them. Then I sniff all the corners where nervous dogs have peed. One corner smells like cat. I spend a long time there, studying up on cats. I'm glad I touched that one, so I know what it's like. Sometime, I'd like to lick one, too. Just to see how it tastes.

When I'm done smelling, I sit down and look at my two people. Jessica is awfully pretty—she's even prettier since she had her time as a dog. Dr. Max is wearing his white coat and tennis shoes, so I think he'll probably want to take me for a walk later. In the park. Or the square. Or maybe the beach! But now they're kissing again, so I settle back to wait. And wait. I hadn't thought kissing could go on so long. I hope they'll hurry up and get down to business. Now that they're finally going to mate, my new family can get on with really important things. Like walks. And eating hot dogs. And snuggling on the sofa and going through doors and licking cats. Good things like that.

Dr. Max is taking us for a walk. I'm in front of the two of them, leading the way. I take us to the square, because there are often other dogs there. It's funny, though—as we get close, the sky turns strangely dark. I feel cold, even under my fur. Jessica shivers. She leans against Dr. Max and he puts an arm around her.

"That's strange," he says. "I didn't see any storms in the forecast."

I look back at Jessica. Our eyes meet, and we both decide at the same moment to stop walking.

"Why don't we stop here," Jessica says, pointing to the big gate that marks the entrance to the square.

"Zoë can sniff around. I, uh, I think we'd rather stay far away from Spitz if the weather's bad. You know."

She and Dr. Max start smooching again, so I sit down and watch the sky. It swirls around getting darker and darker. Rain splashes near my paws. I hear a rumble of thunder, and then I notice something moving in the middle of the square, close to Spitz's doghouse. Foxy is there, leashed up to his woman. She's yelling and shouting something at Foxy, something that sounds like, "Why can't you be more like Zoë? The whole town loves her now—she's perfect! Why can't you be perfect?"

I hear Foxy bark loudly, like he's shouting back. He tugs against the leash, as if he wants to go somewhere else. Then a flash of lightning makes everything white and bright. I see them both topple. My eyes get too blurry to keep watching.

When I can see again, the woman and Foxy are far apart. Foxy is staring at his paws, lifting them one after the other like he has gum on his pads. Or like he's confused by them. The woman looks back and forth from her hands to her feet. And to her hands again. Then she tries to stand up and falls over on her face.

I look up at Jessica. She's looking at me. And we both smile our secret smile.

TOR

Award-winning authors
Compelling stories

Please join us at the website
below for more information
about this author and other great
Tor selections, and to sign up for
our monthly newsletter!